MW00954971

Campus Chronicles:

Kamaria & Kyree's

Story

by Cion Lee

Campus Chronicles:Kamaria & Kyree's Story ©

2023 by Cion C. Lee.

All Rights Reserved. This book or any portion cannot be reproduced in any form unless granted written permission by the publisher, except for the use of brief quotations in book review.

This book is a work of fiction. All settings, characters,names,events,real people, living or dead, are in place to give the book a sense of reality. Any similarities to real life such as characters, places, names, or descriptions are entirely coincidental or a product of the author's imagination.

Chapter 1

Kamaria Laurent

January 10, 2020

I banged my head into my microeconomics textbook in frustration. The loud bounce music coming from the next room was the number one reason I'd begged my parents to let me live off campus for my last semester. I planned an entire detailed presentation for them on why I deserved it, and listed valid reasons. Getting straight A's from the moment I'd started attending the University of Baton Rouge back in 2016 was one of my leading reasons. According to them that was what I was supposed to do and I didn't deserve any privileges for the bare minimum. My hopeful spirit was crushed, so I didn't even bother to point out how I hadn't gotten into any trouble and stayed focused. If a perfect grade point average didn't impress them, then good behavior wouldn't either. That was confirmed when they went on to say that a solo off campus apartment was out of the question for me, but they were willing to let me move into the on campus apartments. I was disappointed because the East Campus apartments were set up just like the dormitories I'd been staying in. But it was a step up, so I accepted the offer. Unfortunately, I was back in a dorm-like situation with girls I didn't click with yet again.

Making friends was something I lost hope on a long time ago. Although Baton Rouge was only an hour away from my hometown, New Orleans, I still looked forward to a fresh start as a freshman. College was going to be my chance to redeem myself from the dork I'd been in highschool. Of course, I'd always be a nerd at heart and the voices of my parents in my head was a constant reminder that school came first. But I wanted to indulge in campus fun as well as make some lifelong friends. My favorite auntie even had me excited to meet boys because she went on and on about how most of her friends had met their husbands in college.

Let's just say, the first few weeks of college killed the fairytale I'd formulated in my head. The first set of girls I was paired with in Mary Louise hall weren't the friendliest no matter how nice I was. They'd smile in my face but there was a lack of sincerity there. One time I put my shyness to the side and asked them if I could go to a party with them after overhearing them talk about it. There was awkward silence before one of them spoke up and said there was no room in her car for me...as if I wasn't capable of driving my own car. I shouldn't have taken it so personally, but my feelings were hurt. For weeks I'd suspected they didn't want to be seen hanging with me because I was the opposite of them, and that was confirmation for me. They were all petite girls who pop culture would call "slim thick." The tallest one was about 5'5. They were glamorous in every way, never leaving the dorms without their hair or makeup perfectly done, and they always rocked perfectly put together outfits that showed off their frames. My auntie had spoiled me with a lot of nice, designer clothes before I left for college, but I was big on being comfortable. I was also taught by my mother to cover up what God cursed me with. Her words, not mine.

I'd taken after my father in stature, so I stood over most girls at 5'10. My weight was something I'd struggled with since elementary school. I could vividly remember my mom putting me on diets so I could lose weight, but I just seemingly got bigger. It got to the point where my mom just gave up and started buying me bigger clothes. That's when she let up a little on ripping into me about my size, so I became content with wearing larger clothes. For as long as I could remember, girls never wanted to be my friend and boys never wanted to talk to me, so I didn't know why I thought college would be some big turning point for me. My best bet was to do what I'd been doing since grade school; focus on my studies and stay out the way. By the end of my freshman year I was secure with being introverted, and that hadn't changed. I didn't even play myself by trying to get to know my roommates this semester. I politely introduced myself to them, we went over house rules, and I learned that they were seniors just like me. It didn't shock me that I didn't know them already because I kept to myself. UBR was a large campus so it would probably be impossible to know everybody, and I only ever talked to

8

people who had the same major as me. That was only when I had to do group projects and things of that nature.

"Thank you,"I breathed in relief, as the ear bleeding music finally stopped. A few minutes later I heard the front door slam. They'd been going out every other night since we'd moved in after Winter break. At times like this I'd question if I was doing too much by studying this hard only a week into the semester. Deep down I knew I wasn't. I was getting a B.S. in Accounting, and even though I was gifted in math, I would still get tripped up sometimes. I never allowed myself to fall behind because I always stayed ahead of the curve. I studied even when I didn't have a test coming up. I stayed ready so I never had to get ready.

An hour later, I finally closed my textbook and laptop. My stomach was growling, and this seemed like the perfect time to cook because I was home alone. I got up, put on my Tory Burch slippers and made a beeline for my door. When I opened it, I almost jumped into next year. I could've sworn I was home alone, but I was so wrong. My roommate, Clarissa, was still here and the way she was smiling at me was making me feel weird.

"Uhhh, can I help you?"My eyes danced around.

"You sure can,roomie,"she replied in the countriest accent ever. She had Shreveport, Louisiana to thank for that. "So, this boy I've been dating is about to come over, but he's bringing his friend with him."

"So why do you need my help?"

"I need a wing woman. Just keep his friend company. Nothing too crazy."

"I don't think so,"I said firmly.

"Oh, c'mon! All you have to do is make light conversation with the nigga."

I wanted to explain that the thought of making light conversation with a man scared me. Making light conversation with anybody scared me. I'd never been the outgoing type. The thought of being rejected was terrifying, so I didn't put myself out there like that.

"And what if he wants more?"

"I doubt he'll want more,"she cackled. "Y'all would just keep eachother company while me and my boo do our thing. C'mon…help me out, roomie to roomie."

As much shit as I talked about not needing or wanting friends, my beautiful and popular roommate asking me for a favor made me feel good. I was no dummy, so I knew she was only in my face so she could use me to her benefit. But maybe this could open the door to a genuine friendship. It would be pretty pathetic if I left UBR with no friends or exciting stories to my credit. Like the saying goes, better late than never.

"Okay. I'll do it,"I agreed, putting my nerves on the backburner.

"Great!" She looked down at my clothes. "Are you gonna change?"

I looked at my big basketball shorts, with my oversized Marvel t-shirt.

"I guess I could put on some cute sweatpants?"

"Sweatpants?" Her face turned up. "No, Kamaria. Do you have shorts or something?"

"Um, I have them…"I swallowed nervously. "But my legs are really big and my bu-"

"Girl, please,"she waved me off dismissively before inviting herself into my room. She walked over to my dresser and pulled a drawer out. She started pulling skimpy stuff out that I only wore to bed, while I questioned what I'd gotten myself into.

Kyree Pierre

"Nigga, I told you I gotta be at the club by 11. I knew I should've driven my own shit,"I complained. I'd been throwing legendary parties at UBR since my sophomore year in 2016. My hard partying was the reason why I barely made it through my first year, but I bounced back from that. I quickly became a pro at balancing academics and the social scene. It was all about time management, and right now my best friend, Shad, was playing with my time. Like any other red blooded man, I loved pussy. But I didn't let it dictate my life. Shad couldn't say the same. We were supposed to be heading to our off campus apartment to get some rest before tonight. But he got a call from some girl and practically rushed to her apartment.

"It's only 8. I just need like 30 minutes,"he chuckled.

"That's sad."

"Nigga fuck you. I ain't tryna make love to this hoe."

"Wait, is this the girl you took out to eat last weekend?"I recalled.

"Yup."

"Still selling dreams,"I shook my head. If my intentions were to only fuck a girl and go about my business, I didn't take her on dates and pump her head up. Niggas complicated things for themselves by doing shit like that, and sure enough, Shad always had female drama.

"Ain't selling shit. She was hungry and so was I. I'm not a stingy nigga, so I paid for her meal. It ain't my fault if she looked deep into that shit."

"So what, I'm supposed to wait in this car for you?"

"No, you gon kick it with her roommate."

"Fuck no! I ain't tryna be set up, Shad."

"I said kick it. Not marry the bitch. Besides, the two roommates I always see her with are bad as fuc-"

His words cut off when his phone vibrated. I watched him read the screen and then burst into laughter before he looked at me apologetically.

"What, nigga?"

"So, her two fine roommates went out. You gon chill with the other one."

"How she look?"

"I meannn, I only saw her in passing once. She's cute…"

"But?"

"She big as fuck."

"Yea, I'm good. You don't need me. Go in there by yourself and shine my boy."

"If you don't come in now it'll look bad."

"I could care less. This is some childish shit anyway. Why do you need me to keep a bitch company just so you can get some pussy?"

"I don't. I told her I was leaving the Union with you, so she figured you would need something to do while we did us. Fuck it. I'll tell them you got sick or something,"he shrugged carelessly, before climbing out his car. I watched him walk to an apartment, knock, and a few seconds later the door opened. The girl greeted him with a big hug, before pulling away and looking around. At times like this I wished I was an asshole, because I would've sat in the car guilt free. But I never liked making anyone feel bad. Just because bigger girls weren't my type it didn't mean I had to make a stranger feel like they weren't worthy of my presence. I would hate it if somebody played on me like that. So I got my tall ass out of the car, and slowly jogged to the apartment.

"Oh, he doesn't look sick to me,"the girl tittered. "Hey, I'm Clarissa."

"What's up,"I nodded. "I'm Kyree."

"I know who you are,"she smirked. Not even on no cocky shit, but I wasn't the least bit surprised that she was giving me flirtatious vibes even though she was supposed to be messing with my homie. Aside from being popular on campus, girls had been on me since elementary school. My mom always went on and on about how handsome I was and I thought she was just talking until girls my age started saying it. It wasn't long before I got to a place where I saw it myself. I'd always stood over most people, so the fact that I'd peaked at 6 '5 didn't come as a shock. I just wished my height came with some God given talent, but the varsity basketball team in highschool is where my glory days in sports ended. It was cool though because it was never a passion of mine. It was just a hobby my parents put me in to keep me busy amongst other sports like football and baseball. Being a highschool athlete had a nigga fit and ripped. I still frequented the gym often to maintain my athletic body.

"Kamaria, come over here,"Clarrissa waved her hand to someone I couldn't see because I hadn't entered the apartment yet.

"No, if he doesn't want to chill with me then he doesn't have to. I can get back to studying."

Having one of my own, I was used to New Orleans accents. Unlike most girls from my city, hers had a sweet, angelic undertone to it. Little bumps formed on my arm, as I nudged Shad's back so he'd enter the apartment. I had to see this girl with the perfect voice.

"Kamaria, the boy is here so ob-"

"I can speak for myself,"I said, once I was in the apartment. Kamaria was standing far away from us all with her arms crossed. I don't know what I was expecting, but I wanted to punch Shad in his shit for the way he described this poor girl. Okay, so she was bigger than any girl I'd ever talked to or dated, and she honestly wasn't my type. I liked them a lot shorter and on the slim side. She was what my uncles would call a Stallion. It was all on display in the black tights she wore with a white beater. She had long, big ass legs, bone crushing thighs, wide hips, and arms that were a clear indicator that she got down in the kitchen. Her midsection was far from flat, but it wasn't outrageously big. It went with her proportions. Body aside, she was a pretty dark brown girl. Her face was chubby and round, making her look like a cute babydoll. Her lips were full and pouty and her pretty brown eyes had this innocence about them that I was drawn to.

"Okay, so you healed in like five seconds?"She snapped.

"Honestly, I didn't want to come in at first but only because this was sprung on me. It's nothing against you personally, love. I don't mind sitting here and getting to know you."

"Oh,"she uttered, appearing stumped.

"We're gonna go to my room. Y'all have fun,"Clarissa giggled, as Shad dry humped her from the back.

"That boy a fool,"I chuckled, before looking over at Kamaria. Her nervous energy wasn't hard to miss. I found it humorous, but I didn't laugh. "You mind if I sit?"

"Oh, of course not. Can I get you something to drink o-"

"Thank you, but I'm good. I just had Popeyes at the Union. Unless y'all got alc."

"Alc?"She asked, looking lost.

"Alcohol,"I laughed in disbelief. "You don't get out much, do you?"

She rolled her eyes, before sitting on the chair next to the sofa.

"Why you sitting way over there?"

"Because this is where I'm comfortable."

I nodded. "Well I guess it's best if you stay there then. So, were you really studying?"

"I mean, this is a university right? Everybody should study."

I smirked at the fact that she had a smart mouth. I fucked with that because that timid shit would get boring real fast.

"Yea, but it's Saturday."

"Like you said, I don't get out much."

"I was asking you a question,"I chuckled. "But thanks for answering it. So you a freshman or sophomore?"

"Neither,"she giggled. "I'm a senior."

"Swear?"

"Swear."

"Damn, and I thought I knew damn near every senior. What year did you start going here?"

"2016."

"Dang…I started in 2015 and I've never seen you. That's crazy."

"Or you've walked past me countless times."

"Nah, I would've noticed you."

"Doubt it,"she mumbled. "So what's your major?"

"General Business."

"Interesting. Are you graduating this year, super senior?"

"Super senior? Oh, you got jokes,"I nodded, resulting in her laughing. A huge, pretty smile accompanied by the whitest teeth overcame her face. Yea, she was more than cute. She was beautiful.

"A nigga started off rocky, but yea, I'm graduating this year."

"Perfect. It's not about how you start the race but how you finish it. Graduating in five years is actually the norm nowadays."

Her encouraging words made a nigga feel like he was doing something right in life even though she didn't say much.

"What about you?"

"I've been on the dean's list since I got here, so yea…I'll be graduating on time."

"That's what up, baby. I guess not having a life paid off."

"Yea, that's what I was telling my Aun-wait, what?!"She shrieked, as I laughed my head off. She picked up a sparkly throw pillow and tossed it at me, but I caught it.

"Aye, don't take that personally. I just had to get my lick back."

"Yea, okay,"she laughed, showing that she didn't take my joke to heart. I liked that.

"Since you pretty much got this semester in the bag you might as well start having fun. College is a once in a lifetime experience, and yea, school comes first but you gotta have fun too."

"Me and fun don't really go together."

"Fun is my best friend. I practically run the party scene here. If you're my friend I can show you a good time."

She nodded her head. "Okay."

"Yea?"

"Yea, I don't see why not."

We continued talking about everything under the sun from our hometown of New Orleans, Louisiana, what part of the city we grew up in, and why we chose UBR. Apparently her upbringing was a lot different from mine. Her parents were both doctors, she attended private school, and grew up in an East Over mansion. I was from the Calliope projects, but my parents moved us out after Hurricane Katrina to a middle class area in Gentilly. My mom was a manager at a hotel, and my dad had his own popular snowball stand. For most of my life I hadn't wanted for much and they were always willing to help me, but they didn't have an excessive amount of money to blow. That's why I used my popularity to my advantage and started throwing parties for profit because being broke was for the birds. The conversation was flowing so well between us that I was aggravated when Shad exited Clarissa's room. I wasn't ready to leave, but I still said goodbye and got her number on my way out.

"Man, that bitch was loose as fuck."Shad complained the moment we made it to his car.

"So you not coming back?"

"Hell n- wait, you want to come back?"He chuckled. "You fucking with big mama?"

"Nigga grow up,"I spat, as he laughed hard. "That girl is not even that big."

"I mean, when I saw her she had on some big ass clothes that did nothing for her so I saw what I saw. But she *big fine*, for sure. I can think of some niggas who would find her attractive. I just didn't think you would based on your track record."

"She was cool people. I could see us being homies,"I said, keeping it light.

"Well you don't need me to come back over here with you if that's the case. Cause Clarissa got one hitter quitter pussy."

Chapter 2

Kamaria

I rushed into the union, anxious to get out the blistering
cold. Ice cold days in south Louisiana weren't common, but
when they happened it was like a snow storm for us all who
weren't used to it. There were already talks about them giving
us a few days off because of freezing temperatures that could
result in icy roads. We weren't prepared to handle that type of
weather, so for safety reasons they'd shut us down. I never
complained about a day off, so hopefully the rumors were true.

I went straight to my favorite food spot in the union
called "Refresh" so I could grab a loaded baked potato and a
salad. It wasn't super packed since most people opted for
Chick-Fi-La, Popeyes, or Canes. I didn't really indulge in fast
food too much, although Canes was a guilty pleasure of mine.
I was in and out of Refresh in five minutes, and looking for a

place to sit alone. Looking for a solo table upstairs was a waste of time. It was a known fact that the calmest areas in the union were downstairs. I'd even taken naps on couches that were ducked off on the lower level. As I was walking to one of the back staircases, I saw a group of people coming up the stairs. My heart skipped a beat when I noticed Kyree. He was all in some pretty girl's face grinning from ear to ear, so he didn't notice me. Of course he didn't notice me. He'd walked past me plenty of times and never looked twice. I told him this last weekend and he acted like the thought was preposterous. It was evident that he was just being nice to me because he never used my number that he asked for. This was *Kyree*. A notorious party boy and ladies man. I wasn't even in the mix and I'd heard about him. His physical appearance said a lot too. The nigga looked too good for words. His smooth, peanut butter skin, sharp jawline, smoldering cheeks, soft looking pink lips, nice teeth, pretty smile, honey brown eyes, and brown and blonde ombre shoulder length locks made him pretty much perfect and out of my league. I wasn't extremely insecure at all. When I looked in the mirror I couldn't say I was ugly or had a terrible body, but I was a realist. The super attractive, model-like guys didn't go for girls like me. I'd accepted that a long time ago, but for some reason I thought me and Kyree hit it off well enough to at least be friends.

"Ou! Girl, I like that bag and I've been looking for it! Where'd you get it?" A girl in the group looked directly at me, so it was safe to say she was talking about my new Gucci backpack that my Auntie Sana got me as a gift for Christmas. She was a successful lawyer with no kids, so she was always spoiling me.

I smiled back at her. "I'm honestly not sure. I'll have to ask my Auntie because she got it for me.

It seemed like the entire group stopped when she acknowledged me, and that included Kyree. He leaned closer, like he was just noticing me. I was pretty sure I didn't look any different from the other night. I was in public, so I presumed I looked better. I wore a black trench coat, a black graphic t-shirt, tight black joggers, original brown UGGS, a Gucci scarf, and a Gucci baseball cap over my fresh straight sew-in that I had pulled back into a ponytail. I woke up not wanting to deal with my hair, so I didn't.

"Kamaria?"Kyree squinted. "Girl, I ain't even see you. I see you tryna be all incognito and shit."

"You know her?" The girl he was flirting with, scoffed. She reminded me of the famous rapper and sex symbol, Rubi Rose, but she was nowhere near as overtly sexy as her and she had auburn hair. She was dressed like a typical "hot" girl on campus in yoga pants, a cropped sweater, a jean jacket, and Nike sneakers.

"Yea,"he smiled, making my cheeks burn. "This my homie, Mari."

I stifled a smile at the impromptu nickname he'd given me. I'd never had a nickname before, so I liked it. It made me feel special.

"Hey!"

"Hi!"

"Wassup!"

Everybody gave me friendly greetings in unison, except the girl with the orange hair.

"You want to sit with us?"Kyree asked.

"Um, I wa-"

"Girl, come on!"The girl who'd inquired about my bag grabbed my hand and pulled me along, taking me by surprise. "I'm Essence by the way! This is Tysean, Lark, Dale, Zion, and Mary."

Mary. That was the name of the girl who had to be Kyree's girlfriend because she was eyeing me like she had a problem. Everyone else offered warm smiles, so I ignored her weird energy. They already had food from a Chinese spot that was downstairs. I'd eaten there before and the food was good, but it did not agree with my stomach. Kyree walked straight to a table by the large glass window, giving off the impression that they normally sat there. I typically passed up this area because it was always loud and packed. It was definitely a hot spot for popular students who wanted to socialize. Now I was being thrown into the mix and being forced to socialize. Shockingly, I wasn't too nervous. I already knew Kyree was nice, and almost everybody else seemed cool too. So I was just going to go with the flow and not psych myself out.

"Girl, you're an Accounting major? So, you're like really good at math then?"Essence asked in fascination.

"I mean, she's made it this far, so I would assume she's good at math,"Tysean said in jest. He seemed to be the funny one in the group, and he was easy on the eyes. His brown complexion, big lips, and dimples were yummy.

"Everybody ain't able,"Lark groaned, while twisting her pretty hair that was down her back. I was good at deciphering real and fake hair, and her thick black tresses appeared to be all natural. She was a few shades lighter than me, so her hazel eyes really popped. "Me and Essence have been taking the same math class for the past two semesters."

"Hoe, don't be telling my business,"Essence scoffed, making everybody laugh, including me.

"What math class is this if you don't mind me asking?"I asked.

"Statistics."

"I passed that class two years ago and I saved all my notes. I can give them to y'all."

"Girl, I fucks with you!"Lark exclaimed.

"Do you have to be so loud?"Dale clutched his ear. As an introvert I was a pro at recognizing another one right away. I questioned how he'd gotten cool with them until Lark revealed that he was her older brother by a year.

"You know your sister is ghetto,"Kyree smirked.

"Says the nigga from the projects,"Lark tittered.

"Alright, with yo' country ass."

"Country?"Lark and Dale repeated as if that were ridiculous, but their accents were strong. Their "twangs" were heavy.

"Dallas is a major city, nigga. You got us messed up,"Dale said, suddenly having a whole lot to say.

"And? So is New Orleans,"Kyree threw back.

"Boyyyy, that small ass hick town!"Lark shrieked.

"Alright bitch, not too much,"Essence held her hand up.

"Girl, you from Kenner, so stay out of that,"Zion said. She'd let it be known already that she was a Baton Rouge native.

"It's all the same shit to anybody from out of town, so like I said, not too much on New Orleans."Essence sassed.

"Man, just because ya mama named you Essence don't mean you automatically gotta go up for New Orleans,"Lark said.

"I'm saying,"Dale cosigned.

"It really don't matter what y'all saying. At the end of day y'all still some cowboy boot wearing, bull riding, hillbillies."Kyree went in, propelling me to burst into laughter.

"Oh, that's funny?"Lark questioned with her head tilted to the side.

"I mean, when it comes to my city I'ma ride."

"That's what I'm talking bout,"Kyree held his hand out for me to slap it, and I obliged.

"So that's how you know her?"Mary spoke up for the first time since we'd sat down. She'd been sitting there with a dry look on her face, exuding ugliness. "Because y'all are both from New Orleans?"

"Yea,"he lied with a grin. "We're old friends, right, Mari?"

"Rightttt,"I giggled, going with it. Besides, that was a better way for him to say he knew me over the real reason.

"What part of New Orleans are you from?"She asked me.

"The East,"I replied evenly. I wasn't feeling her vibe, so I wasn't going to play nice. My shyness didn't translate into being a pushover or doormat. I demanded respect from people because I gave nothing less.

"Oh, so you're a rich, suburban girl."

I laughed. "What would give you that assumption?"

"Because I know about The Ea-"

"Then you're ill-informed, sweetie. The East has a lot of rough parts. In fact, most people lock their doors when they drive through. I'm pretty sure a girl like you would get car jacked by some kids with ease. However, the part of the East I'm from is nice. My parents worked hard and I've been fortunate to have a good upbringing."

"So the answer to my question was yes,"she rolled her eyes.

"You asked me a question? Because the tone of your voice said you were making a statement based merely off of ignorance and nothing more."

Essence choked on her water, while Lark, Zion, and Dale laughed. Kyree looked at me in awe like he didn't expect me to go there. People always assumed that I could be tried. They didn't know that my parents threw me to the wolves early. For most of my life I went to predominantly white private schools. I learned how to gather bitches early on in life with just the power of my tongue.

"Ignorance?! Ain't shit igno-"

"Mary, chill out,"Zion cut her off. "It's not that deep, and you started with her."

"I didn't do this girl nothing!"

"You were on some passive aggressive shit, and it didn't go over her head like you assumed it would. Let it go,"Kyree ordered. His word was seemingly enough, because she went back into her dry ass bubble. The conversations died down a little as everyone dug into their food forreal. I didn't like eating in front of other people, so I was holding back on my chicken caesar salad.

"So how's your week been so far?"Kyree leaned over and asked me.

I put my fork down. "Boring and cold. I just wanna climb in my bed this weekend and sleep."

"Damn, and I was gonna hit you up about some parties."

"You partying in this weather?"I raised an eyebrow. I didn't see how anyone could even have fun in the freezing cold.

"The party's inside, love,"he grinned. "Besides, I ain't letting a little chilly weather make me miss out on money."

"So you get paid for every party you throw?"

"Hell yea. Otherwise it's no benefit to me."

All the partying he did made perfect sense to me now. It was a job for him.

"Well I'll definitely be willing to go out with you on a warmer weekend."

"You better mean that. Don't be giving me the round around."

"If you really plan on hitting me up then I'll go."

"You think I won't?"

"You didn't this week,"slipped from my mouth before I could catch it. I instantly felt desperate, but the smile that overcame his face put me at ease.

"Yea, well, there were no parties this week so I saw no need to hit your line. Since I see that you just wanna talk with a nigga then I'll definitely text you."

"What?" My face got hot as my stomach bubbled. Now he was thinking I was sitting by the phone waiting for his ass, so I definitely looked desperate. "Calm down, it's not even like th-"

"You hot?"Kyree frowned at me as I fanned myself with my mini notebook.

"A little."I downplayed it, even though I was starting to burn up.

"Take your jacket off,"he suggested. "We're right by the heaters."

I didn't plan on removing my jacket when I got dressed today, but if I continued sitting here with it on I'd start sweating and I didn't want that. So I stood up, and slipped it off.

"DAMN! Good googly moogly!"I heard a deep male

voice say from behind me, followed by laughter and other cat

calls. I was sure they were harassing some poor girl, but that

had nothing to do with me. I put my jacket on the back of my

chair neatly.

"That ass is huge!"

"That's the BBW Drake must've been talking about!"

"Say, sit down,"Kyree said in a demanding tone that

confused me. I was about to sit back down anyway, so I

offered no objections as I slipped back into my seat.

"Girl, you got a body on you, huh?"Essence smiled,

before poking her tongue out.

"Huh?"

"Huh?"Lark mocked me, resulting in a few snickers.

"You ain't slick, tryna hide all that ass under that trench coat.

Based on the reaction you just got, ion blame you. These

niggas is thirsty around here."

"The reaction?"I questioned in bewilderment, and then

it hit me. Those cat calls were for me! I'd had a huge butt

since I was about 11, but my mom always made it seem like a

bad thing. I wasn't completely sheltered, so I knew modern day society glamourized big butts. But they had to be on a certain type of girl with a certain body type. Since I didn't fit the bill I never saw my body as desirable. Everyone's reaction had me in a state of shock, and I could feel something inside of me shifting. I just couldn't put my finger on it. I did know that I wouldn't be in a rush to put that trench coat back on.

"Maybe you should put it back on,"Kyree suggested. "These lames ass niggas be doing too much."

"No, it's too hot over here."I politely declined. I felt good about myself and I wasn't ready for it to end.

"Oh, you hot?Well maybe you should take this off!"

That weirdo bitch Mary reached over the table and pulled my hat off. I hadn't bothered flat ironing my leave-out this morning, so I had a bad case of hat hair. It was an unspoken rule to never remove a black girl's hat, and she just maliciously violated it. I was out of my seat in less than a second, and both of my hands were mushing her face roughly. Maybe she thought I only had a mouth on me, but she had me fucked up. She wouldn't be the first girl that I had to tussle with because they thought they were going to bully me.

"Oh, shit!"Kyree shouted, before pulling me away.

"Did she just put her hands on me?!"Mary shouted in disbelief.

"I mean, you touched her first,"Zion rolled her eyes as she snatched my hat from her. She rushed over to me to put it back on my head as Kyree held me from behind. I had no idea why he was restraining me. It wasn't like I was trying to get at that bitch. I didn't regret what I'd done, but I didn't want things to escalate. I wasn't about to get expelled for a bitch I barely knew. I seriously didn't know what her problem was, but I hope she learned that I wasn't the one.

"Can somebody bring me my stuff?"I asked, calmly.

"You scared to come back over here, nappy head hoe?!"

I laughed. "Yea, I got a head full of nappy, healthy ass hair and I love it. Better than being edgeless with thin hair. And scared? You clearly just saw that I'm far from that, stupid bitch."

She had a silky hair texture but it looked like she'd dyed it one too many times and applied a little too much heat. Her edges were thin and her roots were fried.

"Whatever, fat ass!"

Now that could've hurt me, but it was so unoriginal. My family had been calling me fat since I was 8.

"Mary, just walk away. You're embarrassing yourself for no reason,"Essence begged, as Lark gathered my backpack, food, and coat.

"Walk away?! Tell her to walk away! Y'all supposed to be my friends and all up her ass!"

"Friends?! We cool and all, but you fucking Kyree don't make us friends. At this rate you won't be sitting with us no more. This drama is so childish,"Essence said.

"Fuck all y'all! Kyree, lose my number."

"I never use that shit anyway,"he muttered, as she stormed off in the opposite direction. He looked down at me. "You good?"

"Yea...but keep her away from me."

"Shit, I'm keeping her crazy ass away from me. She think we go together or something."

"I'm sure you have something to do with that."I smirked.

He grinned, before licking his lips. "I'm an upfront guy, so that's impossible."

My heart skipped as I held his gaze. Someone clearing their throat tore our eyes from one another.

"Here,"Essence handed me my things. "Sorry about that, girl. She is not a friend of ours. That's one of Kyree's many flavors."

Hearing how she casually referred to the many girls he had was scary. Would us hanging out mean that I would have more run-ins like that? It wasn't worth it considering this boy didn't want me like that anyway. I'd be in drama for no reason at all.

"Chill, Essence, before I get my nigga Shad on you."

"Shad not my man,"she tittered. "Let me get your number, Kamaria. Cause I need those statistics notes."

I exchanged numbers with her, and said goodbye to everybody. Through all of this, Kyree was posted up behind me with his arm still around me.

"Can I move now?"

"Oh, shit,"he chuckled, before dropping his arm. "My b, whatchu finna get into?"

"Well I had one more class but I'm not in the mood."

"Awww, don't let that bullshit make you skip. She was just hating."

"On what?"

He gave me a look as if I was playing with him.

"Why you think?"

"I honestly don't know, but I can stand to miss this class. Over 60 people are in it and attendance never gets taken."

"Well, I'm done for the day. Let's go do something fun…that's my way of apologizing for that bullshit that just took place."

"I told you I just wanted my bed, Kyree."

"You can have that after I take you somewhere,"he smiled cutely, making him hard to resist.

"What do you have in mind?"

"Movie Tavern. We can eat and watch a movie."

I wasn't going to tell him that Movie Tavern was one of my favorite spots in BR. I loved a fancy movie theater.

"That sounds cool, but I just ate."

"No, you picked at your food like you was scared of it. You gotta still be hungry, so I gotta feed you. Let's go." He patted the small of my back, urging me to walk ahead of him. One side of me was doing the most and over thinking this shit like it was an actual date, but the other side of me knew not to read into anything he was doing. Like Essence said before, he had plenty of flavors so I was certain he didn't have an appetite for me.

Chapter 3

Kyree

February 7, 2020

You would think someone had died with the way my mama was blowing up my phone, but I knew better. She hadn't talked to me since yesterday morning and it was brief. Looking down at my phone I saw I had a series of 12 missed calls over the past two hours. I'd been sleeping and my phone was on "do not disturb", serving its purpose. Before my mama put a missing persons flier up on Facebook for me, I quickly called her back on Facetime.

"What the fuck do you have going on, Mr.?!" She questioned as soon as the call connected, making me laugh.

"I was sleep, crazy lady."

"Crazy?! Boy, don't get fucked up by getting beside yourself, nah. Why the fuck you so tired anyway?"

"Hmmm, let's see…maybe because I'm a full time college student and it's my last semester."

"You know what the fuck I mean, smart ass. We haven't been talking as often as we used to. Your daddy said the last time he spoke with you was a few days ago."

"I mean, do we have to *talk* everyday, mama? Lawd…"

She looked momentarily stunned until a knowing look washed over her pretty face. Most people would swear up and down I looked just like my mother until they saw me next to my father. That's how I wanted my kid to be; a perfect combination of me and their mom. Kids weren't something I was anticipating until I reached my thirties though. I had shit to do, and being tied down with major responsibilities wasn't on my goals list.

"Kyree Genesis Pierre, who the hell is she?"

Laughter escaped my mouth. "What?"

"Who's the fast tailed little girl that got you acting brand new with the lady who gave birth to you?"

"Fast tailed?"I chuckled. "I ain't heard that one in a minute."

"Hold up,"she squinted. "Are you at her place?!"

"Huh?"I uttered in confusion. How could she possibly know where I was?

"If you can huh then you can hear! Unless you re-decorated with pink and blue curtains, fuzzy throw pillows, and a bedazzled lamp then your ass is not at home."

"Wowww,"I threw my head back. Women really noticed every fucking thing.

"Wow, my ass. Go ahead and tell me who she is, Kyree. Now."

Before I could find the words to respectfully tell her to mind her business, the door swung open. Even though I'd seen her multiple times that day, I still froze up. Kamaria was my friend and I planned on keeping things platonic because I enjoyed her company. But I couldn't deny that she was looking good. She was simple in a black and yellow Off-White workout set, black Vapormax, and a black Louis Vuitton tote bag. I'd noticed weeks ago that she had a thing for designer shit, but as we got closer I saw that she wasn't really consumed by them. Her family had money, so her wardrobe merely reflected that. She wasn't obsessed like some niggas and females I knew.

Besides, Kamaria could probably wear a potato sack and make it look good with her body. She expressed to me that she was always taught to hide her body so she wouldn't draw attention to herself, but those days were seemingly over. As the weeks went by, she wore shorter jackets, tighter jeans, leggings, and figure hugging workout gear that showed off her thick ass shape. I was cool with all walks of life on campus, so I heard niggas inquiring about her first hand. I was also able to kill their dreams on the spot. Since we were cool, I was looking out for her like a good friend would. These niggas wasn't on shit. All they wanted to do was have bragging rights about laying her down. Kamaria had flown under the radar for the longest, so her mystique was alluring. I loved witnessing her new budding confidence first hand, and I was kind of selfish when it came to her friendship. However, I knew I wasn't being overbearing because I'm sure she would've said something. She seemed to enjoy my company just as much as I enjoyed hers.

"I got you some food,"she held a Canes bag, making me smile. She was by far the most thoughtful girl I'd encountered. She also picked up on small shit. Only people that had known me for a long time knew that I had to eat something whenever I woke up or I would get hangry.

"Is that her?!"

Shit. I forgot my nosey ass mama was on the phone.

"Ma, chill,"I laughed. The terrified look on Kamaria's face was humorous.

"Can I see her?"She asked. "As a matter of fact, give her the phone."

Kamaria shook her head "no" vehemently, making me laugh harder.

"She's scared? Tell her I don't bite."

"She can hear you, lady."

"So she gon be rude and not come to the phone?"

That seemed to knock the fear out of her. She sat my food down on the bed, before sitting next to me and putting her head in the camera's view.

"Hiiii,"she said timidly with a small wave.

My mom's eyes seemed to brighten up at the sight of her, and my chest swelled with pride. I thought the world of my parents, so their approval on anything meant a lot to me. It was never the deciding factor, but it held a lot of weight.

"Mama, this is Kamaria. Mari, this is my mom, Mrs. Pierre."

"Well aren't you a pretty little thing!"My mom exclaimed.

"Thank you,"she smiled.

"You're welcome, baby. And don't pay my son no mind. You can call me Ms.Nette."

"I thought you said you don't let nobody who was born in the 90's call you by your first name?"I questioned, repeating a line she'd told my first girlfriend who I took to homecoming in 9th grade. She ripped poor Quisha's head off because the girl called her "Ms. Lanette." Now she was allowing my friend she just laid eyes on for the first time to call her by her nickname.

"Kyree, don't question me,"she hissed. "Anyway, Miss Mari, how old are you?"

"21, but I'll be 22 in April."

"Are you graduating this semester?"

"Hopefully."

I looked at her sideways. "Ma, she's tryna be modest. She's been on the dean's list for four years straight. She's graduating this semester and at the top of the class, I bet."

"Kyreeee," she whined. One thing I noticed about her is that she hated hyping herself up. If she didn't want to do it, then that was her prerogative, but she couldn't stop me from bragging about her.

"That's amazing, baby! I see you got brains to match that beauty. What do you plan on doing after college?"

"Well, my degree will be in accounting so I'll have plenty of options as far as jobs go."

"Ok, Kyree's degree is in business. Maybe you can help him with his books," she grinned, and I shook my head. My mama always went on and on about how the woman I needed to be with would elevate my life in every way possible, including financially. So she was undoubtedly taking this shit and running with it.

"If he ever needs help I'll be there."

"Oh, really?"

"Yea, that's what friends are for."

"And that's all y'all are?"

Kamaria looked at me, and it was evident that she wanted me to take over this interrogation.

"No, don't look at him, baby. I'm talking to you. Are y'all really only friends?"

"Y-yea."

I wasn't sure what her hesitance was about because for the past month we'd kept it strictly platonic.

"You let all your friends take midday naps in your bed?"

That was my que to step in.

"Alright, mama, that's enough. Forreal."

"Oh boy, please! I'm just tryna get some clarity."

"There's no clarity to be had because we've both made it clear. We're friends. The end."

"Hmmp, well the definition of friends must've changed from back in my day."

"Really? Because I could've sworn dad said you and him were strictly friends at first."

"Strictly friends who've been married for 24 years with three kids. I rest my case. Now let me finish talking to my future daughter in law."

I think she was making it her mission to embarrass me and leave Kamaria flustered, and it was working. We were both mortified but for different reasons.

"Mama, I'll holla at you later,"I said, as I prepared to hang up.

"Wait! Mari, I want you to come to New Orleans with Kyree for Mardi Gras."

"Oh, I'll be there anyway. I'm from New Orleans, too."

"I knew I heard an accent there, but I wasn't sure. Okay, then it's settled. I'll officially be meeting you soon."

"I look forward to it."

"Likewise."

I shifted my eyes because my mama never used words like that in her life with her ghetto ass. I ended the call and immediately started apologizing for my mother's behavior.

"I'm sorry about that. That lady be doing the absolute most."

"Most parents do,"she giggled. "But she had me scared as fuck for a minute."

"Yea, but she liked you. I could tell."

"I liked her too."

"So it's all good then,"I concluded. "Can we go back to my apartment tonight?"

My apartment was more spacious and so was my bed. We'd spent the night with each other more than a few times, but it was always at her place for convenience. She lived on campus, so it was easier for me to get to class from her spot. Her place also felt more cozy. The down side was the full sized bed that came with the dorm style apartment. My apartment was off campus and I had bought my own king sized bed. It would also be more quiet and private over there because I had one roommate opposed to three.

"Ummm…"she scratched her neck. "What did you have in mind for tonight?"

I looked at her weirdly. "Same shit we always do. Watch disney plus or netflix, study, talk shit…why you acting brand new?"

"I'm not, it's just…well, if you don't have any real plans set in stone then I'm gonna go out with Essence, Lark, and Zion."

My heart dropped. Essence and them were my girls. I fucked with them the long way, but I didn't know how I felt about Mari hanging with them. I'd witnessed how they partied on multiple occasions and they went too hard for her to keep up.

"I mean, you sure? I know you prefer staying inside and shit. That's why I didn't throw a party today."

That wasn't really true. My load in school had gotten bigger and harder, so I only started throwing parties on Saturdays. I used my Fridays to finish off all my school work from the hectic week, so I could enjoy the rest of my weekend with no worries. Now the one person who I looked forward to spending my Friday evenings with was trying to ditch me for people I'd introduced her to. I was salty and jealous.

"I don't prefer staying inside, sometimes it's just the best option depending on my homework load or upcoming tests. I'm caught up on everything right now, so I want to finally go out with the girls. Besides, they've been asking me and I'm always coming up with excuses so I'm starting to feel ba-"

"You've been out with them twice before."

"Yea, with you and other males in the mix. We've never had a real girls night. *I've* never had a real girls night. I want to experience one."

I could've continued hating, but that wasn't even like me. I'd never tried to control what a girl in my life did, and I wasn't about to start now. She had every right to go out and enjoy herself. Although my friends were wild I was positive they wouldn't have her on no bullshit.

"Then go have fun."

"So you're not mad?"

"What would I be mad about?"

"I don't know. I know how you like for us to hang out on Friday nights, so I didn't kn-"

"It ain't no pressure about that," I hastily cut her off, even though I felt my chest tightening. To know that she deliberately made plans even though she was aware of what we usually did, bothered me. She basically said fuck me. "I'll

find somebody else to chill with tonight. You go have fun."

A look crossed her face and I didn't know what to make

of it.

"Ok,"she stood up with a heavy breath. "Well you have

fun tonight, too."

Kamaria

In my four years of being at UBR I'd never stepped foot

into a party. In hindsight that was probably for the best

because if I'd experienced a fraction of what I was

experiencing tonight I wouldn't have been nearly as focused

on school. Essence kept fixing me some fruity drink that I'd

fallen in love with. Not only did it taste good, but it was giving

me an indescribable feeling. My body felt all warm and I felt

the sudden need to move my hips to the music. I never

danced in my life, so I probably looked foolish, but I wasn't conscious of that. I had no more inhibitions. I just wanted to have fun.

"Mari, you too fine to be dancing like a white girl,"Essence giggled. "And you from New Orleans! You gotta come better, friend."

"Teach me!"I screamed over the bounce hit "Sit on Dat" by VickeeLo with laughter. If I was sober her words would've made me stop dancing altogether, but I found everything extremely funny.

"Grab onto something with your hands and make them ass cheeks fight!"She instructed. It was a good thing the kickback had started resembling a house party over an hour ago or everybody would've noticed me trying to learn how to dance. Everybody was seemingly under the influence and in their own little worlds as they had a grand ole time. Nobody was worried about me, so that gave me infinite courage to really put Essence's tips to use. I held onto the wall and mimicked exactly what I'd seen other girls in my city doing, but never had the balls to try myself. I always thought I'd look stupid, so I saw no point in trying.

"What?!"Zion screamed, before slapping my ass. I took that as a sign that I was doing good.

"You better fuck it upppp, Mari!"Lark shouted.

"That's my bitch!"Essence hollered, as I turned things up a notch by moving my ass in a circle. I didn't know if it looked good, but I could only assume it did based on their screams and other commentary I was hearing. It was a lot of "ouuus" and "ahhhs," and that boosted my confidence tremendously. I was dancing and I didn't look crazy! It was a miracle! It wasn't long before some guy came up behind me and I was dancing on him. I'd obviously never done anything like this before, but I wasn't scared. It could've been the liquid courage or the fact that I liked what I saw when I turned around to get a glimpse of him. He was a hottie with a body, resembling a darker and buff version of Clarencenyc. Time seemed to get away as I danced to song after song with my new dance partner. Even when the DJ stopped spinning ass throwing music, he still stayed by my side. We were jamming to some NBA YoungBoy song that the whole party seemed to know. I knew of him because he was a popular artist straight out of Baton Rouge, but I'd never checked out his music. I was an R&B head, but I had to admit the song was cool. I was jamming with the nameless cutie as he rapped it from word to word.

"I feel like I'm Gucci Mane in 2006. All these diamonds, dancing on my fucking neck cost like four bricks. And the way that I be toting on that strap, don't make no sense. He a million dollar nigga but be posted in the bricks, ayy. It make no sense, yeah..."

"We've been hanging tough for the past hour and I haven't even gotten your name yet,"he laughed, showing off his pretty white teeth.

"Righttt, we've just been dancing and haven't spoken more than two words to each other,"I giggled. "I'm Kamaria."

"Nice to meet you, Kamaria,"he held out his hand, taking me by surprise. "My name is Daniel. Do you attend UBR?"

Based on the way he was just going off to NBA Youngboy I thought he was a little bit more rough around the edges, but he spoke clearly with no obvious accent.

"Yes."

"You must be a freshman,"he guessed. His eyes wandered to my body for a second before he looked back up at my face. That sort of thing would've normally made me feel self conscious but his eyes read that he appreciated everything he saw.

"No,"I giggled. "I'm actually a senior."

"Really? I'm currently a senior at LSU. I'm surprised I haven't seen you on the scene in the past four years."

"Yeaaa, I've mostly been into my books."

"So have I. I just got accepted into LSU's law school."

"Congratulations. I'm sure that wasn't easy."

"It wasn't, but I still made time to have fun."

"Everybody can't split focus like you,"I said in jest to mask my annoyance. It was nothing against him but I'd already gotten this speech from somebody else and I wasn't trying to think about him right now.

"You seem to be splitting focus just fine tonight,"he smirked.

"My girls dragged me out,"I laughed.

"Blame them,"he nodded. "But you more turnt up than all of them combined."

"Well honestly, I made a vow to enjoy my last semester to the fullest. I don't want to regret not enjoying college to the fullest. Ya know?"

"It sounds like the perfect plan to me. Can I be a part of you enjoying this last semester to the fullest?"He grinned.

"We can be friends,"I giggled.

"Just friends?"

"You heard me,"I batted my eyelashes. I wasn't sure when I learned how to flirt but it was coming naturally when I needed it the most.

"Okay, I can handle that for now."

"For now, huh?"

"Yea. I'm a very straight forward man, so I'm letting you know now that my goal in getting to know you is to make you mine. I don't play games, Kamaria."

"Neither do I, so I guess it's good you ran into me. We'll just have to see about me being yours though,"I said confidently, when my heart was thumping in my chest. I'd never had a man this attractive straight up say that he wanted me…*ME!* I was flattered and scared at the same time, but I couldn't let him see that.

"We'll definitely see, Kamaria,"he smiled, before flicking my chin. "I'm about to go get a drink. Do you want anything?"

"No, I think I've exceeded my limit for the night,"I chortled. Even if I hadn't I wouldn't let a stranger fix me a drink.

"Smart girl,"he smiled. "I'll be right back."

When he swaggered off, Zion stepped over to me with a big smile.

"Mari, do you know who that is?!"

"No,"my eyes danced around. "Should I?"

"That's Daniel Sanders. He's been popular in BR since high school. He used to have all the girls in a frenzy…shit, he still does!"

"You went to highschool with him?"I asked, hoping to get the inside scoop on him.

"No, I only ever saw him around and through social media. He's a local celebrity girl, and you have his full attention. I'm so happy for you, mamas,"she held her chest like a proud parent.

"Relax,"I tittered. "It's hardly that serious."

"Okay, I just better be in the wedding. I'll be the flower girl."

"I can't with you, Zi."I laughed so hard that my stomach ached.

"Bitchhhhh,"Essence stepped over to us with big eyes.

"What?"Zion asked.

"Kyree is responding to my stories on Instagram losing his damn mind over you."She pointed to me, making my heart drop.

She stepped between me and Zion to show us what she was talking about. I thought she may have been exaggerating, but she wasn't. Kyree was responding to almost every story Essence had posted of me.

"Wtf..."

"Y'all down bad. I can see her ass."

"Why would she wear that? This got y'all all over it because she don't even dress like that. Smh."

"Where y'all at? Y'all got my girl out here bad. I'm coming get her."

Suddenly I was conscious of my outfit, as I pulled down my high waist jean shorts that I'd paired with a pink Chanel t-shirt and Chanel sneakers. It was a 65 degree night in February, so I took advantage of that by wearing something more revealing. Since we were only attending a kick back/ house party I kept it casual but cute. My versatile sew-in was in a cute ponytail, showing off my Chanel earrings, and I also wore a small pink Chanel crossbody purse. All my pricey items were courtesy of my Auntie. She'd be so proud if she saw me right now, and I was happy about my outfit too until I saw what Kyree said. I knew these shorts were kind of risque when I put them on, and I felt my ass falling out whenever I walked or danced but I also liked what I saw when I looked in the mirror.

"Bitch, don't let him get in your head. You look the fuck good, and he knows it too!"Essence twisted her neck.

"Yea, he's just hating because he's not here with you."

"Well…maybe I should call him. I don't want him to be mad at me. Or maybe you can tell him where we are so he can co-"

"Mari, no,"Essence said firmly.

"Why?"I heard myself whine. Kyree was my friend and I valued that. I didn't want him to be mad.

"For one, it's a girls night so he needs to fall back,"Zion folded her arms. "We don't play about inviting niggas out on our girls nights, Mari."

"Amen,"Essence cosigned. "And you like that nigga too much."

"He's my friend."

"Bitch, please,"she huffed. "You like him more than a friend and he likes you more than a friend. I would encourage y'all to stop playing but Kyree is full of games, and I don't want you looking like a duck."

"What do you mean?"

"You don't need to be catering to him when he's not even making it clear to you what he wants."

"But I'm not making it clear either, so can I really hold it against him?"

"YEA!"They answered in unison.

"You're the prize, Mari! As the man he needs to chase you and let you know what it is!"Zion explained while tilting her head to the side.

"Okay, so I can't enjoy him as a friend in the meantime?"

"Of course you can,"Essence scoffed. "A real platonic friend…not like a friend you have feelings for because there's a clear difference. As long as you do that he'll continue to play games."

"How's he playing games though?"I squinted. I couldn't help but feel like they were being a tad bit dramatic. Yea, Kyree had me friendzoned but I didn't think there was malicious intent behind that. He could've been scared to take things to the next level just like I was.

"Because he's in my dm's going off about you having fun but he's laid up with Mary. The proof is all in her close friends."

My heart plummeted. He ran back to that evil bitch after she came at me crazy over him? Maybe I'd been giving Kyree way more credit than he deserved. I heard the whispers about how he was a dog and how no girl's heart was safe with him. The more I got to know him I felt like it was all a bunch of gossip that carried no validity. Maybe it was time for me to wake up.

Chapter 4

Kyree

February 12, 2020

"Kyree, you heard me?"

His mouth had been moving and words were coming out but I definitely hadn't been listening. My mind was all over the place. I was frustrated with myself for not being prepared for a pop quiz in my Management 3830 class. I liked to stay ready for anything, so I was disappointed in myself for not being on point. Then the party I was supposed to be throwing this weekend had to be canceled because the club I was having it at had gotten shut down due to health code violations. Finding another venue this short notice was out of the question, so I was shit out of luck and losing out on money. Worst of all, somebody I'd gotten used to making my days better was acting weird with me. I didn't know what the fuck Kamaria's problem was, but ever since her ass had attended that party this past weekend she'd been acting funny with me. The routine that we'd fallen into didn't seem to be a thing anymore and I was starting to think it was throwing everything else in my life off. I stared down at our most recent text message thread in my feelings because she'd brushed me off about hanging out *again.* She gave me some bogus excuse about having a study group, but she was so cap. She didn't like studying with other people. Anytime we studied together I'd have to be dead silent so she could focus. I was tired of the bullshit, so I straight up asked her if she had a problem with me. She had the audacity to lie and say no. So now I was sitting in the quad, waiting for her ass to walk out of the math building. I knew her schedule like I knew my social security number. We were going to get to the bottom of things today.

"Kyree?!"

"What, Shad?"I finally acknowledged him, not bothering to mask my aggravation. I would've preferred being alone right now, but my friends didn't know how to read the room.

"Nigga, I was trying to tell you that you should just move the party to our apartment."

"Man, hell no. I ain't having no randoms in my shit."

"*Our* shit,"he corrected.

"Right, we both signed leases with our names on it so why the fuck would we throw a big ass party there and be held responsible for whatever potentially goes wrong?"

Tysean chuckled. "Yo, he got a point."

"That nigga be thinking too hard,"Shad mumbled.

"Or maybe you don't think enough,"Dale laughed.

"You know he don't be using his whole brain all the time,"Ty tittered.

"Aye, fuck all y'all,"Shad spat, only resulting in more laughter.

"Y'all niggas some clowns,"I shook my head as the laughs settled down. That was my way of showing appreciation for their silly banter because it did help me forget all my problems momentarily. I'd met all of them my freshman year. I came to UBR with no home town friends. I mean, there were a few girls I'd graduated with who attended UBR, but I didn't know them like that. I was an athlete all four years of highschool, so most of my close friends were scattered all over playing sports on a collegiate level. I even had some friends who'd made it to the major leagues. I was nervous about moving away from home and meeting new people, but I'd always been a people's person,so it wasn't shocking when I started making friends immediately at summer orientation. The first person I met was Shad because we were assigned roommates at the three day orientation. He was a BR native, and he seemed to know everybody. We hit it off right away and through him I met a lot of people. I left orientation with several associates and hoes thanks to him. We kept in touch for the rest of the summer, and he even came to New Orleans to hang out with me a few times before school started. Of course we naturally decided to be roommates. The freshman dorm we were in was split into four sides, and that's where we met Dale and Tysean. We were all different, but freshman year had a way of making lifelong friendships. We saw each other at our lowest, but we also had bukoo fun. I didn't think we'd be graduating at the same time because college was unpredictable like that. Just because you started with someone it didn't mean you'd finish with them. However, Dale and Tyseans engineering majors took them five years. Then there was me and Shad who got carried away with our social lives and it affected our grades. Ultimately, that was water under the bridge now. We'd bounced back and we were graduating soon. No one could tell us shit.

"So you just gon give up on the party?"Shad questioned.

"Nigga, you ain't worried about Kyree's party. You worried about them pills you not gon be able to sell at the party,"Ty said, exposing the real reason he was so hard up.

"What?"He sucked his teeth. "Nigga, I'ma get these pills off regardless."

Shad was the pill man on campus. Whatever anybody needed, he had it on deck. There'd been plenty of times I purchased shit from him myself to make myself relax whenever I had a big test or something. He was the real deal, and he'd managed to make a killing while keeping it on the low. My parties were crucial to him because that's where he made a lot of his money.

"Then you gon have to do that this weekend, playboy,"Tysean quipped.

"Nigga where the fuck is my J's I been asking about since Christmas?"Shad countered. Ty was in the business of reselling popular tennis shoes, and made thousands a week off of that shit. Ty's grandparents were well off, so he got a loan from his grandpa to start his business and he hadn't looked back since. Everytime new sneakers would drop, he'd buy them in bulk and then resell them for double or triple the price they retailed for. People loved to complain about how people like him were ruining the shopping experience for sneakerheads, but that didn't stop their dumb asses from spending money with him.

"Obviously not in your possession. Nigga you missed the drop and I ain't restocking no time soon."

"I should report you. I'm sure what you doing is illegal anyway."

"Shad, you should be the last nigga talking about something being illegal,"Dale laughed. "Y'all niggas need to be thinking bout y'all futures."

"Mannn, this nigga get a paid internship with a Software company and all of a sudden he want preach to us. Wasn't you just the weedman around here?"Shad asked with his fingers on his chin as if he was really trying to remember.

"That was so long ago…I mean, who really remembers?"Dale waved his hands around as if he couldn't recall. Truthfully, he did sell weed during his sophomore and junior year. He used his lowkey work study job in the library as a coverup, and it worked out perfectly. He bowed out gracefully on his own once he felt like he'd made enough to get him through his final years of school. Now he was solely focused on his future which would be 100% legit.

"I think it's evident that I'm the only one who's stayed on a clean path so far,"I said just to agitate them.

"Good for you, nigga. You want a cookie?"Dale sneered.

"Yea. You got any with weed in 'em?"I jested, making Ty and Shad double over in laughter. Dale was in the middle of a good comeback for me, when we were interrupted.

"Hey, hey, hey,"Essence walked up with Zion.

"Wassup, y'all?"I stood up to give them half hugs. Before meeting them, I never had strictly platonic girl friends. I met them in my sophomore year through Lark because she was Dale's little sister. They were always around, so we all just got really cool. Essence and Rashad had even dated off and on. They were currently off, but they still argued like they were on. I could always count on them to be my personal form of entertainment.

"Be careful about who you hug, bro,"Shad said, after I sat back down. See, he was already starting.

"What, nigga?"I grinned. I was preparing myself to laugh because I knew whatever this fool said next would be hilarious.

"You don't want nobody coming to you as a man over this one,"he pointed at Essence.

She sucked her teeth and rolled her eyes. "Shad, suck out my ass with a straw!"

"You just say anything,"he looked at her in disgust.

"And you don't?! You the one starting with me, but that's nothing new!"

"How I'm starting with you because I'm warning my nigga about you. He don't need to be in no shit."

"No, you're being petty. It's not my fault you and my new trade exchanged words."

"Man, what?"I laughed.

"Oh, your boy ain't tell you?"She blinked her eyes, with her hand on her hip. "This ignorant ass nigga took a picture of me sleeping and sent it to someone I'm dating."

"How he get a picture of you sleeping though?"Dale scratched his head.

"Yea, that was my first question too,"Zion gave her a disappointed look.

"Look, all that is beside the point! He was being messy!"

"I just thought the guy should know,"Shad shrugged. "Now all of a sudden I gotta watch my back because he gon whoop my ass. So like I said, Kyree, don't be hugging her in public or else you gon be watching your back, too."

"Shad, you gotta be stopped,"Ty laughed hysterically.

I laughed too, but I didn't have anything to say. This was classic Shad and Essence. They'd date other people but always find their way back to each other, so I always chose to mind my business. I had more pressing matters to discuss with Essence anyway, and I hadn't been able to catch up with her or any of the other girls this week.

"Say, Essence, have you seen Mari today?"

"Yea,"she replied flatly.

"Okayyy, where is she?"I asked, while looking at her strangely. Her demeanor had shifted and all of a sudden she was being dry with me like I'd done her something.

"You have her number. Hit her up and ask her to link,"Zion suggested.

"Mannn..."I uttered. My suspicions were being proven true. Kamaria was mad about something and they were all in cahoots about it. I felt betrayed in a way because I thought me and Kamaria were real friends. If she had an issue with me then I should've heard it first. I also introduced her to my friends, and she'd seemingly hijacked them from me. I was supposed to have their loyalty first, but they'd obviously picked their side.

"Exactly,"Essence pursed her lips and rolled her eyes. "Niggas…"

"Niggas?"I repeated in derision. "What the fuck is really going on?"

"They then corrupted Kamaria and got all in her head. That's what. I told you to keep her from round them,"Shad shook his head. He'd never told me that, so he had to be saying it just to get under Essence's skin and it worked.

"Boy, fuck you! I sure did put *my* friend up on game! She don't need to be pressed over no nigga who's laying up with the next bitch! Especially a bitch who came at her wrong."

"Yo…what the fuck are you talking about, Essence?"I glared at her while trying to control my anger. I did still consider her a friend, afterall. But I seriously felt derogatory words on the tip of my tongue that I wanted to aim at her. While I'd been being graceful by staying out of her business with Shad, she'd inserted herself into *my* business with Kamaria.

"You know what she's talking about,"Zion twisted her neck. "You was laid up with Mary but talking down on Mari for having fun with us."

"I wasn't laid up with no fucking Mary! Where y'all get that from?!"

"Her close friends, nigga, so don't try to lie,"Essence said.

"The fuck I gotta lie for?! I was in New Orleans on that night!" I unlocked my phone and went to my camera roll. I scrolled to the photos and videos I took with my family that night. My mom had cooked dinner and my twin sisters were home for the weekend too. Kyana and Kyomi were three years younger than me and in their sophomore year at TSU. Like me, they preferred to spend their weekends at school so they could party. It was rare that they drove home, and they always did it in the spur of the moment. I was laying down when they called me as they were passing through BR. I had them swing by my apartment to pick me up and I drove back home with them. My mama cooked baked chicken, red beans, and cornbread. We were also throwing back her famous homemade hurricanes. That's why my dumbass had started replying to Essence's instagram stories that featured Kamaria. Granted, I meant almost everything I said but I would've controlled myself if I were sober. She wasn't doing anything wrong by enjoying herself. I wanted to be there with her, but it wasn't something I was entitled to and I understood that. When I returned home the next day she seemingly switched up. I thought maybe she felt a way about the things I said to Essence about her, but I went back to look and I didn't say anything too bad so I was lost. Finally, I had answers. Essence's stupid ass had told her that I was with Mary and that was a blatant lie.

"I know what I saw, Kyree,"Essence stated. She was clearly trying to stand on the mess she'd created, but she didn't have a leg to stand on. I could tell by the look on her face that she knew she'd fucked up.

"I haven't fucked with Mary in over a month. I bet she was posting old shit…and yo' duck ass fell for it,"I spat, before standing up. A huge crowd of people were exiting the math building, and Kamaria had to be in it. I knew where she was all along, I only asked Essence to fish for information. I got exactly what I bargained for and it made me realize these hoes weren't my friends like I thought they were.

"You then done it now,"I heard Shad taunting Essence as I stormed off.

I spotted Kamaria from afar as she walked away from the quad in a hurry. She was dressed in a black Nike jogging suit that did her body justice. She had on a black and pink Von Dutch trucker hat, a pink MCM tote, and black fur boots. She looked fine as hell and she was dressed appropriately for the 63 degree weather. I had on a Nike jogging suit myself in gray with black and white dunks, and my Palm Angels backpack. It was funny how we weren't on one accord but we still complimented each other well.

"Mari!"

She stopped for a second, before speeding up again. Was this girl trying to run from me? I did a quick jog to catch up with her. To ensure that she wouldn't go anywhere, I jumped in front of her. We were outside of the quad and standing on the sidewalk across from the Union.

"So you really gon avoid me?"I asked in disbelief.

"No one's avoiding you. I just have somewhere to be."

"Oh, forreal? They gon kick you out of the study group if you late?"I asked sarcastically.

"They might,"she replied, with her eyelashes fluttering. Her attitude brought a smile to my face unwillingly. I wanted to be mad at her for hearing bullshit about me and just running with it, but I missed her too much.

"Man, look…since you playing, I'ma cut straight to it. I wasn't with Mary on Friday night. I was at home. I know you think you saw proof, but I have proof that I was picked up by my sisters around 6:30 and I slept in New Orleans." I gave her my phone where I had my camera roll already on display. I recorded and took pictures from the moment I got in the car with Kyana and Kyomi.

"Whatever Mary posted was bullshit, and I bet she did it for attention," I continued to explain as she examined the evidence. "I'm really disappointed in you though."

"Me?!" She exclaimed after looking up at me.

"Yea, you. We supposed to be friends, bruh. If you thought I did something you didn't like you could've come straight to me."

"Okay, you have a point and I can't dispute that. But I can say the same for you, Ky."

"What?"

"You pretended like you were cool with me going out when you obviously had an issue with it. I was out there bad, huh?"

I sighed heavily as she threw my drunken rant in my face. I started to blame it on the alcohol, but that wasn't me. I had to own my shit.

"Alright, I felt a way because you were having fun without me."

"Really, Kyree? That's so childish."

"It is, but it's also real,"I grabbed her hands and pulled her closer to me. "You were my friend first and I don't be too excited about sharing you…but I gotta get used to it I guess."

"You sure do, *friend*."

I eyed her closely. She should've been smiling by now since I cleared things up and admitted to my wrongdoings. Yet it still looked like she had something on her chest.

"Wassup, Mari?"

"Nothing."

"Nah, something's on your mind. I can tell."

"Nothing is on my mind that I feel like I have to tell you." She removed her hands from mine.

Beep! Beep!

I looked up and saw a familiar face sitting behind the wheel of a red Jaguar.

"Wassup, Kyree?"The guy behind the wheel nodded.

I looked at him trying to gauge who the hell he was.

"It's Daniel…from LSU,"he divulged.

"Ohhh,"I nodded. He'd jogged my memory. We had mutual associates and we'd partied in the same circles on more than one occasion. "Wassup?"

"He's here for me. Excuse me,"Kamaria said meekly, as she moved around me and twisted to the passenger side of his car.

I wanted to say so much but my words became lodged in my throat. Kamaria was dating this nigga? I had no right to feel any way about it because we were just friends…but everybody knew I had feelings for her ass. And I don't care how innocent she pretended to be. She knew it too. That's why she was lying to me about her plans instead of just being straight up. I'd never been more blindsided and hurt in my life. The whole time I thought she was distant because of fake news, when she'd really been distant because she was dating somebody. I stood there with my head fucked up as she drove off with that lame ass nigga. If that's what she wanted then she could have it. I was good.

Kamaria

"So how does a girl like you know Kyree?"Daniel asked a few minutes into the ride. He tried making small talk about my day as well as his but I could tell my interaction with Kyree was on his mind. I guess he couldn't hold back any longer.

"A girl like me? I'm not sure what you mean…"

"I think you do. Y'all are polar opposites."

"Are we?"

"It seems that way. You're a Dean list student who's about her business. He's a super senior and a party boy. What do y'all have in common to be friends?"

"Wait,"I held my hand up, while sporting a frown. I may have been annoyed with Kyree at the moment, but I'd never allow anyone to talk down on him in this manner. "You should know better than anyone that it's very common to not finish college in four years. Most people take five to six years to finish. It doesn't matter how long you take as long as you get the job done."

"That's true, but we all know that Kyree's reason is because he was partying too hard and probably slacked off. His major doesn't call for five or six years."

"How well do you know Kyree?"

"I've been seeing him around for yea-"

"Exactly," I sharply cut him off. "You don't know why he's graduating in his fifth year, and it doesn't matter. He hasn't flunked out and he gets good grades because he's smart...just like me. But that's irrelevant, you shouldn't judge those who do drop out or can't finish. College isn't easy, so we should applaud those who stay, no matter how their path looks"

Daniel smirked. "Are you sure you and him are just friends? You're defending him kinda hard."

"Would you allow someone to just make ignorant comments about your friends? Let me know, because that says a lot about your character."

An amused smile spread across his face, before he started laughing.

"What's so funny? I'd like to laugh."

"Relax,"he chuckled. "I'm laughing because I would've never guessed you had all this fire in you. You be acting all timid and shy most of the time."

"I guess that means you don't know me all that well yet."

"You might be right, and I hope you don't think I was being serious about Kyree. I just wanted to see where your head was at with him. If you claim y'all are just friends then I'll respect that."

"Uh-huh,"I uttered, before pursing my lips with doubt. I was not convinced. To me it looked like he'd put his foot in his mouth and now he was back tracking. Since I'd been enjoying the past few days in his company, I wasn't going to harp on it. It wasn't in my personality anyway. I could let things go pretty easily. That's why the fact that I was stuck on Kyree was annoying. He'd officially friend-zoned my ass and I felt crappy about it. I was hoping that Daniel could distract me from him, but no, he wanted to further discuss him. I was currently thinking of a subject to switch over to, but thankfully, Daniel beat me to the punch.

"You had a test today, right? How'd it go?"

I didn't hesitate to dive into that topic. Daniel enjoyed talking about school just like I did, and it was probably because it was something we both excelled at. He also liked to talk about things like life after college, politics, and ways to make our community better. Honestly, I could barely get a word in those conversations but I didn't mind letting him rant because he seemed passionate about that stuff. He said his ultimate goal in life was to make the world a better place, and I could definitely see him doing that. He kind of put a stain on the way I viewed him once he started judging my friend...but I was going to let that go.

"I can't wait until Mardi Gras break, though,"I said, after telling him how I think I aced my test. "This last semester has been working on my last nerve."

"There's only a few months left. You got this,"he coached. His phone started ringing, so he picked it and looked at the screen. "Man, what the fuck she want..."he muttered to himself, surprising me. The last time I heard him curse was when he was rapping those NBA Youngboy lyrics at the party

I'd met him at. It wasn't just his choice of words though, his vernacular and demeanor had shifted.

"What the fuck you want? I'm busy!"

I looked out the window with a startled face. He was disrespecting the hell out of whoever was on the other end of that call.

"Mannn, I'm not tryna come over there. I got somebody with me, and we bouta go get something to eat."

He'd taken me on a few dates since we'd met, and I'd been to his apartment twice. He never tried anything, but we kissed each other goodbye yesterday. It was nice, but it was also PG because I pulled away prematurely. I swore I'd kick the kiss up a notch today but now I was having second thoughts because he turned me off by talking about Kyree. I was really trying to let that slide though…

"Damn! Y'all can't do shit without me! Is y'all slow?! Why y'all let the nigga in anyway?!....What?! No, the problem is, you a dumb ass BITCH! Fuck, I'm on my way over there right now,"he growled, before ending the call. "Alright, bye Mama."

My eyes almost popped out of my sockets. He was speaking to his mother that way?! What the hell was going on?! I wanted to ask, but I didn't feel comfortable doing so. I clearly didn't know who the hell I was riding with. This man had morphed into someone else when he answered the phone. He went from Martin Lurther King to Suge Knight. I was scared that I might say the wrong thing and he'd shape shift on me too.

"Hey, I'm sorry about that, Kamaria,"he apologized. I looked at him in amazement because he switched right back to the cool, calm, and collected version of himself I'd been getting to know. "My family tends to bring out the worst in me. That's why I try to stay away. Do you mind if I pass by my mother's house, right quick?"

"Not at all,"I answered quickly, still a little scared. I had a half a mind to demand that he bring me back to campus, but I sat back and enjoyed the ride. I couldn't think of one good reason for him to be speaking to his mom that way, but I also wasn't in his shoes so I was trying my hardest not to judge. I was aware that I'd grown up sheltered and that everyone didn't have the same story.

"You sure you're alright?"

"Yea, uh-huh,"I giggled nervously, while scrolling through my phone. I was positive that my answer wasn't convincing, but he didn't press the issue. He whipped through the BR streets, like he was on a mission. I tried to calm my nerves, but they got worse when I saw the neighborhood he'd entered. Growing up in New Orleans, I'd seen low poverty areas but I'd never spent an extended amount of time in one. At least with New Orleans, I was familiar with the different hoods. In Baton Rouge I spent the majority of my time on campus. I'd only started venturing out recently and it was with people I'd deemed trustworthy after getting to know them. I'd only known Daniel for about six days, which meant I didn't know him at all. I did not want to kick it in the hood with him. Anything could happen, and I wasn't sure if he'd make my safety his number one priority.

He pulled his car in front of a one story, brick home where a bunch of people were hanging out. There were kids, teenage boys, men who appeared to be around Daniel's age, and young girls in skimpy attire despite it being cold outside.

"WHY THE FUCK Y'ALL HOES NOT ON THE STROLL?"Daniel barked at the girls, and most of them jumped in fear.

"It's not busy right now, daddy,"one girl timidly responded.

"I don't give a fuck! If two cars pull up within two hours y'all need to be out there to catch them. I see why my money be looking funny now! You hoes playing! Get the fuck from in front my house and go to work!"He barked in their faces. They all shuffled away with the quickness. I wanted to feel bad for them but my mind was reeling at what I just witnessed. Was this man a PIMP? What in the secret-life of the law student was going on around here?!

"Deezy, you ain't have to do 'em like that,"a guy laughed.

Deezy? Who the fuck was Deezy?

"Fuck them raggedy ass bitches,"he grumbled. "Where the fuck my dumb ass mama at?!"

A lady with a bright red wig and cheetah robe on bursted out the front door and onto the porch. "NIGGA YOU GOT ONE MORE TIME TO CALL ME OUT MY NAME AND I'MA SHOVE YOU BACK UP MY PUSSY WHERE YOU CAME FROM!"

"Mannn, *fuck you* with that Ronald Mcdonald ass wig on. Where that nigga at?!"

I could've rolled out the car, into the street, and into traffic. Why were these people talking to each other like this?

"His drunk ass then passed out on the couch after trying to steal the crack that I was bagging up."

"Oh, he was fucking with my product? I got something for that ass,"he nodded, before storming back to the car. I didn't know what he was getting, but he headed for the trunk.

"Daniel, stop that foolishness! That's your daddy in there."

"Fuck that junky ass nigga! Nobody told you to call me to come get him!"

My heart dropped when I saw him walking back to the house with a gun in his hand. He had that in the trunk this whole time?!

His mom must've felt me staring because she looked over at the car. I looked away to avoid making eye contact with her, but it was too late. "Who you got in the car with you, baby? She got a cute face. She think she too good to speak?!"

"Yea, she is too good to speak,"he replied snappily.

"Oh shit!"One of the men exclaimed. "I'm just noticing that bitch in the car! That hoe pressure!"

Damn…did I have to be a bitch *and* a hoe?

"We putting her to work? Anybody who comes across my threshold either selling pussy or cooking crack,"his mom said. My heart dropped because I didn't hear a hint of humor in her voice. If I wasn't fearing for my safety before, I was certainly fearing for it now. My thoughts were racing too fast for me to keep up with. My hands shook as I texted Kyree my location and "COME GET ME NOW!" in all caps. He wasn't the only friend I could've hit up, but he would come the fastest. Friendzone or not, he didn't play about me. I didn't play about him either which is why I was hesitant about dragging him into this nonsense, but I had to get the fuck away from here.

"Bitch, chill your money hungry ass out! She ain't doing none of that! That girl in college, making something of herself unlike y'all bums!"

My mouth fell as he insulted everybody out there.

"That's why ion be coming around here unless it's to collect my money! I'm tryna do better, get my degree and shit, and y'all be getting me outta character! I'm finna be a lawyer! Ion got time for this bullshit!"

"You sure do be in character because you be acting your ass off. You wannabe book worm ass nigga. Like you wasn't just fussing at them hoes for chilling out here instead of being on the track..don't be acting all righteous with me,"his mom spat, before twisting her neck. "Go get your daddy out my house, so you can get the fuck from around here with that saditty ass bitch. She still ain't spoke to me. I should go over there and whoop her ass."

"I WISH THE FUCK YOU WOULD! I'll slap that wig off yo' head!"He shouted in her face, before storming off into the house. Several seconds later, he was dragging a frail man outside who was kicking and screaming a bunch of obscenities.

"Turn me loose, Daniel! I was taking a nap! Get the fuck off me before I get up and beat your ass! I can take a nap in my house, nigga!"

"Nigga, you don't live here no more! My mama told you not to come back after you tried to sell every piece of furniture in there for some rocks!" Daniel bashed a gun over his head.

"Daniel!"His mom screamed in horror, but that didn't stop him from beating his dad with the pistol. She faced some of the men who were hanging in front of the house. "Get his ass off this man before he kills him and go to jail!"

They all crowded around Daniel who was seemingly relentless, and I saw that as my chance to make an escape. I got out of the car and ran for my damn life. I wasn't even aware that I could move so fast until that very moment. I ran and ran until I was a few blocks away and spotted a corner store. I slipped in just as my phone started ringing. It was Kyree. I quickly answered, out of breath and all.

"H-hello?"

"Yea, I was calling you because your location moved. I had to make sure, but judging from your voice I can see that lo' didn't lie. You good? What the fuck is going on?"

"Too much to explain over the phone,"I breathed.

"You at this yellow corner store?"

"Yea."

"I'm outside. Come on."

I hurriedly moved outside, and got in Kyree's car.

"Let's go. Now,"I said urgently. I don't know why I was paranoid because I hadn't done anything. I just wasn't sure if Daniel would feel slighted about me fleeing his attempted murder scene. His mama had already expressed wanting to fight me. I wasn't ashamed to admit that I didn't want any smoke with those crazy ass people.

Not needing to be told twice, Kyree pulled off but not without asking questions.

"Somebody was fucking with you?! Cause that nigga can get clipp-"

"No one did anything to me."

98

"You wanted to get away for a reason, Mari."

"Because Daniel is not who I thought he was. Why would you let me get in a car with a law student who moonlights as a pimp slash drug dealer?!"

"WHAT?!"He whipped his head around, and the car swerved. He quickly regained control of the car and refocused on the road. "Daniel does what, now?"

"So you didn't know?"

"Fuck no! I thought his lame ass just went to school like the rest of us! He tried to get you to do something?!"

"NO!"I shouted, before taking a deep breath. I didn't know where to start with this story, but I had to tell him. I didn't need his imagination running wild. I started running everything down, not skimming back on any details. By the time I finished the story, he was pulling into the parking lot of my on campus apartments. He killed his ignition, and just sat there after I wrapped up the story. I was anxious to get his take on the course of events, but his silence was scaring me.

"Say..."he shook his head. "I understand you gon date and all, but you gotta vet these niggas out better."

My eyes furrowed. It sounded like he was blaming me and I wasn't with it.

"Excuse you?"

"I ain't stutter! You had no business being in the car with a nigga you just met over the weekend at a fucking kickback! You drive your own shit and y'all meet at mutual public places! Does he know where you stay?! Have you been to his shit?! Man, that could've gone so left! You lucky he wasn't completely sick in the head by forcing you to hoe for him."

"Okay!!! In hindsight, I see how there's some things I could've done differently to avoid this! But I don't need you rubbing shit in my face right now! My life just flashed before my eyes!"

"Mari…answer my questions."

"What questions?! Sorry, I couldn't hear shit past you blaming me!"

"Has this nigga been here?!"

"As my friend, that's not your business!"

"Oh, so that's how you coming?"

I crossed my arms and looked at him in silence.

"Alright, well as your friend, I don't want to see you hurt. I don't know what type of time that nigga on. So I need to know if he knows where you stay."

"Don't worry about it, *friend*."

Daniel had never been to my place. I would always have him pick me up from a public spot on campus. But I wouldn't give Kyree the satisfaction of answering the question.

"Bruh,"he chortled. "You green as fuck, but you still smarter than most."

"Ok...your point?"I blinked.

"You know I have feelings for you, Mari."

My breath was momentarily snatched away. That coming out of his mouth was unexpected. I didn't know how to respond. As much as I wanted him to be forthcoming with how he felt about me, I never thought about how I'd handle it.

"Oh, you don't got nothing smart to say in response to that?"

"I-I...I don't know what to say,"I finally replied.

"Just like I don't know what to do with how you got me feeling,"he ran his hands over his face. "I've honestly liked you since the first night we chilled together…but I was lying to myself at first."

"Because it's not cool to like the big girl, right?"

His face screwed up. "What?"

"C'mon…you know you're ashamed. I'm not like any girl you've ever dated befo-."

"Stop,"he held his hand up. "Me wanting to suppress my feelings for you has everything to do with *me.* Kamaria, I hate whoever gives you these insecurities about your looks because they should be nonexistent. Because you're pretty as hell and fine as fuck. How can you not notice how proud I am to show you off whenever we're together? And I never told you this…but niggas be constantly reaching out to me to get at you. I be shutting all that down on some hater shit though. I ain't even gon' lie."

My face was warm as I giggled at his last statement. My stomach would not relax as I felt things I'd never felt before.

"So what's the problem, Ky? If you like me and I like you, shouldn't it be simple?"

"It should be, but I didn't want to ruin what we've been doing."

"What do you mean?"

"You're right, you're nothing like girls I've dated in the past,"my heart dropped, until he continued talking. "You don't try to be somebody you're not to impress others, you have real goals, you don't let superficial shit consume you, you're smart as hell, and I can tell that you like me for me. Not because I'm well known or some other dumb shit. I fuck with our friendship hard, so I don't want to mess it up."

"How would you do that?"

"Mari, I've been in a few relationships and I ruined them all. I'd rather have you in my life as my friend than not have you at all."

"...I get that, but if you like me as much as you claim then you wouldn't do anything to hurt me, right?"

"I would never want to,"he professed, while grabbing my hand. "But I just...I don't know. I'm not confident in relationship me, and I know I'd have to come correct if we were to date exclusively."

"Alright,"I sighed heavily. "Well, we can still be friends. But we have to chill on doing relationship-like things. I respect how you feel, but I have to get a hold of my feelings if you don't want more."

"Who said I didn't want more?!"

"It sounds like you're saying that."

"But I'm not. I'm just letting you know that I'm scared of that next step. It doesn't mean that I'm not willing to take it."

"Kyree, don't say things you don't me-"

He cut me off, by gripping my jaw and pulling my face towards his. Our lips collided, and my heart would not keep still. Every emotion that was missing from the kiss I shared with Daniel was suddenly present now. I grabbed the back of his head that was covered by his locks, and deepened the kiss. Before yesterday, I'd only kissed one guy. It was the prom date that my mom had gotten for me. He was a college student and the son of my mom's best friend. That kiss was nice…but this, it was different. It was like he was infatuated with my lips. He wiggled his tongue into my mouth and in between my legs got warm. I crossed my legs tightly as I felt a tingling sensation in my center. It felt so good that it scared me. We tongue kissed for what felt like minutes, before I had to pull away for air.

"You still think I'm saying things I don't mean?"

I looked at him, completely speechless, propelling him to laugh.

"Why you acting like that was your first kiss?"He chuckled, and then he instantly grew serious. "Wait, don't tell me that was your first k-"

"Kyree, don't be ridiculous,"I laughed. "I just kissed Daniel yesterday."

"You what?!"

I stopped laughing while thinking why the hell would I say that. I meant to think it to myself but it just slipped out. I was so used to Kyree being my friend that I was comfortable saying anything around him. I couldn't do that anymore if we were exclusively dating.

"Nothing,"I laughed nervously.

"Ain't shit funny,"he snapped. "You need to block that weird ass nigga."

"I'm going to,"I rolled my eyes. "I have no desire to talk to him anymore."

"Yea, you better not."

"Anyways, are you sure about this exclusive dating thing? Can you handle that?"

"I know I can't handle you dating other niggas, so I can only be fair and give you the same thing in return."

I nodded. "Okay, I can live with that."

"Good, now let's go inside and lay down. You and your drama wore me out today."He shook his head before climbing out the car.

I had to admit that today was quite eventful for me. But I didn't even care about the Daniel fiasco anymore because I got what I wanted in the end. Kyree had finally professed his feelings for me, and we were now dating. I would go through all that again for this outcome.

Chapter 5

Kyree

February 14, 2020

I walked back and forth in Kamaria's kitchen with my phone to my ear, as I called my mom for the umpteenth time. She needed to answer asap because I needed her for something very important. Normally, she'd be up early so I didn't understand why she wasn't answering. I'd already called her twice. I thought I'd have to hit my dad's line, but she finally answered.

"Hello?"She yawned.

"You was sleep, Ma?"I asked the obvious question.

"What the hell do you think? Kyree, what are you doing up at 7 AM?"She asked groggily.

"Why you still sleep at 7 AM?"

"Boy, you know I go into work later on Friday and you fucking with my rest. What do you want?"

"Ma, I need your recipe for french toast."

"Are you serious? That's why you blowing my damn phone up?"

"Now you see how I feel when you blow up my phone. Forreal though, I need that."

"Why you need my french toast recipe all of a sudden? I've been making it since you were a baby, and it's never been your favorite. I then taught you how to make everything you actually like eating."

"C'mon ma...I need it because I'm making Mari a Valentine's Day breakfast."

She cackled. "I knew it. I just needed to hear you say it. You making breakfast for all your friends or something?"

"You childish."

"Oh, I'm childish?"She tittered. "I'm asking what needs to be asked, and if she's as smart as I think she is she'd be inquiring about these things too."

"Ma, you talked to her on the phone like once. You don't know her like that."

"So she's okay with just being friends?"

"Nah,"I chuckled.

"So what are you going to do about it?"

"I already did something about it, lady."

"Are you telling me you finally have a girlfriend?!"She squealed in excitement.

"Finally? Man, don't do me that. I've had girlfriends before."

"Yea, your last attempt at having a girlfriend was when you first started college and you were trying to hold on to poor little Hailey,"she said, bringing up someone I dated for two years and some change. We started dating in our junior year of highschool and it ended a few months into our freshman year of college. I was never faithful to her but I became sloppier with more freedom. She attended Grambling, so it just made it easier to do my thing. She broke up with me in an attempt to scare me straight, but it backfired because I kept it pushing and never looked back. In hindsight, I realized I was never really in love with her. I was just comfortable with her and had grown attached, but once she set me free I realized I needed to be alone. "You did that girl so bad. Don't do the same thing to this girl because you'll end up hurting yourself too. I see how she has you doing things you've never done."

"Let's now focus on the past. I'm not the same person I was back then."

"You better not be if you call yourself being in a relationship. I really need to meet this girl now."

"We'll be out there for Mardi Gras."

"That's too long from now. Why can't y'all come tomorrow? I'll cook."

"Tomorrow's too short notice,"I lied. It wasn't like I could say I had plans for Kamaria that included a hotel room that I had booked for two nights. Well...I could say that but I didn't feel like being lectured about things I already knew like being safe and using protection. I'd never had an issue with that before thanks to one talk with my dad when I was in 8th grade.

"How about Sunday then?"

"I'll let you know, mama, but I need the recipe now. Kamaria always wakes up around 8 AM, and I want to surprise her."

"Awwww,"she gushed. "My baby is really growing up. Alright, I'll text you all the steps so you can look at it and don't miss anything. It's simple anyway."

"Ok, cool."

"Oh yea, don't forget your cousin Cambrie is having a Masquerade party for her 23rd birthday the Saturday before Mardi Gras. I'm kinda aggravated that she decided to have her party on the same night as Endymion, but I guess her birthday is more important chile..."

I laughed because it was no secret that my mom loved all the popular parades that took place the weekend before Mardi Gras.

"I bet if it was the night of Bachus you'd be saying something different."

"And you know it,"she tittered. "But I'ma let you go so I can text you this recipe. Love you, baby. Talk to you later."

She texted me a few minutes after we got off the phone, and she was right, it was easy. Doing this at my own apartment would've been more convenient because I wouldn't have had to get groceries delivered to cook breakfast. They had stuff in the refrigerator but since she had three roommates I didn't know what was for who, and I couldn't ask her. So to avoid any trouble I just got my own shit. On the menu was french toast with powdered sugar, bacon, scrambled eggs, and hash browns. It was a simple breakfast which meant I was done in no time. It was ten minutes to 8, so Kamaria was probably shuffling around in her sleep right now and on the verge of walking up. So I put our plates on a red tray I'd purchased from a party store along with a bunch of other Valentine's Day shit, and I made my way to her room.

I tried entering the room silently, but was stunned to see her standing in the middle of the floor recording my entire setup while sporting a happy puppy dog face. We locked eyes first and then her eyes went to the tray in my hand. She wasted no time panning the camera down to the tray. My plan had gone up in flames.

"C'mon Mari," I groaned. "I was tryna surprise you."

"I'm surprised!" She shrieked, as she looked around at the red and pink balloons that floated in her room. She had three gift bags on her desk and a life sized V-Day teddy bear in the corner. "This is so sweet, Ky. Put the tray down so I can hug you."

"That's all I get?"I chided, as I placed the tray on her bed. She practically ran to me, and I took her by surprise by lifting her off the ground.

"Kyree! You can't carry me!"She giggled.

"Wanna bet?"I pecked her lips. "Wrap them legs around me."

She gazed into my eyes and did as I said. I held her up with ease, and then I kissed her deeply. We'd been doing what we called dating exclusively for two days now and I couldn't keep my lips off of hers no matter where we were. Our friends weren't letting us live that shit down either, but most of the time I didn't even pay them any attention. I was just focused on Mari. She seemed happy, so I was happy.

"You following my lead today?"I asked her after we'd stopped kissing. Our heads were pressed together.

"As long as it doesn't interfere with my classes."

"Nerd,"I teased.

"And proud of it,"she smirked, before kissing me again.

"You ruined my surprise, bruh."

"The surprise was not ruined just because I woke up a few minutes earlier than usual,"she giggled. "I wasn't expecting this at all."

"Yea, but I wanted to bring you breakfast in bed…have music playing in the background. The whole nine…and I wanted to record your reaction."

"I'm glad it didn't go that way because you would've been recording me with crust and shit in my eyes. Good thing I did wake up first to brush my teeth and wash my face,"she giggled.

"I don't find nothing funny though,"I joked.

She laughed. "We can still have breakfast in bed and listen to music."

"You right…and I still got bukoo surprises in store for you, so it's all good. I picked up her remote off her bed, while still holding her.

"Ky, can I get down now?"She asked with a stifled smile.

"In a minute,"I replied, as I made my way to her Spotify. I clicked on her love song playlist and shuffled it. A song I'd grown to like because of Kamaria came on first. It was called "I Want You Around" by Snoh Aalegra. I associated the song with our friendship and now it was even more relatable with the change in our relationship.

"You love this song, don't you?"She giggled.

"You know I do,"I kissed her.

"Awwww!"

I turned and saw all her roommates; Clarissa, Angie, and London.

"This is too cute!"London shrieked.

"Must be nice…"Angie said with a stiff smile as she scanned the room with her eyes.

"You did all this, Kamaria? Cause this is nice,"Clarissa grinned. Their fakeness wiped the smile I just had for Mari right off my face. She'd already told me that she wasn't close with her roommates at all. However, I'd been witnessing them trying to get close to her for the past month. To put it bluntly, they'd been kissing her ass. They were always complimenting her, asking to borrow her handbags and shit…and to my dismay, she'd allow them to. They'd also been inviting her out. Thankfully, she never accepted any of those invitations. Mari may have been green, but she wasn't slow. She knew their asses weren't 100% genuine, but I think a part of her felt good to feel accepted so she didn't ponder on the sudden switch up from them.

"Why would she do this for herself?"I questioned, not holding back the hostility in my tone. I felt like she was trying to play Kamaria, and a female like her had no business trying to play anybody. She consistently got fucked and ducked.

"*You* did it?"She marveled. "Chileee, that's what's up. Teach me your ways, Mari."

"Ain't nothing for her to teach you. Either a nigga wants to do it for you or he doesn't,"I said.

"Well tell me something then,"she laughed awkwardly before walking off.

"Can I see what he got you, girl?"London asked.

"Uhhh, maybe later. I haven't even looked yet,"Kamaria responded, as I finally let her down.

"Okay, well girl I'm wearing your LV shoulder bag tonight for my date, so put it on my bed."

Was this bitch *telling* her that she was wearing her shit? Never being one to let people I fucked with get walked all over, I started to speak up, but Mari beat me to the punch.

"I'm sorry, are you asking?"She blinked her eyes rapidly. That alone made the energy in the room turn stale.

"She definitely asked,"Angie butted in, while eyeing Kamaria like she was strange. "Why you acting weird like we don't always share stuff?"

"Who is *we*? And I'm not acting weird, baby. It just sounded like she *told* me she was going to wear my bag. My understanding of the English language is top tier. I know what I heard."

"Yea, you heard right,"I cosigned. Shit, she needed to know she wasn't tripping and that they in fact were.

"Look, yes or no? I'm not bouta beg for no bag,"London snapped. I could tell they thought Kamaria was a pushover, and that was laughable.

"Good, bitch! I could care less. It won't be me without a bag tonight. The fuck?! Bye!"She marched over to her door and slammed it in their faces.

"Bitches lose a lil weight and think they too much!"

The look on Kamaria's face didn't go missed. That bitch's dumb ass comment had gotten to her, but she brushed it off.

"You heard that hoe, huh?"

"Yep, and she can go straight to hell."

"Then don't let them be in your face no more. All that new energy they've been giving you has been fake."

"Fake?!"London shouted from the other side of the door.

"Girl, leave it alone. It's not that deep,"Angie attempted to whisper.

"Yea, fake! And I ain't lost no weight! I'm still the same 195 pounds I've been since the beginning of this school year! You must like what you see, bitch!"

"Alright, that's enough,"I laughed, before pulling her away from the door. "Let's eat. Fuck all them hoes. They some haters."

———————

Kamaria

Despite the drama from my weird ass roommate, my Valentine's Day morning was perfect. After we ate breakfast, I opened my gifts. Kyree got me a Gucci Dionysus GG Supreme mini bag, pink Gucci slides, gold Tom Ford lock heels, and the latest iPad because I broke my old one. I'd never had someone to call my own, so the fact that I was experiencing this in my first real relationship was special. Nobody was going to dampen my mood. Not even my mother and she had come close. I posted a picture of my decorated room, my breakfast, and a picture of Kyree on my instagram story with the caption "my Valentine." I attached the Snoh Aalegra song to all the posts. Somehow this got back to my mother despite her not having an instagram. She wasted no time texting me about it while I was in my first class. She never called me during the day because she'd be at work.

You don't need to be spoiling a man to get him to take you seriously. You're the prize, Kamaria.

That shit stung because it was the second time that day somebody made it seem like I was unworthy of being dotted on. Yea, I had caught Clarissa's shade. I was far from stupid, and I was sick of people thinking I was. My kindness was constantly being mistaken for weakness. That's why I didn't hold back on my response to my mother.

I know I'm the prize, and I'm grateful to be with a man who realizes that. It's unfortunate that you'd assume that I was pathetic enough to roll the red carpet out for a man before he rolled it out for me. It says a lot about what you think of me.

After I sent that, she responded quickly and what I read didn't surprise me. It was the norm. More underhanded insults and brushing my feelings under the rug.

Kamaria, you took that wrong. You never told me you had a boyfriend, and I would never assume that about

you of all people. He's a handsome young man. I hope his intentions are pure. I'd like to meet him when you come home for Mardi Gras break.

I understood why Daniel had cursed his mama out now because I wanted to do it so badly at that moment. But I chose not to respond to her instead. Everytime she called or texted me she left me feeling low. I couldn't recall the last positive conversation we had, and that was sad. She wanted me to be perfect and that was why she was constantly criticizing me, but the shit was getting old. Maybe I wasn't what she imagined for a daughter, but I could only be me.

By the time my last class rolled around, I had pushed my mom to the back of my mind and I just wanted to meet up with Kyree. He said he had the rest of the day mapped out, but after the morning we shared I didn't know what else he could possibly do for me. I had yet to give him my gifts and I already felt like they were mid compared to what he'd done. Kyree loved Nike sneakers so I got him two pairs of Dunks I heard him say he wanted. I wanted to get three, but I thought that would be pushing it. If only I'd known what he had in store for me I would've gone all out.

As I was walking out the building of my last class, someone walked up behind me and put their arms around my waist making me jump.

"Get out your phone."Kyree laughed, before kissing the side of my head. "What got your attention anyway?"

"Nothing." I quickly turned my phone off, because I didn't need him to see that I was trying to see what the Mall of Louisiana had in stock so I could get him something else. I had to skip class yesterday to drive to New Orleans to get his dunks, but I wouldn't be able to get that far away from him today. He was all over me.

"Why you was on Ulta's website? You need makeup or something?"

"Uhhh, yea,"I lied. I was really looking up what colognes they had so I could buy him one or two. "Can we go to the mall?"

"We can…but I got something else in store for us first."

I didn't bother asking what, I just allowed him to lead the way. The first place he took me was a popular crawfish spot, and as a New Orleans girl crawfish was truly a part of my heart, so I appreciated it. We ate crawfish while enjoying a fruity alcoholic drink that the place sold. After that we went to a spa where we enjoyed couples massages and a mud bath. We already had a buzz from the crawfish place, so we were all laugh's and touchy feely in the mud bath. He bought a simple black bikini for me that left nothing to the imagination. Whenever I did have to wear a swimsuit I opted for highwaisted bottoms, and keeping my cover-up on was a must. However, I had unlimited confidence in this skimpy black string bikini. I'd even taken mirror pictures when I changed in the locker room. My stomach may have not been flat, my breasts were humongous, my thighs were huge, and I had a lot of ass but so what. I actually liked what I saw in the mirror, and that was all that mattered. The way Kyree looked at me when I joined him in the mud bath made me feel good too. It was like I had an epiphany and realized that all the bullshit people fed me about my body just wasn't true.

"Stoppp,"I giggled, as Kyree made me straddle his lap

and he grabbed two handfuls of my booty to do so.

"You don't want me to stop."

He licked my lips before slipping his tongue into my

mouth. He was so right. I didn't want him to stop and my

pussy was doing that weird beatboxing thing again. I had been

sipping on a glass of Champagne, so I wasn't going to run

from the feeling this time. I sat my pulsating center right on the

thickness between his legs that seemed to be growing rapidly.

"You feel that?"

"Mhmm,"I muttered, to avoid the unusual sounds that

wanted to come out of my mouth. I was softly humping his

hard on, and the arrogant grin he bore made it clear that he

was aware of what I was doing. At 21 I was still a virgin for

obvious reasons. Well, I had a situation after prom. Things got

heated after my first kiss and that led to my date going down

on me...and we almost had sex. But I chickened out much to

his dismay. I was still scared of going all the way, but I was so

ready. I didn't want to run away from what Kyree was making

me feel, and I really could care less that we'd only been dating for two days. We had a special bond since the day we met, and I was confident about taking this next step with him.

"Uhhhh,"escaped from my mouth unwillingly, as the thumping between my thighs quickened and my legs shook.

Kyree paused and I watched his eyes light up.

"Mari, did you just cum?"

"I-I think so…"

"You think so?"He raised an eyebrow before laughing. I instantly felt self conscious because I was so inexperienced that it was embarrassing. I was dealing with somebody who probably ran through girls that could do tricks on the dick. Then there was me…unsure about the heavenly feeling his dick had given me.

"It's alright, baby,"he kissed me passionately, making me forget everything I was just worrying about. "I got you. I promise."

I wanted him to expound on that, but he didn't. We stayed in the mud bath a few more minutes before getting out and heading for the showers. Our lips were permanently locked as the shower rinsed the mud off of our bodies. I was becoming obsessed with the way Kyree was groping every inch of my body.

"Alright, we gotta go,"he chuckled. "You have an appointment at 6 pm, and we have dinner reservations for 9. If you still want to go to the mall we have to move because it's already 3."

"We have dinner reservations? And what do I have an appointment for?"

"That's for me to know and for you to find out."

"I might need to get something to wear. I don't think I have anything going-out worthy."

"Mari, you got bukoo clothes with the tags still on them. Stop playing..."

"I might want something new though."

"Alright, well come on. You lucky the Mall is right down the street from here."He turned the shower off and grabbed a towel to dry off.

"No, you're lucky."

"Smile, Mari."

I looked up, and he snapped my picture as I was picking up my towel. I was sure he'd capture nothing but my ass that had devoured my string bikini.

"Damn, you look good…"he said as he gawked at the photo.

"You're not supposed to have your phone in here."

"I'm a grown ass man. What they gon do? Take my shit?"

"Ignorant,"I shook my head.

He walked up behind me, and all I felt was his stiff member in the crack of my booty. I think he was making it his mission to keep my pussy wet at this point.

"Moveee,"I whined, as I stood up straight.

"Smile,"he put his camera in my face and his tongue to my cheek. I couldn't help but smile big, as he captured the photo.

"Stick your tongue out,"he directed. Of course I did it, and he stuck his out too, connecting it with mine. He took another picture with our tongues touching like that, and his hand was around my throat. The sexual tension between us was so thick that it could be cut with a knife. I couldn't wait for tonight.

Kyree

"You look so beautiful, Mari," I said, as I sat in front of her while she was getting her makeup and hair done. Although I wasn't fucking with Essence ever since she stirred up that unnecessary drama, I still reached out to her to see who did the best hair and makeup in BR. She sent me a list of people, and it was like pulling teeth to get somebody for a house call on one of the busiest days of the year for women. But having money always made a way, and luckily I had that to spare. I was nowhere near where I wanted to be financially but I was doing better than a lot of people my age, and I didn't take that for granted. Throwing parties gave me the luxury to handle my responsibilities with ease and splurge. I'd treat myself to some things, but I made a habit out of saving my money or pouring it back into my parties to make more money. I could definitely get used to spending it on Mari. I'd been enjoying it thus far, and she expressed how thankful she was everytime, making me feel even better.

"Do I really? I'm kinda scared because the last time I got my makeup done was for prom in 2016...and yea, it scarred me for life."

"2016 makeup was interesting,"the MUA, Chyna, laughed. "I was just looking at my old work saying makeup has come so far from five or four years ago. But girl, you look gorgeous, and you have great skin which gives me the perfect canvas. Just trust the process. I got you."

"Okay..."Kamaria said hesitantly. I held back laughter because she still wasn't 100% sold, and I knew why. She told me that she liked experimenting with makeup, but she steered clear of mua's because it was a fine line between polished makeup and clown makeup. She claimed she hated her prom pictures because her makeup was too extra, but Chyna was getting her right. Essence's makeup was always nice, so I knew her recommendations would be on point. I had to pay Chyna a squeeze in fee, an after hours fee, and a traveling fee to do Kamaria's makeup. What would've normally been a $100 service was now $400...and I wasn't even going to speak on how much I had to pay Traci, the hairstylist, to come out. I didn't regret a thing though. They were getting my baby right. Kamaria had taken out her sew in at the beginning of the week, and she had a head full of natural hair. It reminded me of my moms hair with its curly and kinky texture. It seemingly stopped at her shoulders, but when Traci started blowing it out and flat ironing it, it came down to the middle of her back. Kamaria described a style to Traci that she wanted and I was unsure of it because I couldn't picture it in my head, but as she was finishing I couldn't help but praise what I saw.

"Your hair is coming out nice, Mari."

"Yea, you look so good,"Traci amplified. "I love these pin curl up-do's."

So that's what it was called. It reminded me of a hairstyle my mom used to wear back in the day, but it didn't look dated. She had two loose straight strands of hair framing her face, and it complimented her well. Her makeup was natural, per her request, and she had these light pink lips lined in brown liner that made me want to grab her face and kiss her.

"Alright, I'm all done,"Chyna said, before handing her a hand mirror.

"Wowww,"Kamaria's eyes brightened as she stared at herself.

"Talk to us, girl,"Traci grinned.

"I look fucking gorgeous. Thank y'all so much,"she beamed. Now it was my turn to smile. It made me feel good whenever I heard her speak highly of herself because she rarely did it. I wanted to hear her popping her shit on a regular basis, but we could do baby steps for now.

Traci and Chyna took pictures of their work, I paid what I owed them, and they were on their way. It was now 8 pm, so we had to get dressed in a timely fashion to make our 9 pm reservation at Stroubes. It was a popular Southern steakhouse that also specializes in seafood. I'd made the reservations weeks ago because I'd been planning to bring Kamaria here. Even as friends I wanted to spend my Valentine's Day with her, so I was happy that it was deeper than that now.

"You gotta let me take your pictures before we leave,"I gawked at Mari as she exited my bedroom. She got a red two piece set from some BBL fashions store in the mall, but Kamaria's *real* curves were perfect for those types of clothes. I wasn't in the store with her when she got the outfit but she relayed how the gay salesman had bucked her up to get a mini skirt. Apparently, she never wore skirts because she was always told that she shouldn't. She told me that she just got comfortable wearing shorts. That bothered me because she had the most perfect long and thick ass legs that were made to be shown off. The proof was right in front of me as she sauntered over in her red mini skirt that was paired with a strapless red lace corset top. She had on the gold Tom Ford heels I gave her earlier that day, gold hoops, and a dainty LV heart shaped necklace.

"We're gonna be late."

"We good. It's only 8:20. I got at least five minutes to snap you up. C'mon,"I slapped her butt. She went straight to a back shot for her first pose. "Man, turn around."

"Why?"She giggled. "I thought I looked good."

"You know your ass looks good. Go ahead, and do that pose. It's staying in my phone."

"Don't hate,"she chortled. I took a few more pictures of her from the back before she turned to face me. That's when I noticed the bag she was carrying. It was a red Dior saddle bag with gold hardware. It matched her outfit perfectly.

"You really be putting that shit on."

"That means a lot coming from you,"she smiled. I took pride in dressing everytime I left the house whether I was going to class or partying. I complimented her well tonight in black dress pants, a black turtleneck, a Burberry red trench coat that I left open, on my feet were red LV loafers, and I had the matching belt. I already had every item in my closet, so throwing it together was easy. Kamria had put together her fit last minute and that deserved applause because she looked drop dead gorgeous.

"Ain't nothing special about this old shit I got in. Let me praise you without back talk."

"Ky, this outfit was $40. You bought these shoes and got my makeup and hair done. Oh, and this purse is a Vintage piece from the year 2002 straight out of my mama's closet,"she revealed. "She was going to give it away when she was cleaning out her closet last year but I snagged it. So I don't deserve that much praise."

"Man, fuck all that irrelevant information. I bet if anybody else put this shit on they wouldn't look like you."

The corners of Kamria's face turned up, even though I could tell she wanted to fight it. "Alright, I'll let you buck my head up in peace."

"What I'm saying is valid though,"I maintained, while she continued posing for my camera. After we finished up, we got ready to go. She went to my room and returned in a red trench coat of her own with a few gift bags. I had more gifts for her too but they were in the trunk of my car. When I opened the passenger door for her and got her into my car, I went to retrieve one of the gifts. Pure bliss took over her face when I got in on the drivers side, and handed her a big red bouquet of roses.

"Awwww, thank you!"She leaned over and gripped both sides of my face, forcing my lips to poke out, and then she kissed me. "I would've never guessed you were so sweet."

"Don't act like today is the first time I've ever done something nice for you."

"It's the first time I've known your true feelings behind your actions though."

"Mari…c'mon, you knew what it was."

"Incorrect. I had an idea, but I was basically playing the guessing game. I didn't know anything for sure until you told me."

"I get that, but the fact still reminds me that I've always done nice things for you."

"You have, but you know you're on anything level today. Stop the cap."

"Stop the cap?"I repeated with laughter. "Alright, don't be stealing my lingo now, girl."

"Your lingo? I could've sworn that was like Atlanta lingo or something."

I cut my eyes at her. "Oh, that's how you coming?"

"You know people from New Orleans ain't never said that shit until it became popularized on social media,"she laughed.

"You might be right, but I never heard you say it until now. It's okay to admit that I influence you, baby."

"Kyree, bring your arrogant ass back down to Earth,"she giggled.

"Kyree?"I questioned with disdain.

"That's what your parents named you, right?"

"Okay, you showing out. Keep that energy,"I nodded before turning up the radio. "You" by Lloyd featuring Lil Wayne was on, and it was a major vibe. We both started singing at the same time.

"Stop, wait a minute. The way you move that girl you done got my heart all in it. And I just wanna be with you tonight. Girl, please...I'm a player, yeah, it's true. But I change the game for you. I wanna see what it do..."

The car ride to the restaurant was filled with laughs and singing love songs. If my friends could see me right now I'd get clowned for the rest of my life because I was not acting like myself. I hadn't been acting like myself ever since I'd met Mari. She naturally made me switch up, and I didn't want to go back. Her presence felt like a gift that I wasn't even worthy of.

"Ky…"Kamaria glared at me. We'd arrived at the restaurant and after I helped her out of the car I went to the trunk to get the rest of her gifts.

"What? What's the problem?"I asked, genuinely oblivious.

"You got me more stuff?"

"Oh…"I looked down at the bags in my hand like I was just noticing them. "Yea. That's a problem?"

"Yes,"she whined. "I feel like I didn't do enough for you."

I smacked my teeth. "As a man I'm supposed to do more."

"I think it should be equal…"

"Reciprocity is major in any relationship, but this shit is brand new…it's perfectly okay for you to receive everything I'm offering. And it's not like you didn't get me anything. It's all good, Mari…I swear. You think too much,"I chuckled, before closing my trunk. I strided over to her, grabbed her hand, and led her into the restaurant.

We arrived right on time, and we were seated immediately. We scanned the menu, and discussed what we wanted. We were used to eating out together, so it wasn't surprising that we both wanted multiple appetizers and were willing to share. That's usually how we did it. We put in our order for appetizers and main courses at the same time. Kamaria surprised me by ordering an alcoholic beverage. She'd been drinking all day when I could never get her to do so in the past.

"Whatchu know bout lemon drops?"

"I went to lunch with Essence last week and tried one. It was good. Do you have a problem with me drinking?"

"No, I was just curious to know when you got into it because you've been drinking all day."

"This is about to be my third drink today, don't be so dramatic,"she rolled her eyes with a smile.

"I'm saying though, you refused to drink the first few times I had you outside so I figured you don't be on that, forreal."

"Orrr, I was being cautious because I was hanging out with new people."

"Ya' know…that makes a lot of sense."

"Yea, I have a lot more sense than you think,"she winked.

"I never said you didn't have sense."

"But you never miss a chance to call me green."

"Does that offend you? Because I'll stop if it does."

"No, it doesn't offend me. I probably haven't been exposed to the things most people my age have been exposed to, but I'm not completely clueless either. I know how to take care of myself."

"That's evident, and I don't doubt that for a second. I just know how sweet you are and I don't want anybody taking advantage of that or trying to change you."

"Change is inevitable. I'm going to always be me, but that nice shit makes people try me more than they'd try anybody else. That's why London came at me the way she did this morning. I'm too nice."

"Fuck that. Don't change who you are for fucked up people. If somebody gets out of line just put them back in, like you did London…and Mary,"I chortled, as I had a memory of her mushing her in the union.

"You don't have any more hoes that will try me, do you?"

"Nah, and I definitely won't have any after tonight." I turned my phone around where I'd just posted the pictures she took in my apartment on my Instagram page. The photos were posted five minutes ago and already had 200 likes and a lot of comments. Essence and them were the main ones hyping her up in the comments. I hadn't scanned the rest of them yet, but everybody was loving her.

"You posted me?"She gawked.

"That's a problem?"I eyed her strangely.

"Yes! You could've sent me my pictures first and let me scan them! I would've picked my favorites for you to post. And don't you think I should've posted my own pictures first?"

"Mari, please, these are *my* pictures. I took them and they're in my phone. Good luck getting them."

"Hater,"she groaned.

Our appetizers and drinks started arriving shortly after, and we wasted no time diving in. We were trading dishes back and forth, and feeding each other left and right. The food here was definitely hitting.

"I'm going to need a gym membership fooling around with you,"she said after eating a NOLA BBQ Shrimp.

"What you mean?"

"You know what I mean. You always got me stuffing my face. I'ma be 200 pounds soon."

"So what's wrong with that?"

"Really?"She tilted her head.

"Yea, really. You realize most of your weight comes for your height and that big ass you're carrying around, right?"

"My stomach could be a little smaller though."

"Then we can hit the gym up if that's what you really want. I go at least three times a week, but real shit, ain't nothing wrong with your body so I'ma keep feeding you. We obviously like to eat and that ain't nothing to be ashamed of."

"See…that's easy for somebody with a fast metabolism to say."

I laughed. "You sound like my mama. She swears her metabolism was fast until she had me and then I ruined her body."

"What? Your mom looks fine."

I'd shown her plenty of pictures of my mama for her to see that she was on the slim but curvy side.

"And so do you. Let me find out you fishing for compliments."

That statement stumped her into silence before she bit her lip.

"Actually…can I be honest? And don't judge me."

"I would never do that."

"Okay, anytime I'd eat around my family when I was growing up I'd have to deal with comments about my weight. So I guess it became natural for me to talk down on my body whenever I know I'm eating a lot. I swore I'd stop doing it but I can't help myself sometimes."

"You said your *family* made comments about your body?"

"Yep…mainly my mom."

"And your dad?"

"He'd make little comments here and there. He wasn't as worse as my mom but he never defended me, and whenever he'd notice my feelings were hurt he'd say some shit like 'your mom's only looking out for you.'"

"So nobody took up for you?"I was astonished. No wonder why she had insecurities and went so long covering up her body. It made me proud that she'd come out of her shell in such a short amount of time because a girl as beautiful as her didn't need to hide from the world.

"My aunt did whenever she was around, but she worked a lot so she could never be around 24/7. Everybody in my family is slim. I don't know who I got my body from. The only notable thing I got from my parents is my height. So yea, I had it rough and it did a number on my confidence."

"You've come far though. Have you thought about telling your people how they affected you?"

She laughed as if the notion was preposterous.

"It would be a waste of my breath."

"Have they at least changed?"

"Hmmm, it's not as bad as it used to be. I honestly got smaller from when I was a kid because I was really chubby."

"So was I and a bunch of other kids…but go on."

"Well none of my cousins were, so I was constantly compared to them. My mama would put me on diets, force me to work out, and she'd lock the pantry at night so I wouldn't sneak snacks. I guess she felt like her hard work had paid off when I got 13 and I lost a little weight. I think it really just had a lot to do with me getting taller and shedding baby fat, but no one can tell her that. Anyways, they don't overtly talk about my weight anymore. My dad has completely fallen back from doing that, and our relationship has gotten better. My mom is a different story."

"How so?"

"Take today for example. Somehow she saw my instagram stories from this morning."

"Uh-oh, what she said about me?"

"Nothing, but she automatically assumed that I did all that shit for you. Like I was buying your attention or something."

"What?! What kinda fuck shit is that?"

"Ky, ignorant ass people always assume that heavier girls have to pay to play. It's sick. Even Clarissa threw shade, hinting at that."

"Yeaaa, I caught that but I ain't want to bring it up,"I scratched my head.

"I can catch a sneak diss really fast, so you didn't have to bring it up. Today was the first time I was accused of basically being desperate, and it coming from my own mother hurt my feelings. But I'm used to it."

"That don't make it right, Mari."

"I know that, but what can I do about it?"

"Mannn, if I was you I'd keep my distance. No cap."

"That's still my family at the end of the day."

"I hear you,"I nodded. I couldn't hate on her mindset because my family was my world and I couldn't imagine coming up off of them. But my family also didn't sound as fucked up as hers. Still, I wasn't going to vehemently convince her to cut her family off. That was something she'd have to decide on her own and with nobody else's influence.

"And guess what?"

"What?"

"My mom wants to meet you."She divulged.

"You know I'm not too good at biting my tongue right?"I countered.

"These days I don't really bite mine either, so that's all good."

"Cool,"I chuckled.

"She'll most likely be on her best behavior around you anyway...hopefully."

"Yea, let's speak positivity into that meet up. Good thing we don't have to worry about you meeting my parents. They already like you because they know how much I like you. My sisters might give you a hard time."

"Really?"She panicked.

I laughed. "They're just protective over me, so they gone have bukoo questions for you. It's nothing you can't handle though, and I'ma be right there to intercept if they go too far."

"Okay,"her eyes shifted. "As long as they're nice…so am I still meeting them during Mardi Gras break?"

"My mama wants us to come this weekend."

"What?!"She exclaimed.

"Chill,"I laughed. "I told her no for tomorrow and that I'd think about coming on Sunday. Why do you sound scared? I told you that you're good in my parents book."

"That may change once they meet me. Who knows?"

"That won't happen, Mari. Shit, you might wanna meet them this weekend so you can get them out of the way before you get to my sisters. Everybody all at once might be a lot."

"You're doing a terrible job at easing my mind."

"My b,"I chuckled. "You talked to my mama though. You know she likes you, and my daddy gon go with whatever she says. He's super laid back. So what do you say? Sunday dinner in New Orleans?"

"...okay,"she bit her lip, making my dick jump. Her innocence was so sexy. I couldn't wait to take her to the hotel that I'd paid Lark and Zion to decorate. I would've done it myself if I had time.

We went through the rest of dinner further discussing our childhoods, and learning more about each other. We'd had countless talks before about our lives before UBR, but we hadn't unpacked everything. Hearing about all the things Kamaria had to overcome on her own made me admire her so much more. Life had pressured her but she'd come out shining like a diamond, and I already knew people would hate her new found confidence because they felt like she had to be insecure. I was more than ready to take on the world with her.

Chapter 6

Kamaria

"Damn, Mari,"Kyree muttered in the midst of our steamy tongue kiss as we rode the elevator up to our room at the Watermark hotel. I didn't know we'd be ending tonight at a hotel room. I would've been content with going back to one of our apartments but this was a welcomed surprise. There'd been this new trend all over social media called "princess treatment" and I'd definitely gotten it today. When this year began I would've never imagined this in my wildest dreams. Despite rubbing me wrong today, I was grateful that Clarissa had connected me and Kyree.

"Goodness,"I uttered while breathing heavily. Kyree had started licking and kissing on my neck while playing with my booty. My red lace thong was soaked and it'd been that way since the middle of our dinner. Before our entrees came, he moved his seat next to mine so he could kiss me and feel me up. My head was so up in the clouds to where if he wanted to have sex in the middle of that restaurant I would've happily obliged. The gifts he got me made it even worse. I'd heard my aunt say on several occasions that her love language was receiving gifts. I didn't understand that until now. Kyree got me a baby black Givenchy Mini Antigona Lock bag with the marching shark lock boots that I was sure I'd have to get stretched to fit my legs. I'd heard countless thick girls say they weren't big leg friendly. Regardless, I was still happy to have them and I looked forward to squeezing into them. To top it off he got me the prettiest Tiffany toggle bracelet and matching necklace. We were watching Mean Girls one day and I told him I always wanted one because of Gretchen. I couldn't believe he remembered that. I gave him my gifts last and I'd been worrying for no reason because he loved his Dunks. I also got him Dior and Valentino cologne because he loved to smell good. Now that I knew how he was coming I'd definitely spend more on him in the future. Ultimately, the night had been a dream and it wasn't over yet.

"Mari,"he chuckled because I eagerly pulled his lips back to mine after he pulled away.

"What?"I whined, with my arms around his neck and my body pressed against his.

"The elevator is open, that's what,"he grinned, before kissing me one more time and grabbing my hand. Our fingers locked as he led me to the room. When we got to the room he gave me a sneaky smile and I automatically knew there was another surprise behind that door.

"Close your eyes,"he directed. Anxious to see what else he'd done, I closed my eyes with no argument. I heard him unlock the door and then he led me inside. He then slipped my coat off after he took his off I'm assuming.

"Open your eyes now,"he said, after he closed the door. He was no longer holding my hand.

"Oh my goodness,"I gasped when I laid eyes on the suite. It was beautifully decorated. There were pink and red heart shaped balloons floating. Fake candles that looked like the real thing were all over the room as well as rose petals.

Potential by Summer Walker was playing on the smart tv, setting the mood.

"Mari, you about to cry?"He asked in amazement. That's when I noticed why he'd dropped my hand. He was recording me. I blinked my eyes and realized they were indeed wet. I quickly got it together, and held back.

"I really didn't think this day could get any more perfect,"I gushed, before flinging my arms around him. "I appreciate you so much Kyree."

"You appreciate *me*?"He appeared stunned. "Come here, girl..."

He grabbed me by my waist and slipped his tongue into my mouth. He backed down into the bed, never breaking the kiss, so I fell with him. I was half way on top of him, with one of my legs propped up on his body. My mini skirt had risen over my booty and I felt a drift but Kyree took care of that right away. His large hands brought me an abundance of warmth.

"Fuck,"Kyree vented like he was frustrated. He started fumbling with his belt until it was off and then he undid his zipper. "You got my dick hard as fuck, Mari."

I didn't know what to say in response to that, but my pussy responded to it.

"You heard me?"He pressed, as he kissed me again. His lips effortlessly coasted from my mouth down to my neck and to the top of my breasts that were threatening to pop out of my bustier.

"I need you to talk to me, baby."

"What do you want me to say?"I whispered, suddenly shy. I was convinced that I wanted to go all the way with him, but talking to him about it was another thing. I wasn't bold enough yet to say the nasty stuff that he could make sound so good.

"Tell me what you want,"he demanded, while peppering wet kisses along the top of my breasts. He had my pussy throbbing and he hadn't even gone near it yet.

"I want you to make this feel good for me..."

He stared at me for a few seconds, before pressing his forehead against mine.

"This is your first time being here, isn't it?"

I was wondering if he'd ever ask me about my v-card status. He probably just assumed I wasn't since everybody usually got that out the way in their teen years. I guess he couldn't ignore the obvious anymore.

"...Yea."

I noticed something change in his eyes, but I couldn't pinpoint what.

"You sure you want to do this with me?"

"I can't imagine a better person to do it with."

"You better not be imagining another nigga to do it with..."He smirked, making me laugh. "Forreal though, are you really ready? You been holding out for so long, I don't want you to feel ru-"

"I don't feel rushed. You said it yourself. I've been waiting forever, so I've had a lot of time to think of what I would want my first time to be like. This is as ideal as it gets."

He pressed his lips into mine, kissing me deeply. He moved his head back and looked into my eyes. "You said you want me to make it feel good?"

I bit my bottom lip and nodded.

"Talk."He ordered in a tone that made my pussy clench.

"Yes. I want you to make it feel good. I always hear horror stories about how the first time is always painful. I don't want that for me."

"Aw, Mari…"he chuckled like I'd said something hilarious. "I can't promise it won't hurt at first…but I can make everything leading up to penetration feel perfect. Lay all the way back, baby girl."

I loved when he called me Mari, but he'd called me two other pet names tonight; baby and baby girl. They were basic as ever but it made me weak in the knees and I didn't want to stand up. When I was laying back, he came out of his shirt revealing his ripped chest and buff arms. He had such a basketball player's body. It only made sense that he played in highschool. I wasn't prepared for him to start stripping me and I didn't have time to get ready. He had my skirt and top off in less than a minute, leaving me bare chested and in nothing but my thong. Before I could overthink and become self conscious, I looked at Kyree's face. The love, lust, and admiration was evident and that knocked any doubt out of my mind.

"You fucking perfect,"he voiced, while grabbing two handfuls of my breast. All my life I'd heard how my boobs were *too* big with negative connotations, but I never saw an issue with them. They were in fact big double d's, but they sat up in a way that was rare for big boobs. Honestly, I felt like God had blessed me in that department. They only got in the way when I couldn't wear certain tops.

"Ouuu,"I mewled when he sloshed his tongue over my hard nipples. He was alternating between both breasts like he didn't want one or the other to go without attention.

"O-ohhhh,"my head tilted back as the feeling I got while I was humping him in the spa overcame me. He didn't have to ask what it was this time because he knew.

"Damn, baby,"he uttered in disbelief but it was like he was gassed about it. He had every right to be too. Just like I'd heard girls say that their first time was painful, I'd also heard that they didn't cum. Meanwhile I'd already come from him merely sucking on my titties. He was definitely keeping his word and making this feel good.

"Is you ready? Is you ready, baby? You seem ready. You seem ready baby. Girl tonight I won't be selfish. It is all for you. Girl, my bad, I just can't help it. Girl, you taste so good, lovin, feel so numb..." Wus Good/ Curious by PND was playing as he placed kisses down my body. He was stopping at certain areas and tongue kissing them. He did it to my stomach, my hips, and he blew my mind when he licked my toes after kissing them. It was a good thing that I just got a pedicure the day before because he really sucked on them like it was his midnight snack. He was definitely making me curious about what was next. I had an idea when he slowly peppered wet kisses back up my legs before dragging his tongue near my vagina that was still covered by my thong.

"Kyreee," I moaned. He had actually started french kissing my pussy through my panties.

"You wet as fuck, Mari. Good fucking girl…"he ripped my panties down the middle in the smoothest way ever, before finally formally introducing his mouth to my pussy.

"Ohhh shitttt,"I bit down on my lip hard. He had opened my legs as wide as they could go, so my pussy was spread all the way open. He was a pro at this because he knew the exact spot to focus on, and he had me losing my mind. I had a grip on his dreads because I was using my hips to grind into his face. He played with my titties in the process and that just made me wetter. Because of him I realized that my boobs were sensitive and liked a lot of attention. The more he tweaked my nipples and flicked his tongue across my aching center the more I let go. I was holding onto that feeling again, but this time was different. It felt more powerful like I was on the brink of exploding.

"Stop playing and gimme that shit, Mari."

His words were like a greenlight for me and I finally released what I'd been holding back.

Kyree

This girl had squirted and that shit took me by surprise. It wasn't one of those dramatic, fake porn squirts because if it was she would've got me in the eye. That's how close I was to her pussy. I was all in that muthafucker like a tampon, and I'd gladly stay there after tasting her. When I saw her fat ass pussy print beneath her thong, I knew I was going to have fun with her ass and I'd done that. The reward was her sweet juices that she'd just squirted out. I had to show my appreciation to her by licking it up.

"Kyyyy,"she whined, while trying to move my head. She was undoubtedly still sensitive down there but that wouldn't deter me.

"Chill out,"I growled. "Let me enjoy the fruits of my labor."

"Oh God…you're trying to kill me,"she whimpered, as I continued to clean her pussy up with long flickers of my tongue. "Why are you trying to kill me?"

"So I didn't make you feel good?"I asked, when I came up to her face to kiss her. I tongued her down so she could see why I wanted to stay down there.

After kissing her for a little while, I couldn't take it anymore. My dick was straining against my boxers and begging to slide up in something warm and tight, specifically Kamaria. I stood up to take off my pants and boxers. When my dick sprung out, Mari looked like she saw a car wreck in real time. I wasted no time trying to assure her that it would be okay.

"It's gon be alright. It'll only hurt for a second."

"Why don't I believe you?"

She was smart. My dick was nine inches long and thick with a mushroom head. It was probably going to hurt the whole time because she'd never taken dick before.

I laughed as I got back into the bed, and climbed on top of her. I watched her catch a chill when my bare dick touched her wet and juicy pussy. I usually didn't do shit like this because I deemed it as childish, but I wasn't in a rush for her to be in pain. In fact, I'd rather watch her enjoy herself. That's why I rubbed my dick against her clit. She was moaning like it was the best feeling ever, and I couldn't stunt, that shit felt good to me too. Her fat pussy lips felt good coating my dick and her wetness made gliding against her easy.

"Yessss,"she chanted as her eyes shut tight and her legs shook. My baby came again. She was three for three. I gave myself an invisible pat on the back.

"You ready for me, Mari?"

"Yea…"she replied weakly, still coming down from the orgasm.

Before she could overthink it, I lined my dick up with her hole and pushed my way in. All the air seemingly left her body, as she laid there as still as a rock. She was having a natural reaction to being in pain. Getting my dick wet was the least of my concern at that moment, I just wanted her to feel better. I noticed how she got aroused the most whenever I played with them big ass titties, so I kissed all over them. That got a few moans out of her, so I ventured deeper into her.

"Uhhhh!"She gasped with wide, tearfilled eyes.

"Should I stop?"I asked. The last time I broke somebody's virginity was in highschool and ole girl took it like a G. Mari had me feeling like I was slowly killing her and it was fucking me up. I couldn't even fully bask in how good and snug her fucking pussy felt.

"No…I'ma be okay…it's just big,"she sniveled.

"I'ma mold you to me, baby. Watch,"I pecked her lips and then double backed for a nasty tongue kiss. While she was distracted, I plunged the rest of my dick into her.

"Kyree!"She screeched.

"I-it's in my baby,"I stuttered. I had broken her in and felt it. I was her first. That shit made me feel *proud*. No matter what happened moving forward nobody could take this highest honor away from me. "You feel it?"

"Hell yea I feel it,"she whispered, as a tear rolled down her cheek. I kissed it away before I started to thrust in and out of her slowly. I'd had my fair share of tight pussy in the past, but I never had a pussy that suffocated my dick and submerged me in what felt like an ocean. She was snatching my shit and it was the best feeling in the world. I was already thinking of more things I could buy her because she really deserved the world for what she had between her legs. It was lethal.

"This shit so fucking wet, Mari...it feels like it was made for me,"I grunted as I rocked my dick in and out of her.

"It was,"she moaned, while running her fingers through my locs and her legs were wrapped around my torso. For the first time since I penetrated her I realized she was enjoying it.

"Yea? This my pussy?"

"Yesss!"

"Scream that shit then. Let everybody on this floor hear you,"I gritted while fucking her at a faster pace. I was trying to thug it out, but I was holding on by a thread. I blamed her for having good pussy and giving me ownership of it.

"This is your pussy, Kyree! Only yours!"She screamed. I got a few more pumps in before I lost the battle with myself and nutted. I gazed into Mari's eyes longingly for a few seconds before I realized what I was doing.

"Ohhhh shit,"I quickly pulled out and released the rest of my nut on the face of her pussy. "My bad, Mari..."

When I looked back at her, she was looking at me nervously.

"What's the matter, baby?"

"How was it? Did you like it?"

Laughter escaped my mouth at that ridiculous question.

"Liking it would be an understatement, love. My dumb ass forgot to put on a condom, and I slipped up and nutted in you. I never do reckless shit like that. So I think it's safe to say I loved it and you're my future wife, so start planning our wedding."

"Wait, what?"She giggled.

"Yea, I figure we should graduate first, get an apartment or condo together, get situated into our careers, and then we'll get married and have a family. Shit, we might be having that baby first because the first half of my nut definitely went inside of you."

"What?!"

"Chill, I'm just playing,"I laughed to ease her mind. "One lil time ain't gon do nothing."

"Kyree, I paid attention in health class. One time is all it takes, which is why I'm going get an Ella pill tomorrow."

"The fuck is an Ella pill?"

"Something for bitches my size."

"Whatever man, as long as you know you that you're going to be my wife and have my babies then we good."

"Okay,"she huffed with a smile. I could tell she thought this shit was a game, but it really wasn't. I could show her better than I could tell her just how serious this was.

Chapter 7

Kamaria

February 16, 2020

I was not the same. I had been bitten by the love bug and there was no undoing it. I hadn't left Kyree's side since losing my virginity, and I dreaded the time we'd eventually have to separate. If I could follow him to class and sit in his lap during his lessons I probably would. That's how deep my feelings had gotten for him. He wasn't making it any better by being just as clingy. Like right now, we were driving in his car and he was holding my hand and kissing it every other minute. At every red light he'd lean over and kiss my lips. Why would I want to be apart from him?

"We almost there, Mari. You good?"

"I'm nervous as hell, but I'll be okay."

"I got you," he kissed my hand again, making my heart flutter. "You look beautiful, baby."

"Thank you,"I smiled as if it wasn't his umpteenth time telling me this today. I felt good about my outfit, hair, and makeup. My bun from Valentine's was ruined on Valentine's Day, so I threw on a bone straight wig with a middle part I had that was in excellent condition. I put a leather baker boy cap on over it that went perfectly with my leather over the knee boots and Givenchy purse. My outfit was really simple consisting of jeans and a black and white Fendi sweater. I wanted to be fully covered since I was meeting his family, but I still didn't want to lose the sexy I'd been gaining. I think I found a fine balance today. My makeup was natural as usual, and I took a page from Chyna's book with brown lip liner and pink lip gloss combo. Not to be dramatic, but that shit made me feel and look like a new woman.

"Twitter is so funny,"I laughed, as I scrolled through quotes from my Valentine's day post. I'd only posted my gifts but the post had gotten over thousands of retweets. "Ky, somebody said you must sell drugs for a living."

"That's fucked up,"he chuckled. "I ain't gon lie though, before I started getting to my own bag I used to wonder how college students had bukoo bread to blow."

"Yea…I could say a lot about my people, but I'm so glad they take care of me financially."

Majority of my schooling was covered by academic scholarships, so my parents were willing to help me out when it came to living. They made great money as neurosurgeons, so I would get a monthly allowance of $1500. For a college student with no real bills that was more than enough. I also had multiple credit cards to use at my leisure. Outside of necessities, I never spent a lot of money. I took myself shopping at the beginning of every season for new clothes, but I didn't overdo it. When it came to my high-priced designer items, I'd accumulated those things over time on my parents' dime. Then there was my aunt who loved spoiling me whenever I got all A's or did anything remotely impressive. Most of my really expensive stuff came from her. I recognized I had it great financially because a lot of my peers were struggling. Getting an education and living in the real world was costly.

"Yea, that's a major blessing. My parents were doing all they could to help me out but they couldn't maintain the house, take care of my sisters, and fund my whole life. The most they were able to do during my freshman year was send me a few hundred a month. I appreciated it, but I had to make something shake so I could live the way I wanted to live."

"You probably wouldn't be satisfied with what my parents send me per month, either."

"How much do they send you?"

"1500 dollars"

"Yeaaaa..."he laughed. "I would've thought that was major a few years ago, but the rent for my off campus apartment is $1200 alone."

"Even with a roommate?"I marveled.

"Hey, you get what you pay for."

I had to admit that his apartment was really nice. It came with every amenity you could think of, and it was spacious. His room was on a completely different side than Rashad's, giving them both privacy.

"Then I got my baby,"he patted the wheel to his black 2018 S-Class Benz. "The maintenance on this is expensive. Thank God I don't have a note."

I got my car when I turned 16, and it was a white BMW truck. I didn't even choose the car. I wanted a yellow Kia Forte really badly. My mom would turn up her nose whenever I suggested it, but my dad made it seem as if he'd get me that car. So I was very surprised to walk outside to a BMW after my birthday dinner. I couldn't say anything because I'd look extremely ungrateful complaining about getting a foreign car. Besides, the vehicle *was* nice.

"Yea, my car is paid off too but I'm responsible for the upkeep and it's not cheap. Plus, that little fucker is a gas guzzler."

He chuckled. "You got a nice ride though, and didn't you tell me that you got that when you were 16? Man, you should've seen my first ride at 17. Nobody could tell me shit though because I had wheels."

"Yea, I got it when I was 16, but it was my mom's choice. She deliberately went against what I wanted,"I laughed.

"What, you wanted something out of their price range?"

"Nope. What I wanted was actually significantly cheaper. My dad seemed to be cool with what I asked for, but I know my mama got in his head like she always does. The next morning after they gifted the car to me she asked if I liked it, and I said yea…and that wasn't a lie. It is a nice car."

"It just wasn't what you asked for."

"Right. My thing was why pretend like I had a choice when I really didn't? Anyway, when I said yes she was like 'good, because no child of mine was going to ride around in what *you* wanted.'"

"Damn, what did you want?"

"A Kia!"

"What's her beef with Kia's?"He chuckled.

"If I had to guess I'd say she didn't like the fact that I didn't want a luxury vehicle. She likes to keep up appearances, and give Facebook and our family a show."

"Damn…well, how about I get you a Kia as a graduation gift?"

"Ky, I am *not* 16 anymore. I don't want that damn car."

"Okay,"he laughed. "So what's your dream car now?"

"A G-Wagon."

"Damn, well I guess I better get to hustling and throw some more parties."

"That can always be my push present. No pressure."

"Yo' push present? Oh, so you warmed up to having my babies, huh?"

"Yup. One day."

If a stranger was witnessing this conversation they'd think we were both delusional. We had a four day old relationship and had already agreed to having kids together. Now I knew what my grandma meant when she said love turned people into fools. I didn't know if I was in love, but whatever I felt was strong and I wanted it forever.

Kyree

I told my baby that she had nothing to worry about, and I meant that. When we got to my parents house the first thing my mom did was welcome her with a great, big hug. My dad followed suit, but I wasn't feeling how she looked at that nigga with stars in her eyes. He was the older version of me, but she needed to chill out. Anyways, dinner was going well. Of course my mama had a million and one questions, but Kamaria was handling them with ease.

"So do you know how to cook, baby?"

"Only the easy stuff. Nothing like this,"she gestured towards the mashed potatoes, crab macaroni, and lamb chops my mom had cooked. "I'd love to learn though."

"I love to teach, so we might just make a good pair."

"Be careful, Mari,"my dad butted in. I wanted to tell him that she was Kamaria to him, but that would've been ridiculous. "She's a drill sergeant in the kitchen."

"Don't listen to those lies, Mari,"she tittered. When she stopped, she just stared at her face as if she was trying to see something.

"Mama, stop being weird."I called her out.

"Boy, hush! This girl is just glowing."

Kamaria beamed."Aw, thanks. I used Fenty Beauty foundation and Trophy Wife highlighter. It works wond-"

"Baby, I am *not* talking about your makeup."

My dad bursted into laughter. "Son, how'd you get this sweet girl to give *you* a chance?"

That was a nice way of him saying that I was too advanced for her. Maybe I was, but she was mine now. It was too late to backtrack.

"So are y'all using condoms?"My mom blurted out.

My dad choked on his wine. "Really, Nette?"

"Yes. I wanna know. Cause I don't want any grandkids from Kyree until he's out of college."

"I don't want to have kids anytime soon myself,"Mari said.

"Not wanting them is one thing, but are y'all doing anything to prevent it?"

For the first time since dinner started, Mari looked over to me for help.

"I'ma assume y'all are not using condoms,"my mom concluded.

"Chill out, Mama. She's going to get on birth control."

After we got her a morning after pill we discussed it, and she made an appointment with her doctor. By next week she'd be on birth control. I'd also been doing a good job at pulling out since Valentine's day.

"Chileee…"my mom look at my dad. "Didn't I tell you, Kylo?"

"You told me,"he nodded.

"What are y'all talking about?"I questioned. They were doing too much.

"I told your daddy that Miss Kamaria here had his son's heart in her pocket,"she tittered. "I ain't mad at it though. I just want y'all to be smart."

"I will be,"Kamaria spoke up.

"Damn,"my dad laughed. "I guess she can't speak for you, son."

"I don't know why, it was *my* idea for her to get on birth control."

She squeezed my hand under the table. I instantly knew that was my que to change the subject. I looked over at her and she was laughing with everybody, but it was a fake laugh. Nobody but me would've noticed it.

"So Dad, did you see the Laker game last week?"I steered the conversation in another direction.

Soon, my dad and I were discussing sports while my mom and Kamaria were talking about their favorite fashion brands. One thing Lanette Pierre loved was her labels and dressing. She would always say she worked too hard to cheat herself and that's why she was always treating herself.

Ding-Dong!

"Who's that?"I asked.

My mom checked her phone. "That's Cambrie. She asked me what I was cooking earlier and asked if she could stop by for a plate. I started to think she wasn't going to come."

My dad got up to go let her in.

"Who's Cambrie?"Kamaria asked me discreetly.

"My cousin,"I responded. Cambrie and I were the same age, so we grew up really close. We weren't as close as we used to be but that was only because I'd been in BR while she attended Grambling. She graduated college last year, so she was back in New Orleans. I was sure if I moved back to New Orleans we'd spend way more time together because she was my dawg.

I turned around when I heard my dad re-entering the dining room because I wanted to greet Cambrie. Right away, I noticed the warning eyes my dad was sending me. I had no clue what it was about until he moved back to his seat. Cambrie wasn't alone. She was here with my fucking ex-girlfriend. I was sure it looked like I'd seen a ghost, and Mari definitely noticed.

"Hey family,"Hailey said with a big, forced smile on her face. I don't think she was expecting me to be here with my new girlfriend. If she did and showed up then that was the messiest shit ever, and she was far from that.

My mom looked surprised, but she still spoke and got up to greet them properly with a hug. I cringed when I heard her refer to Hailey as "daughter in law."

"Is one of your sisters a lesbian or something?"Kamaria whispered in my ear. I ignored her.

"Hey cousin, I didn't know you'd be here,"Cambrie said, confirming what I thought. Even though Hailey and I had been broken up for years she was still close to my family. In fact, she'd been friends with Cambrie first. It wasn't odd that she'd slide to my parents house with Cambrie for a plate of food. What made it awkward was me being here with Kamaria.

"Hey Cam,"I stood up to hug her. When I pulled away I turned to Kamaria. "This is my girlfriend, Kamaria. Mari, this is my cousin, Cambrie."

"Hi, it's nice to meet you,"Mari held her hand out.

"Hey…"Cambrie uttered dryly, and then she shook her hand like she didn't even want to do it.

"So how long have y'all been together?"Hailey questioned, looking directly at me as if I'd betrayed her.

"I'm sorry, I didn't get your name,"Mari said in the sweetest voice but wasn't shit sweet on her end and it was evident.

"Your boyfriend knows it,"Hailey responded in an even sweeter voice.

"But I'm asking *you*. Surely you can tell me your own name."

"Alright,"my mom stood up. "I see where this is going and there'll be none of that in my house. Hailey is Kyree's ex, Kamaria, and while I respect and support y'alls relationship, Hailey will always be welcomed around our family too."

Kamaria appeared to be baffled by what my mom said, and so was I. She had just made her sound way more important than what she really was. That's why it wasn't a good idea to bring everybody around your damn family. Bonds were created and muthafuckers got carried away.

Hailey stood there with a proud smile on her face."Exactly, don't act like we weren't just together or like you

179

weren't hitting my line telling me how much you miss me. You could never stunt on me in front of this big bitch."

Before I could formulate my words to go *in* on her delusional ass, my mom immediately intervened.

"Okay Hailey, now you *do* have to leave. I don't tolerate disrespect in my house."

Hailey's skin turned red, showcasing just how flustered she was. She immediately started explaining herself. I guess she didn't want to get on my mama's bad side.

"Mrs.Pierre, I'm sorry! You know I wasn't trying to disrespect you. I just don't appreciate what's going on here. I was just over here for dinner a few weeks ago s-"

"Man, you popped up over here just like you did today. Don't make it seem like I invited you!"

"I popped up?! Wowww, you really want to show off in front of your new girl. You know your sisters told me to pull up."

I never imagined this night taking a turn like this. Hailey never brought this type of energy even with girls I'd cheated on her with. We'd been broken up for years, so her getting all hype over Kamaria was ridiculous. I wasn't going for that shit either. Kamaria didn't have to say shit because I wasn't letting it go any further.

"No, you reached out to them asking if you could come over and they said yes because they're nice and have no issues with you. But please chill like it's something going on with me and you."

"Kyree, you and I know what went down between us that night! Don't ever play with me like I'm some desperate ass female."

Kamaria

I'd been quiet thus far because the only way to understand what was going on was to listen. I didn't even feel the need to say anything when Hailey called me fat because…well, that was unoriginal and tired. My "fat ass" was sitting next to the man she was pressed like a panini about, so there was really nothing to address. I was more concerned about why she was so mad in the first place. In my mind the only way she'd be in her feelings was if Kyree had been entertaining her recently. Her response had just confirmed my suspicions. Not wanting to jump to conclusions, I waited for Kyree's rebuttal. When he merely smacked his teeth and said "mannn," I decided I didn't need to hear anything else. He was still messing around with this chick, and I was ready to see myself out. With the way I was feeling I would Uber back to BR.

"I'll just see myself out,"I uttered, while standing up.

"Woahhh,"Kyree grabbed my hand. "Where you going?"

I snatched my hand back as if it touched a hot stove.

"Don't touch me. I'm clearly the intruder here. You have unfinished business with this girl, and your mom said she's always welcomed so I'll just remove myself from the equation,"I hissed, before storming off. I heard Kyree, his mom, and his dad calling my name and telling me to come back, but I wasn't trying to hear it. Especially from his mom who'd made her stance clear out the gate. It wasn't until I stepped out onto the front porch that I realized Kyree was right behind me.

"Seriously, where the fuck you going? I brought you here!"

"I'll figure it out,"I mumbled, as I pulled out my phone to call my daddy. He always told me if I was somewhere I didn't want to be to call him. Before I could press his name, my phone was swiftly removed from my hand.

"Excuse you?"I scoffed.

"Look, I brought you here so if you ready to go then we can leave. It's nothing."

"I'm not getting in the car with you."

"Mari…I know you not tripping on what Hailey said back there."

"Oh, you mean how she exposed that she still has dinner with the family and that y'all recently had sex? Noooo, I'm cool with that,"I said sarcastically. "Hell yes, I'm mad! Why would I want to be with you if you're still fooling around with your ex?!"

"Because I'm not! I admit, I've been guilty of entertaining her but it was before me and you. And we didn't have sex recently."

"Really? Because you didn't dispute that in front of her!"

"And that's only because I didn't want to say what *really* went down in front of my parents."

"Yea, whatever,"I huffed. Kyree and I had only been an official couple for a few days, so it was believable that whatever happened between him and Hailey was before us. That didn't take away from how the whole ordeal made me feel though. She was infiltrated into his family in a way that made it apparent that I'd have to deal with her being around. That's not something I felt as though I should have to deal with.

"I'm serious, Mari. As a matter of fact, I'll show you our message thread right now…and I'll block her on everything,"he said, as he went for his phone. He couldn't even get it out of his jeans before the door swung open and Hailey stepped out with his cousin, Cambrie. They both had bags of food in their hands. I guess Nette had to make sure her daughter in law ate regardless of everything that had just gone down. I thought I was overthinking it when Cambrie gave me a dry greeting, but it turns out I hadn't been. Hailey was her girl, and apparently she was close with his sisters too. Thanks to my childhood I knew the feeling of being ostracized all too well and I went out of my way to avoid it as an adult. Now I was being subjected to it all over a man.

"Are you serious, Kyree? You gon really stunt on her like this?"Cambrie asked.

"I'm dead ass serious. I don't have no reason to stunt on no *Hailey*,"he said her name as if he detested it. "Y'all doing the most, bruh."

"That's fucked up and you know it!"Cambrie shouted. "You was just with this girl last we-"

"Man, she sucked my dick when I was blacked out drunk. I passed out in the middle of that tired shit."

Hailey was undeniably hurt as her eyes grew misty. I was on the verge of feeling bad for her until she opened her mouth.

"At the end of the day you let me do it which means you cheated on this fat bitch!"

"Bit-"Kyree started angrily, but I cut him off. He didn't need to speak for me anymore.

"Sweetie, up until a few days ago we were strictly friends. We had never kissed, had sex, nada. I don't know how he used to treat *you*, but he didn't cheat on me. And I can guarantee if I put my mouth on him he wouldn't fall asleep. Oh, and call me another fat bitch. Please, I'm begging you."I clasped my hands, while stepping towards her. The only fights I'd had were against my female cousins growing up, but that was all the practice I needed to slap this bitch silly. Fighting over boys was a no in my book, but she kept coming for me. She was asking for it and she was going to get it.

"BITCH HE NEVER CHEATED ON ME EITHER, YOU BIG F-"

Close enough. I drew my hand back and popped her in the mouth the way my granny used to whenever I got mouthy. The only difference is I used immense force, resulting in her lip busting due to it hitting her teeth. Kyree quickly jumped in the middle of us and pushed her back as she tried to charge at me.

"Kyree move!"She screamed, with tears in her eyes and blood running down her chin.

"Cambrie, take your girl and leave. You know my mama wouldn't appreciate all this going down at her house."

"Really? Your bitch hit her first!"Cambrie shouted, as she stepped closer like she wanted to do something. Kyree pushed her back too.

"I'm still being called out of my name?"I asked in perplexity. I was amped up and Cambrie could get it too!

"Y'all being disrespectful! She ain't do shit to either one of y'all. Hailey if you got beef then take it up with me! And Cambrie, you supposed to be *my* family!"

"That goes without saying! But right is right and wrong is wrong!" Cambrie clapped her hands, making her stance clear. She was rolling with her girl which meant any chance of us having a friendship was dead. I was fine with that even though I had been looking forward to having great relationships with his family. Oh well. Fuck her.

"Fuck that! Move, Kyree! I'ma fuck this bitch up!"Hailey screamed.

"Hey! I know y'all then lost y'all damn minds doing all this bullshit in front my door!"Kyree's dad barged outside along with his mom. "Kyree, you know we don't play this shit."

"Neither do I! Tell them to leave like y'all should've done from the moment they arrived and this stupid hoe was on fuck shit!"

"Kyree,"his mom gasped. "Have you lost your damn mind?!"

"Ion mind helping his ass find it,"his dad rolled his sleeves up.

Kyree took a deep breath as if he were holding on to his composure. It was apparent that he wanted to go off but out of respect for his parents he was trying to hold back.

"I apologize, but all y'all out of line. I'm with Kamaria,"he pointed at me. "I haven't been with Hailey in *years*, so why should my girlfriend have to be uncomfortable to appease her?"

I expected a response from Hailey but she was too busy breathing all heavy and silently crying like a big ass baby. Her lip looked like it was growing fatter and bloodier by the second. I held back a smirk at my handy work.

"Kyree, I'm not trying to appease anybody. I just didn't think I had to treat Hailey any differently. She's been to this house plenty of times since y'all broke up and there's been no drama,"his mom said, making my stomach turn. Was she blaming me?

"Yea, there's been no drama because up until now I never had an official girlfriend. She came up in your house being straight up disrespectful and you really put her on a pedestal as if she's important to come and go as she pleases."

"I didn't do that. I was just saying that this is my house and Hailey has always been welcomed."

"Nette…"his dad spoke up. I could tell he didn't want to insert his opinion, but he was going to anyway. "You may not be trying to do that, but that's how it's coming across. Kyree is our son. We should respect his wishes first and foremost."

"And I agree, Kylo, but up until today he's never said Hailey couldn't come around. If he had I wouldn't have said that."

"So you thought I would be cool with my ex-girlfriend passing through while my current girlfriend was over for dinner?"He squinted at her in disbelief.

"Boy, you know good and well I didn't know Hailey was coming!"

"Could've fooled me,"he mumbled.

"I'm trying to see why that even matters though? This has been my best friend since elementary school. She's *been* a part of this family and that's not about to change for her,"Cambrie looked me up and down in disgust. To my surprise, I laughed.

"That's funny?"She hissed.

"It's *hilarious*,"I tittered, before rolling my eyes. "I could care less that y'all are best friends or if she's a part of y'all family."

"And neither do I. We can't undo the past, but as far as *my* parents' house goes in the future, she's not welcomed."

"Mrs.Pierre?"Cambrie looked at her with the saddest puppy dog face.

"Sorry, baby, but I gotta back my son on this one. And you did show up here cutting up today."

"I apologized for that!"

"Apology accepted, but seeing Kyree with someone else obviously bothers you and I can't trust that you'll control yourself in the future. And I don't want the rest of your pretty lil face getting messed up. "

Her skin turned red with embarrassment."She barely even touched me!"

"Cambrie take Hailey and y'all be on y'all way,"Kyree's dad ordered.

"So my best friend can't come over here no more?"

"Nope, or anything else me or my people throw. That includes birthdays, get-togethers, and holidays."

"Wowww, well if that's the case your girlfriend can't come to anything me or my mama throw. That includes my birthday party! Just like you don't want to make her uncomfortable I don't want to make my best friend uncomfortable!"

A look of disappointment flushed over Ms.Nette's face. "Now Cambrie...Kyree is your *blood.* You should rock with whoever he choo-"

"Nah, it's cool, ma. She picked her side, and I for sure picked mine. Anywhere Kamaria can't be, I just won't be."

Involuntary chills ran up my spine. Not too long ago I swore I would walk away because I couldn't see myself dealing with this messy drama. But I could never turn my back on someone who stood ten toes down for me like this. He was willing to go against his favorite cousin just to stand in solidarity with me. He'd also checked his mama in front of me and his entitled ass ex. Those actions behind his words spoke volumes to how he felt about me. Leave him alone for what? He didn't even do anything.

"So you picking her over me! Your cousin?!"

"Shit, it sounds like you picking Hailey over him,"Ms.Nette tilted her head to the side. To that, Cambrie didn't have shit to say.

"Let's just go, best,"Hailey muttered, while wiping her tears. I watched them carefully as they walked off. I figured they'd still be on go and want to get Hailey's lick back, but they left quietly.

"I apologize, Kamaria,"his dad spoke up.

"Me too, baby. I didn't know things would go left like that, and I want you to know that you're more than welcomed here,"Ms.Nette added.

I nodded my head because I still felt some type of way. Pressing the issue was not an option though. These were Kyree's parents and I wanted to be good with them. It would only affect our relationship if there was beef because he loved his parents. It was still fuck his cousin though.

"And I'ma call my sister and tell her about Cambrie's ass,"she went on. "I bet she be singing a different tune by tomorrow."

"Ma, I swear it's all good. I ain't tripping about going to no party."

I couldn't tell if he was serious or bluffing, but I still felt the need to speak up.

"Ky, you can go to her party without me. That's still your cousin at the end of the day."

Out of the corner of my eye I could see his mom looking at me with a small smile on her face.

"She'll be my cousin until the end of time and until she learns to fuck with you, she ain't fucking with me either. We a two for one special."

His dad chuckled. "Hey, I ain't mad at that, son. I ain't mad at all."

I wasn't mad at it either. In fact, it made me fall for Kyree Genesis Pierre even harder.

Chapter 8

Kyree

February 20, 2020

"Fuck, Mari," I groaned with my eyes closed as Kamaria's dainty little hand slithered under my Nike sweats and inside of my Calvin Klein boxer briefs. One stroke of her hand on my hard dick had me bitching up, and I wasn't even trying to save face. I wasn't ashamed of her seeing the effect she had on me. She continuously moved her soft hand up and down my hardness, and I couldn't help but be vocal. With any other girl I would've been ready to get down to business, but foreplay with her was alright with me.

"If you want to go up there. I'ma show you how but you can't be scared. Listen close and pay attention. And follow the directions. Your gonna make a left on touchin' boulevard. When you see kissin' street. Make a right, keep

straight, and go all the way. And that'll run ya into good

love," Directions by Mario played from my Alexa speaker as I

enveloped her lips in mine, and stuck my tongue in her mouth.

She was speeding up the pace, and I was on the verge of

nutting. I normally didn't like to burst prematurely, but it didn't

really matter because my dick wasn't going to get soft. It rarely

was on soft whenever me and her were alone. That's why she

hated doing homework or studying with me. She was a very

disciplined person and she didn't play about her grades. I

respected that, but I was needy as fuck. She loved being in

my presence too but she could pull away especially if she

needed too for the sake of school. I wasn't the same. Quite

frankly, it was obvious that I was borderline obsessed with her

ass. As long as she was next to me and I could feel her, I

didn't care about shit else. I could just stare at her ass doing

trivial things like her hair, doing laundry, or brushing her teeth.

She'd always catch me and tell me stop being weird before

doing that soft ass laugh that I loved from day one.

Today, I put my foot down and made her ass come

back to my place. I promised to stay off of her and let her

study for her test tomorrow. I had some homework to do myself, so it was easy to keep my word. I guess she was done studying before I finished my paper because she came laid under me as I was typing. Her soft body on mine along with her head on my chest was enough to wake my dick up but I was able to control myself. That was a wrap once she started kissing on me and shit. The five page essay for my Management 201 class wasn't due until after Mardi Gras break. I'd just been trying to get a head start, and I did knock out three pages. Therefore, I had no qualms about closing my Macbook and giving her my full attention. That's what led us into the position we were in.

"You're close aren't you?"She asked. She knew damn well what the answer was to her question. Pre cum was oozing out of my dick.

"I wanna try something,"she said softly while biting her lip in a way that made my dick jump in anticipation. When she started moving to the lower half of body I already knew what was up and I was honored. I was assuming since she never had sex prior to me that she probably hadn't given or been on the receiving end of head either. Based on how she looked up at me with those pretty, innocent eyes I was certain that I was correct in my assumption. When she took me into her mouth I didn't have to assume any further. This was her first time and I could see her figuring it out all over her face. Still, seeing her in the act of having my dick in her mouth was enough for me to bust all over her pretty ass face. I could tell my baby wanted some direction though, so I quickly jumped into teacher mode. I never got tired of showing her the way around the bedroom. When I was done with her she'd be a pro in knowing what I liked, but most importantly, she'd know what she liked. You couldn't learn somebody else's body if you didn't know your own, and Kamaria was becoming more in tune with herself as the days went by.

"Yea…there you go…more spit, make it sloppy…spit on that shit if you have to,"I breathed deeply to control a moan that threatened to escape. I know I said I had no shame but I did have to draw the line somewhere. Her mouth had made it to the middle of my dick and she was just getting the hang of what to do with it. I appreciated how she was taking heed to my tips the minute they left my mouth. She was always so determined.

"You can get more in that pretty little mouth…"

She looked up at me with fear in her eyes, propelling me to crack a smile.

"You can't be scared of that shit, Mari. Ion don't care if you gag or choke as long as you keep sucking that dick."

I wasn't going to mention how her gagging and choking on my dick would turn me on even more. I just let her apply the lesson I gave her, and like the good girl she was she got right to it. My dick was long and girthy so it was no surprise that she was struggling with sucking my entire length, but damn, she was trying her hardest. I was on the verge of nutting just watching her gagging and stroking the base of my dick since she couldn't reach it with her mouth.

"Alright, baby…t-that's enough,"I breathed heavily, as I pulled her off my dick.

She looked at me with a hint of worry in her eyes.

"How was I?"

"You were perfect,"I grabbed her jaw and pulled her up to me so I could tongue kiss her. I was already sitting up against the headboard, so I pulled her into my lap as we kissed nastily. She was wearing itty bitty pajama shorts with no underwear and my white beater with no bra. Now that I thought about it she had to have getting fucked on her mind when she put that shit on. She probably was just expecting me to get it started like I always did. But she had to be the one to get shit popping this time and I liked that. That shell she once had was a thing of the past.

She'd slipped her shorts to the side and climbed right on my dick that was still brick hard and saluting her pussy. I taught her how to ride the day after I broke her in and she didn't need any further instruction. After she got used to sitting on it, she became a natural cowgirl. I'd heard most women complain about riding during sex, but I was starting to think it was Mari's favorite position. Prior to her my favorite position was doggystyle, but a position didn't even matter to me anymore. As long as my dick was deep in her warm, wet, and tight walls then I was in heaven.

"When I lay back, shawty don't know how to act. She ready when the lights go off, she climb on top. Her body rocking, we don't stop. No handle bars or falling off, 'cause 'cause....she ride me like a porn star, she ride me like a porn star. She ride me like a pro. She did this shit before. I hold her tight, no letting go 'til she say she can't take no more. I'm speechless..." August Alsina's Porn Star conveniently played as she moved her body better than the freakiest females I'd been with in the past. She was indeed my own personal porn star.

"Ughhhh,"she moaned when I caught one of her bouncing titties in my mouth. They'd long ago popped out of my shirt. The attention I gave to her aroused nipples must've motivated her because she picked up the pace. Her ass was abundantly bouncing and slapping against my balls. I grabbed two handfuls of both cheeks and started pounding that pussy.

"KYREEEE!"She screamed. I felt her raining down on my dick, and her legs shook.

That did it for me. Her screaming my name or her cumming with my dick in her was like pushing a "GO" button and I was bound to nut. I let out an animalistic grunt as I

nutted for what felt like forever. She sensually locked lips with

me for at least thirty seconds until she realized I was still

nutting. She abruptly pulled away from me.

"Okay, you're doing a lot,"she huffed, before trying to lift

up.

"Nah, this is all for you. Don't fucking play with me,"I

gritted, while firmly holding her hips in place. Her resolve

instantly softened, and right then I knew her ass was gon shut

up and take this nut.

"That's what I thought,"I said cockily. I went on to

tongue kiss the side of her neck.

"Kyreeee,"she whined. "You have to chill with this. I

can't get pregnant."

"You won't,"I kissed her lips. "I'm done anyway."

"Yea, after emptying a gallon of your sperm in me. I just

got off my period."

"Forreal,"I smirked.

She pushed my face back. "You knew that!"

"Why are you tripping? You're on birth control now."

"And you know I'm still getting the hang of those pills. Regardless, you should at least try to pull out."

"Trying to pull out is not an option with you Mari, sorry. If you don't want to get pregnant then I suggest you get the hang of those pills."

"Or I could just stop having sex with you,"she grumbled. I finally allowed her to get up and she got out of bed. She was probably going straight to the shower like she'd always do after we had sex because I always nutted in her. Honestly, I'd never been more consistent with anything so I was proud of myself.

I laughed. "Who you fooling, baby? You the one came your hot ass bothering me while I was being a model student, doing homework early and shit."

"That was payback for all the times you've interrupted me."

"Well shit, feel free to pay me back anytime, my love."

A big grin overcame her face, instantly making me smile, too. I didn't even know why she was smiling from ear to ear, seeing her happy was just contagious for me.

"Why you smiling, girl?"

"I'm your love?"She grinned.

"Mannn,"I laughed. I hadn't realized I called her that. I'd told two girls I loved them in the past but I never really felt anything behind it. It was just something I'd tell them because they told me first. I felt like since they were my girlfriends it was only right. Truthfully, I was just young and doing anything. I didn't know what the fuck love was then. Now…I think I was figuring it out. Referring to a female as "love" was nothing for a New Orleans nigga. That was a term of endearment used for any good looking girl, but putting "my" in front of it made a world of difference. I was claiming Kamaria as *my love.* That was major and it came out so naturally that I hadn't even realized it until she reacted.

"Yea, you my love."

I sat all the way up and pulled her between my legs to kiss her.

"Well you're my love, too,"she giggled, before pulling my hand. "C'mon, let's go shower together."

"Shit, c'mon,"I stood up. I was mesmerized as she led the way to the bathroom in my room and I watched her ass jiggle in those tiny pink shorts. I couldn't help but reach out and slap it.

Funny enough, after she just got done talking shit about not fucking me anymore because I refused to pull out, we ended up going for round two in the shower. And of course I nutted in her ass again and this time I made her verbalize that it was okay for me to do so. When our shower was over she tried to slip in some other pajamas she brought with her, but I made her take her ass to bed with me butt naked. I needed to be able to slide into her with ease whenever I felt like it. She offered no objections, so she was with the bullshit.

"So what's your plans for Mardi Gras?"I asked through a yawn. I was tired, but I felt like talking to her.

"My parents usually go to their friend's mansion on St.Charles and Peniston."

"Ain't that's the bougie white people part?"I quizzed. I grew up Uptown but I'd never been that far down St.Charles for Mardi Gras. Whenever I did walk down I didn't make it past the big McDonald's.

"Something like that,"she giggled. "But New Orleans is a predominantly black city, so it's a lot of us in that area too. My parents' friends are black…but they have a lot of white friends."

"How's Mardi Gras with them?"

"Honestly, a little entertaining. Have you ever seen a white person drunk? It's funny. I'll say that much."

"It don't feel unseasoned?"

My Mardi Gras in the 10th Ward at my granny's house sounded ten times better than watching some white people be drunken fools. My baby deserved better.

She laughed. "I wouldn't know. That's my only experience."

"Well shit, maybe it's time for another experience. Come to my Granny's house with me in the 10th Ward. She don't stay too far away from where everybody be underneath the bridge."

"I thought your people were from the Calliope."

"No baby, *I'm* from the Calliope. My parents moved there when I was like one."

I wasn't even going to bother expounding on that. She didn't need to know that my daddy was a retired drug dealer and that he purposely removed himself from his hood so he could successfully step away from that life. He didn't hide his past from me when I was growing up at all because he said his war stories were warnings for me to never go down that route. He claimed that when he willingly stepped away from the drug game it was hard because he was used to easy money. When he decided to invest into a legit business he missed the thrill of the game and the fast cash. He had to get used to being okay with living a modest life and not being greedy. Even today, my dad wasn't filthy rich but he was financially stable and able to take care of his family. The job my mom had was merely something she had for herself. She contributed to the household in plenty ways but my dad didn't let her touch a bill. That's how it was when they first started living together at age 18 and that's how it would remain until the end of the time. Seeing where my dad was today with his popular snowball stand that had been up and running since 2000 made me proud, and it was the number one reason I wanted to be an entrepreneur.

"Oh, so they're from the 10th Ward?"

"Yea. So you rolling with me or not? I want you to meet my grandma anyway."

"Okay...whew, this break is going to be eventful."

"Who you telling? This Bachus after party I'm throwing at Spades then sold out on online tickets, so I know the door bouta go insa-"

"I'm not talking about your party, Ky,"she rolled her eyes. "Although I am looking forward to that."

Everybody and their mama was looking forward to it. Since I primarily lived and went to school in Baton Rouge, it was rare that I threw a party in New Orleans, but when I did the home city showed major love. The party scene in New Orleans was bigger anyway, so a promoter with my popularity packing out a club was a no brainer. I was definitely moving back home after I graduated and running my bag all the way up. It was bukoo money in my city to be made, and I planned on making it all. My ultimate goal was to own my own club one day. I wanted to finance everything myself, so I had ways to go before I reached that milestone. But I had the patience and determination to see it through.

"Oh, so what you talking bout?"

"I'm talking about me meeting the rest of your family when the last meeting went left. And you're meeting my parents tomorrow…and well, I told you how they are. So I'm nervous about that."

"I'm not,"I chuckled. "It's gon be all good because no matter what happens we gon still feel what we feel for each other and be together. On the real, everybody else can get with it or get lost."

"Ughhh, I envy your ability to truly not give a fuck. I'm almost there, but not fully."

"Just stick with it and you'll get there,"I encouraged, making her laugh. I laughed with her before growing serious. "On the real though, the rest of my family not gon give you problems. I already talked to multiple people about what went down including Cambrie's mama and my sisters. They all flat out said she was tripping and should've been neutral in the situation. She was just riding for her best friend, but if I know my cousin like I think I do she'll see the light."

"I hope so, and not even because I need her acceptance. I just don't want you to have bad blood with someone your close with over m-"

"Shhh,"I put my fingers to her lips. "I'll gladly go against anybody who disrespects you. But shit, she disrespected me too, so it is what it is. I ain't losing no sleep over that."

The universe had a funny way of working because my phone started ringing immediately after I said that. It was on the nightstand charging, so I reached over and grabbed it. We both looked at the screen in amazement. It was Cambrie.

"That is so weird,"Mari giggled. "Let me find out she got this place bugged."

"If she does then she's been getting more than an earful,"I chuckled.

"Answer,"she urged. "And put it on speaker."

I granted her request, while secretly hoping that Cambrie wasn't calling to further fuss about dumb shit. Dumb shit being her friend. I'd been having a good day and I wasn't in the mood for it.

"Wassup?"I answered the phone dryly and on guard.

"You still mad at me, huh?"She had the audacity to ask.

"You serious?"

"I just…I can't believe we went hard on eachother like that. That's not like us."

"It's not, but you made it like that, Cam."

"I know, but cousin you have to understand I was getting Hailey's side and she made it seem as if you'd been leading her on only to pop out with someone else. Hailey has been my girl since before Katrina, and you know I'm protective over her. I thought you were playing in her face and I reacted."

"Okay, even if that were the case you should've directed all your negative energy to me. You decided to disrespect Kamaria instead."

"And I was dead wrong for that. I should've been cordial and respectful because that girl never did nothing to me or Hailey. I was just in the moment and backing my best friend up, but that's no excuse. I really am sorry, and send my apologies to Kamaria too."

"I accept your apology, cousin. But you gotta tell Mari you're sorry yourself."

"....okay. Shoot me her number and I'll text her."

"No need for all that. She's right here and you're on speaker."

She gasped. "Damn! I couldn't get a heads up or something?"

"You didn't need that. Go ahead and apologize to her though. She's listening...."

"Okay....first off, hey Kamaria. How are you?"

"I'm good,"she replied politely. One thing I appreciated about her is how she always reciprocated the energy given to her. My cousin was obviously waiving the white flag and she was receptive to that instead of dragging on the drama.

"That's wassup. Girl, I just want to say sorry for how I came at you. You already know my reasons, so I won't go back into all that. Just know that I have no beef with you and you're more than welcome to come to my party with Kyree if you want. If you're his girlfriend then that means you're a part of the family too."

"I appreciate that, Cambrie, and your apology is accepted. But..."

"I had a feeling that was coming,"she laughed. "If this is about Hailey, yes, she will be there. But she'll be on her best behavior. You have my word and if that means nothing to you then you know for a fact Kyree will be by your side. We already know he's not going to let anybody touch you."

We all laughed because I really refused to let them fight Kamaria after she justifiably slapped Hailey in the mouth. I was glad that Cambrie was finding humor in it now because she was heated at the time it happened.

"I'm not worried about anyone touching me. It's just I don't want any drama. I hate drama."

"Believe it or not I do too, girl. Maybe I can set up a sit down with you and Hailey. If you apologize for hitting her I'm sure it'll be water under the bri-"

"Yo, Cambrie, you then lost your damn mind."

There was no way for me to sugarcoat that. Why my cousin thought it was a good idea for my past to sit down and talk with my present and future was insane. The only reason Hailey's ass was still in the picture was because they were best friends. If that wasn't the case she would've been a distant memory. They didn't have shit to talk about and Mari had no reason to apologize. She gave Hailey a fair warning but she kept on pushing it until she got what she was looking for.

"How? They have no issues so they should be able to be cord-"

"I don't have an issue,"Kamria interrupted. "But evidently Hailey has one with me and it's because I'm with the guy she still wants. That's not changing anytime soon so I doubt she'll want to be cool with me, and after the way she came for me I have no desire to be cool with her. I do understand that she's a close friend of yours though, so I don't mind co-existing seldomly. But as far as a sit down or an apology? Yea, not happening."

"I can't do nothing but respect that I guess. Maybe I

was being too optimistic. Well my invitation has been extended, so I hope to see you both Saturday night. Good night."

"Good night,"me and Mari said together.

After I ended the call I locked eyes with her.

"How you feeling?"

"I'm glad she apologized to us both. It makes me less nervous about being around your family for Mardi Gras, butttt I still don't like her."

I chuckled. "After she suggested that you apologize I don't blame you. Her mama most likely dug in her ass and that's why she made peace. But I'm with you. I'm glad that's no longer a problem for us. Mardi Gras should be drama free."

Chapter 9

Kamaria

Mardi Gras Break- Day 1

I turned from side to side, analyzing myself from top to

bottom. Kyre would be arriving in 30 minutes for dinner with my parents, and I wanted to look good. Not that I had anyone to impress, but if I felt good about my appearance then the rest of the night would go well too. I was trying my hardest to fill myself with as much positive energy as possible because I was sure I'd need it. I even had on my 2000's R&B playlist because it made me the happiest. Tyra B's "Rush" was playing on my tv, and I couldn't get my mind off of Kyree. The fact that I missed him already was ridiculous because we'd only been apart for literally 4 or five hours. I only had one class today, and he had two, so we were able to leave BR rather early at 2 pm. I would've loved to ride with him, but I needed my car during such a hectic time like Mardi Gras, so leaving it behind wasn't an option. So I was forced to separate from my baby sooner than I wanted to. Nevermind that he was actually coming over to my parents house at 7.

"You're giving me a rush, rush. Every time that you come around and when we touch, touch. I can't get enough…"I sang, while brushing my hair that was already flawless. I'd gotten a sew in and closure from the same girl Kyree hired to do my hair for Valentine's Day and she laid my hair yet again. The chestnut brown hair color with blonde streaks was so yummy with my brown skin. I was definitely feeling myself. Essence gave me the inspo by sending me a girl who had the same color on instagram. Usually I stayed away from any color, but I was glad I took a chance.

"Kamaria!"A soft, but strong voice hollered from outside of my room followed by multiple knocks.

I was a 21 year old woman and the hairs on the back of my neck would stand up whenever I was around my mama. I wasn't scared of her but I didn't like the way she made me feel sometimes. I just wanted to be carefree around her and not have any worries. I didn't want to deal with backhanded comments or criticism aimed at my appearance. Why couldn't we just catch up, laugh, and hang out like a normal mother and daughter? I was particularly nervous this time around because I was no longer in the state of mind to just shut up and take whatever she threw at me. I really didn't want to argue with her infront of Kyree, but I wasn't above it. I would give her whatever she gave me, so I was hoping she didn't give me anything negative.

"Come in!"I shouted while brushing imaginary wrinkles out of my Fashion Nova dress. Despite being somewhat of a label whore, I loved indulging in fast fashion because I could get a lot for a little. As a full time college student with no job, that was right up my alley. The black off the shoulder sweater sweater dress was simple yet effective. It was short, but not inappropriately short and it fit my body like a seamstress made it personally for me. I paired it with the Givenchy shark lock boots that Kyree had gotten me. I had gotten them stretched to fit my big legs and I was obsessed with them. I also threw on the Tiffany toggle bracelet and necklace he bought me, along with diamond studs I got from my parents a few Christmas' ago.

"Look who's her-oh,look at you…"

Watching the smile drop from her face when she saw me was mind boggling because I knew I looked good. A big part of me just wanted her to acknowledge that for once, but I was not going to get my wish. For one, it just wasn't in her nature. Secondly, my cousin Kaliya was right next to her. That was the reason she knocked on my door and was in such a chipper mood at first. Kaliya was her big brother's youngest daughter and undeniably her favorite niece. The oldest two, Diana and Lauren, were way older than us. They were in college by the time we were in elementary school, so I didn't grow up with them. My Uncle James had Kaliya with his second wife and they tried hard for her, so they cherished the ground she walked on. We should've been close since we were born the same year and literally a week apart, but it didn't pan out that way. It was hard to get close with someone who you were always being pitted against. Kaliya was beautiful. Her tan light skin was without any flaws, she had soft and wavy hair that flowed down her back, and dainty facial features that included her little button nose and small pouty lips, and squinty hazel eyes. Like everybody else in my family, she had height on her at 5 '9 and she had the perfect model body. With age she got thick in all the right areas, but never too thick. She was definitely the textbook definition of slim thick. None of that was the reason we never got along though. The reason was because my mom would put her on a pedestal while putting me down in the same breath. Maybe it wouldn't have been an issue if it was only mom because I'd never blame anyone for her actions. It wasn't just her though. The same way being pitted against each other contributed to my low self esteem; it made Kaliya feel like she was superior to me. Kaliya had been hyped up by our family her whole life and made to feel like she was the end all, be all. The family was always front and center for anything she did whether it was a pageant, her cheerleading, or one of her track meets that she never won. Everybody had even made a big deal about her move in day at Southern University, and my mom forced me to tag along. We all stayed and helped her unpack and decorate her door. Meanwhile only my parents dropped me off at UBR and they left right away, claiming they had two big surgeries at work the next morning and needed to be well rested for them. That's just one example of the difference in how Kaliya and I were treated. It wasn't just my mother either, it was the majority of my mom's side that did this.

My dad was an only child, so I had no aunts, uncles, or cousins on his side. Just a grandpa and grandma who had both passed away by the time I was in middle school. He had cousins, but they were displaced after Hurricane Katrina. So our family functions were really only my mom's side of the family since she had five siblings. The only one who didn't have kids was my Auntie Sana, and I loved her to death for always showing me special attention that nobody else bothered to. Maybe it was because she understood how I felt to some degree. She was the youngest and the only one with a different father. She had brown skin and kinky hair while my mom and the rest of her siblings were fair skinned with soft and curly hair textures. She stood out amongst them and I think she felt the brunt of that growing up. That's probably why she went out of her way to always tell me I was beautiful and spoil me.

"Wow!"Kaliya marveled. "Did you lose weight, cousin? You look good!"

That was just like her. She always pretended to be this nice person in front of our family, but she never actually gave me the time of day. The thing about Kaliya was that she'd never been overtly mean to me, but she did ignore me or look at me like I was stupid whenever I used to try to engage her with conversation. That started when we were in our pre-teens. Before that, we used to play all the time but we always ended up fighting because she tried to run me. As a child I was timid and insecure, but I wasn't weak and scary. We had one too many fist fights that always led to me getting spankings because I used to mop the floor with her skinny ass. Now that we were adults our relationship was pretty much non-existent. We went to college in the same city but we'd never hung out. She'd been to UBR countless times to party but she'd never invited me out or just stopped by to see me. I hadn't made an effort to go see her at SU either because I saw no reason too. We were cousins, but we weren't friends.

"Nope, I haven't lost one pound. I actually gained a few," I admitted with no shame. I was happy, eating good, and content.

"Oh, well I can't tell. You wearing that dress," she went on, appearing genuine. I couldn't decipher if she actually was or not, but I said thank you anyway.

"Do you think a girl your size should be wearing that dress, sweetie?"My mom asked like she was truly concerned. To my surprise, Kaliya spoke up before I could.

"What do you mean, Auntie Katheline? I think her curves fills out the dress just right. In fact, I can't see a smaller girl wearing it now that I'm seeing it on Kamaria."

"I guess…"my mom frowned. "In my day bigger girls wore things that hide them. People didn't willingly show of-"

"Well those days are over, mama."I snapped.

Her eyes ballooned in incredulity.

"Don't go getting all excited. You know everything I saw is to help y-"

"How is calling me big and telling me to cover my body helping me? It sounds like you're trying to make me ashamed of the way I naturally am. I love my body and I don't have to hide it in huge clothes."

She threw her hands up. "Okay, Kamaria. You're 21 so my days of dressing you are long over. I just don't want you to embarrass yourself."

My blood boiled. She still didn't get it. I wanted to pop off but it would just lead to me being emotional. She'd already made me angry in such a short amount of time. The last thing I wanted to do was start screaming and crying with Kaliya here of all people.

"I like that hair color," she said, while stepping closer to get a better look. When I arrived earlier I had it tied up, so she hadn't seen it yet.

"Thanks," I replied with no emotion. That compliment was about to come with something else. I knew her like the back of my hand.

"I think it would be more suitable for a lighter girl, though. You should get it, Kaliya."

See? I just fucking knew it. She could never let me be great.

"I don't know Auntie, dark skin girls be killing the hair colors. You should go full blonde next time, Kamaria."

I think Kaliya was on a roll to blow my mind today because I didn't even recognize her at that moment.

"Oh God no!"My mom shrieked. "She's way too dark for blonde hair. It wouldn't look right."

I breathed deeply. "Did you want anything, Mom?"

She stared at me intently. "What's wrong with you?"

"Nothing I'm not used to. That's for certain."

"And what's that supposed to mean?"She put her hand on her hip.

"You just keep hurling insults at me. You remember when you used to tell me if I have nothing nice to say, don't say it all?"I questioned.

"I wasn't aware that I was being mean or that you'd gotten so sensitive. I'll keep in mind not to comment on your appearance anymore even though I'm your mother,"she shot back sarcastically.

I rolled my eyes and questioned if it even made sense to go back and forth with her. She was a brick wall and everything I said was bouncing off of her.

"Where'd you get these boots? And is this a Tiffany necklace and bracelet you have on?"She picked up my wrist. "I then told Sana to stop spending all this money on you for no reason. Especially when she doesn't splurge on her other nieces and nephews like this. It's not okay to show favoritism like th-"

"That's rich coming from you,"came from my mouth like vomit.

"Again, what the hell is that supposed to mean?"

"Nothing,"I said, deciding to bite my tongue this time. If I brought up Kaliya she'd just say I was jealous like she'd alluded to in the past. That was bound to make me snap. "Auntie Sana didn't buy me this though. Kyree did."

"That's the boyfriend right?"Kaliya asked while my mom laughed. That rubbed me so wrong, so I questioned her about it.

"Why are you laughing?"

"Because I find that hard to believe. What kind of job does he have?"

I sighed heavily. "I'm sorry you find that hard to believe. You can ask him about what he does at dinner."

"I sure will. Anyways, since James and Karen moved to Houston Kaliya is going to spend Mardi Gras break here.

Maybe you girls can spend some time,"my mom stared at me as if it was my fault we didn't spend time. Kaliya's parents had moved to Houston because they were tired of New Orleans and wanted a change. With Uncle Jame's career as a defense lawyer, he was able to pick up and make the move rather quickly. Usually Kaliya would be right at home for Mardi Gras break, but now she had to pick a family member's house to stay at in the city. It was a no-brainer that she picked my mom since she went out of her way to kiss her ass.

"Yea, we should hang out like we used to when we were little,"she smiled.

"You mean when we used to fist fight?"I blinked in confusion.

She hollered with laughter. "No, definitely not like that. We were a mess, girl. Thank God we've grown from that."

"Righttt,"I replied. I didn't know what to say or how to feel. I was honestly still feeling her out and I most likely wouldn't have her figured out anytime soon. My plans for this break did not include her though. That was for certain. I had plans with my friends and Kyree, and she could not come along.

My phone buzzed on my bed, so I walked around them to get to it. When I picked it up and saw the screen my heart skipped a beat. Kyree was outside.

Kyree

"So Kyree, how much does that little party promoting thing pay? Are you trying to make a career out of that?"Ms. Katheline asked me. I had the utmost respect for my elders, but we were only thirty minutes into dinner and I really couldn't stand this bitch. She was condescending, she talked to Kamaria like she wasn't a fully functioning adult or human for that matter, and her edges were thin as fuck. I could tell she was one of those light skin women with long hair who thought they were better than everyone else merely for those reasons. I also caught on to how she was trying to downplay what I did for a living.

"It's my career of choice for now. It pays enough to where I live comfortably and can look out for the people I love,"I glanced at Kamaria and she stifled a smile. I told her I loved her in so many words without actually saying it yet. A part of me felt like it was too soon since we'd literally just made shit official, but I knew what I felt and the shit between us was real.

"Are you insinuating that you love our daughter, young man?"Her dad, Mr. Lionel, asked with a grin. He was cool and easygoing...but I didn't fuck with him as a person either because I could tell he never checked his wife. Anybody who stood by idly while someone was a terrible person was either a coward or an equally terrible person.

"I'm sure it's not *that* serious,"her mom jumped in. "This is a young man making a lot of money for the first time so of course he's going to spend it recklessly."

"I do love her,"I stated confidently, while grabbing Kamaria's hand. I couldn't even enjoy the steak, garlic mashed potatoes, and sautéed asparagus that their chef had cooked to perfection because this bitch kept saying stupid shit.

"And I don't spend money recklessly, m'am. I was raised better than that."

"I can attest to that. He saves like crazy. I've seen his bank accounts,"Kamaria added. I appreciated her back up because I wasn't going to say all that. It was too close to bragging, and I was taught not to do that.

"That's smart, Kyree. So what's the end goal with you career wise?"Mr.Lionel asked.

"To own my own clubs, but of course I'm going to start off with one."

"Entrepreneurship is hard. Are you sure about that?"Ms.Katheline asked as if she really cared. Weird bitch.

"I don't think anything's harder than going to school for almost 20 years to be a neurosurgeon,"I chuckled, making the whole table laugh. Even her miserable ass laughed.

"It actually took us both 14 years,"Mr.Lionel clarified.

"Close enough,"her cousin giggled. She'd been chilling and only adding commentary here and there. The dinner would've been going a lot better if Kamaria's stupid ass maw wasn't present.

"I guess what I'm trying to say is nothing worth having comes easy, but I know I'm going to succeed."

"You certainly will with that mindset,"Ms.Katheline nodded in approval. "Give my baby girl some of that confidence."

Just when I thought she was about to stop being a petty bitch…

"Your daughter has a lot of confidence. She carries herself perfectly. I don't think someone who lacked confidence could be excelling in life the way she is."I squeezed Mari's hand because in my peripheral vision I could see her taking a deep breath. I didn't want her to give her mama the satisfaction.

"Ha! You should've seen her when she was a little girl th-"

"Alright,"her husband finally butted in. "That's enough of that, Kathy. She's grown now, so there's no need to talk about the past."

"Someone who loves our daughter can't hear about our childhood?"

"Oh, I've told him a lot already. There's nothing else you can really say,"Kamaria said.

"And what exactly did you say?"She asked defensively.

"Nothing but the truth,"she shrugged.

"Mhmm, so Kyree, you're in it with Kamaria for the long haul?"

"Yes, m'am."

"Like marriage and babies?"

"All of the above."

"Oh wow,"she uttered in amazement. "I certainly hope not anytime soon. Kamaria will need to focus on her career, especially since she's behind wi-"

"Behind with what?"Kamaria cut her off abrasively.

"School and your future,"her mom stated firmly. "You should be doing an internship right now. Kaliya, tell us about your nursing internship at Ochsner."

Kaliya didn't get a chance to open her mouth before Kamaria was talking.

"Mom, I did an internship two summers in a row. It was you and dad that said I shouldn't do it during the school year so I wouldn't have to split focus. I don't see how I'd be behind when I had the same internship for two years and my letters of recommendations are singing praises."

"Oh yea, you should be good then cousin. Do you know what you want to do after you graduate?"

"I have an idea, but I'll be happy to just get a decent paying job in my field."

"You're a genius, baby girl, so that will be no issue,"her dad said, before focusing back on me. "Back to this marriage and babies thing though."

That resulted in a little laughter. After Mari got her mama together the energy in the room was cold, so that was a much needed icebreaker.

"Marriage before babies, right?"

"That would be ideal, but it's going to work out however it's supposed to. Regardless, I'm going to do right by Kamaria and give her everything she deserves,"I spoke with sincerity while looking him in his eyes.

He nodded. "I hope you mean that, young man. Y'all just focus on being young and having fun right now though.

You'll never get these years back…and after college life is hard."

"I've heard, but I'm ready for it. I've had enough fun in the past five years."

"Evidently if it took you five years."

"Mom, a lot of people finish college in five years. That's actually more normal than four nowadays,"Kamaria grumbled.

"Yea Kathy, cut it out."

"Oh, I'm just messing around with that boy! He's not upset! Are you, sweetie?"

"No, m'am. I'm not ashamed of finishing in five years because I'm finishing."

"Amen,"Kaliya sang.

"Kyree, maybe we can do dinner with your parents in the future. I have to meet the people who did a fine job raising you,"Ms.Katheline smiled. It was so fake to me.

"Most definitely,"I lied. If nobody brought that up again then it wasn't happening anytime soon. My parents were bound to curse her out after the first backhanded comment she made. That nice-nasty shit wasn't going to roll over with them. Overall, it had been insightful seeing where Kamaria had come from. I could see why she was so in her bubble and had insecurities. I was just proud that all that unnecessary baggage her parents gave her was slowly fading away. She saw her own worth, so they, specifically her mom, didn't have to see it.

Chapter 10

Kamaria

Mardi Gras Day

This had been my best Mardi Gras break yet and I was grateful to be experiencing it before my college days ended. The break starting off with that God awful dinner could have ruined everything, but thankfully it hadn't. It was a minor bump in the road and I made sure I stayed on the go to limit interactions with my mom. Not that I had to try as hard due to her busy work schedule. She'd been working night shifts, so whenever I was out and about in the house she'd be resting. Everything was working out perfectly because I couldn't handle dealing with her for the duration of this break. My parents and I had agreed a while ago that it would be best if I returned home after I graduated college at least until I found a stable job. But I knew for a fact I couldn't do that. I was going to make it my business to have a job lined up and waiting on me by the time I graduated, and if I couldn't find an affordable apartment I'd ask my aunt if I could stay with her. Anything not to have to return to this damn house.

After the dinner I was even more in my head about Cambrie's birthday party, but surprisingly, everything went well. Cambrie had good energy, making me believe her apology was really genuine. Kyree's twin sisters fully embraced me and we chatted all through the night. By the end of the party we were exchanging numbers. The rest of his family welcomed me with open arms too and I honestly didn't see that coming. I thought because Hailey had been around for so long that they'd be standoffish with me how Cambrie originally was, but that wasn't the case and I was relieved. I was ready for anything but I ultimately wanted to hit it off with his family. Hailey was there of course and I didn't miss how she sat at a table the entire time looking salty. I noticed Cambrie going by her several times to cheer her up with attempts to make her get up and dance, but apparently she wasn't having it. She disappeared about an hour and a half into the party, making me wonder about the fate of her and

Cambrie's friendship. I didn't dawn on it too long though because I wasn't that invested and their friendship could crumble to pieces for all I cared. It really wasn't my problem, and I could only hope that my presence at Cambrie's party stopped Hailey from clinging on to Kyree's family so damn much. It reeked of desperation.

Sunday I had an even better time with Kyree's family. He had a lot of cousins around his age from his mom's and dad's side, so they came out for his event at Spades along with his sister's and our friends from UBR. I tried Hennessy for the first time and I fell in love. I drank four cups of Hennessy and coke. To say the least, I had the time of my life. I was dancing to everything and interacting with everybody. Eventually the night got blurry and I woke up in Kyree's bed at his parents house. I was a little nervous at how my parents would react but Kyree had already reached out to my dad to let him know where I was. I was worried about them when it was really Kyree who had an issue with me. He chewed me out about knowing my limits with alcohol and he said it should never get to a point where I had to be carried out the club. I didn't know what the hell he was talking about until his sister sent me a video of Kyree carrying bridal style out of Spades. I was conscious but clearly on my ass. I found the video funny but Kyree was not amused. I could admit that I did overdo it but the night was still one for the books.

Monday was a chill day like most Lundi Gras' were for actual New Orleanians. Kyree and I had lunch together at New Orleans Food & Spirit, and then we went to the mall because I needed something to wear for Mardi Gras. I didn't normally put a lot of effort into Mardi Gras because the crowd my family had me amongst just threw on whatever. They'd be in theme of course, but it really didn't matter to them. I'd learned that 90% of black New Orleans took the Mardi Gras fits way more seriously. They didn't over dress, but they definitely wanted to put that shit on. I realized this when Kyree's sisters and cousin asked me what I was wearing after they'd been discussing their outfits in great detail. Some of them were getting festive shit made, so I wanted to step it up a bit. I gave myself an imaginary pat on the back as I looked in my full length mirror because I did good on short notice. I was thankful that certain stores in Oakwood mall would carry mardi gras stuff around this time otherwise I may have been out of luck. I donned high waisted jean booty shorts that were distressed in the front. Underneath I wore flesh tone dance tights with purple fishnets over it. With the tights my shorts looked less raunchy. I was still giving hips and a lot of ass, but it was more subtle. The real show stopper was my top which was a beaded and bedazzled Mardi Gras push up bra. I was bringing a jean jacket with me in case my boobs started doing too much, but for now they look pretty contained and fabulous. They were sitting up perfectly. I accessorized with a Mardi Gras sequin and feather headband, fuzzy Mardi Gras leg warmers, and white G-Nikes. I had gold sneakers I could've worn, but Kyree insisted that I wear the same tennis as him when he bought them. Wearing fresh white sneakers on Mardi Gras was foolish, but that was his money and he obviously didn't care. He was a lot more simpler than me with his yellow Off White lightweight Jogging suit and white G-Nikes. The weather was ranging from 67 to 75 degrees for the day, so it wasn't too cold or hot. You could pretty much get away with wearing anything.

I woke up at 7 am to get ready for the day, and I was proud of myself for finishing in an hour. As I was loading everything of importance that could actually fit in my small gold Gucci crossbody bag, there was a knock at the door.

"Yes?!"I responded, trying to remove the annoyance from my voice. I wanted to make a speedy exit from the house without being bothered by anyone. My parents usually headed out at 9:30 am, so I thought I'd be in the clear. To my dismay, my mom waltzed in.

"Good morn-Ou, are you putting a shirt over that bra?"

"I wasn't planning on it."I replied, with an unintentional bite in my tone.

"You're going to freeze, and your breasts look ridiculous."

"I doubt it. My weather app is saying it'll be 72 degrees by 10 am and I have a jacket, so I'll be okay,"I explained, choosing to ignore her comment about my breasts. I thought they looked phenomenal so I saw no reason to engage with her. It wasn't like I'd change her mind.

"How do you feel about getting a breast reduction, sweetheart? I think you'd look a lot smalle-"

"Mom, I know this may be hard for you to understand, but I like my body exactly the way it is and I'd appreciate it if you stopped picking at it!"

She looked stunned by my sudden outburst. She crossed her arms and huffed.

"Okay, if you say so...I just came in here to tell you that Kaliya's going with you today."

"Why?"My eyes danced around. "She doesn't normally spend any other Mardi Gras with me."

"It doesn't matter what normally goes on. She'll be going with you today and that's final. It's bad enough you haven't invited the poor girl anywhere all weekend. I don't know what's gotten into you, but you're not acting like yourself. Just because you have a boyfriend and new pals doesn't mean you have to be nasty to your family. Kaliya's waiting downstairs for you."

I was so lost. As far as I could remember this had never been an issue. Kaliya had friends in New Orleans and friends from SU that were most likely in the city today. Why couldn't she just link with them like she always did? Why did she have to be my plus one? Nobody had ever forced her to drag me along anywhere when I was lonely, and believe me I'd been lonely. Those rare times we did end up doing things together I had to be subjected to her snobby friends and be made to feel like an outcast. So I didn't understand how I was being nasty by merely ignoring her when that had become the nature of our relationship because of her. I didn't get a chance to say any of this to my mom because she flounced out of the room, making it clear that it wasn't a debate.

I walked downstairs irritated with the world. I would not let this ruin my day. The bright side was that Kaliya had been cool based on the little interaction we'd had so far, so hopefully that continued as the day progressed. She was sitting on the bench in the foyer and she looked cute, but that wasn't shocking. She always put together nice outfits. Today she wore a Mardi Gras T-shirt that had been cut into a crop top and mini skirt with purple Doc Martens. As usual she had her hair flat ironed and down her back, and she wore the same head band I had on.

"Hey, cousin!"She smiled. "You look cute!"

"Thanks,"I replied blandly. "You ready?"

I would've returned her positive energy but I wasn't fake. She had to have been talking shit to my mom. Why else would she say I was ignoring her or acting nasty? Kaliya had to give her that idea.

"Yea,"she stood up.

We walked to the car in awkward silence. I wasn't hiding that I was mad and she had to have caught on. As we drove the only thing that could be heard was the radio. The mug on my face was still there, and she continued to look straight ahead like she was nervous. I guess she grew tired of the stale energy, because she leaned forward and turned the radio down.

"You alright?"

"Not really,"I answered honestly.

"Is it something I did?"Her eyes danced around innocently.

"I don't know. You tell me. Did you tell my mom that I was ignoring you and being nasty?"

"What?! No!"She exclaimed. "She did ask me what we've been getting into and I told her we hadn't done anything together yet. That's really all. Did she say that I said something?"

"....no. But she came fussing at me about how you had to come with me today and then went on to say that I'm acting differently."

"Yea, no, I didn't say shit to allude to that at all. I did want to come with you today though."

"For what?"I questioned in bewilderment.

"Okay,"she sighed heavily. "I know our relationship has always been...weird. We fought a lot growing up and I always thought you didn't like me, so I didn't like you in retur-"

"Wait, you thought I didn't like you? Kaliya, be forreal."

"I am! Then my dad would always brag about how you were so smart...he still does until this day. If I get a C he's down my back talking about how you've never even gotten a

B. No lie, that made me feel some secret animosity towards you."

"It wasn't really a secret because I knew you didn't like me. After a while you started treating me like I just wasn't there at all."

"And I'm sorry for that. That wasn't fair of me to take how my dad treated me out on you."

Perspective really puts things into place because before this conversation I always thought Kaliya just hated me for no reason or because she thought she was better than me. Now she was telling me she actually had her own insecurities and her dad played on them by comparing us. It must've ran in the bloodline because my mom did the same thing to me.

"I can accept your apology because I've had similar feelings…my mom praising you while putting me down has always bothered me."

I still felt like most of our family put her on a pedestal but that wasn't her fault to bring it to her attention. Perhaps it was because she was the prototype of perfection to them. Whatever it was, it wasn't a reason for me to dislike her. If she was willing to apologize for how she treated me then I was willing to bury the hatchet and move on.

"How about we get to know each other as adults and stop letting people pit us against one another?"She suggested.

"We can absolutely do that, cousin,"I smiled.

"Great, now let's start with having a lit Mardi Gras!"

A few hours later Kaliya's words had come into fruition. I'd only had a taste of a hood Mardi Gras and I never wanted to go back to what I once knew. Kyree's grandmother's 10th ward home was a small three bedroom shotgun house, but it was filled with good vibes and love. His grandma, Ms.Martha gave me the biggest hug that made me feel like I'd known her for years. They had an elaborate set up of food buffet style and every alcohol you could think of right in the living room for easy access. I had two full plates of red beans and rice, fried chicken, mini meatballs, finger sandwiches, and crawfish bread. After taking two Tito's shots with Kyree and his family, we headed for the parade route. It was on the side of

St.Charles I wasn't familiar with, but based on the fun I was already having I knew I'd have a good time. The walk was a little lengthier than what I was used to, but sipping on a Daiquiri made the walk fun.

"Don't drink too fast,"Kyree whispered in my ear with his arm wrapped around my shoulder.

"I'm not going to get drunk,"I nearly snapped, automatically thinking he was still stuck on me getting sloppy drunk at Spades.

"I would hope not after Sunday night. That ain't why I'm telling you to slow down though."

"So what's the reason?"

"Liquor moves through you like water when you down it and you gon have to keep peeing. We gon be a lil far from my grandma's house, and them porta potties nasty."

"I'll be fine, Kyree,"I brushed him off. Everytime I turned around he was trying to school me like I didn't know anything. Sure I was new to drinking but I had everything under control.

When we finally made it to St.Charles and Cilo we had to deal with the challenge of crossing to the left side of the street. The right side of the street was limited to just watching because the parade passed on that side. While people could obviously watch from the left side too, the street was open for people to walk, mingle, and party. We wanted to do all that, so we crossed over after a float passed. Just as we suspected, the left side was lit. Someone was blasting a popular song by a local artist named Stone Cold Jzzle, and Kyree's female cousins instantly started dancing. Too many relatives to count or name had gathered at his grandma's house but at the parade it was eleven of us, including me and Kaliya.

"Oh that's wassup! See when I pull up they show me love! Right before that, they ain't give a fuck!"Fendi chanted along with the song while bending over a little. I'd met her today and she had the strongest New Orleans accent I'd ever heard in my life. Her auburn hair on her brown skin was breathtaking, and she had a deep dimpled smile. She embraced me right away, and I was surprised to find out that she was a year older than me. She looked so much younger. Kyree's dad was cousins with her mom.

"Til I blowed it up. Stone Cold Jzzle man he cold as fuck! Tell the DJ turn the speakers up up up!"Her   younger sister, Versace, bellowed. She had the same strong accent and every other word I heard her say had been a curse word and broken english. It was evident from their names that they were ghetto fabulous and I loved every bit of it. I had met their mother, Peaches, back at Grandma's house and they'd gotten it all honestly. This was the rich New Orleans culture I'd always been deprived of thanks to my sheltered upbringing.

"Ayeee! Don't you throw up 7's with your potna? Yup yup yup!" Cambrie shouted while twerking. Despite being from Kyree's mom's side of the family she and her mom still showed up at his Grandma's house today along with some other relatives from that side. She even called Ms.Martha grandma, too. I thought it was wonderful how both sides of the family were so blended. When my dad's parents were still alive they never really came to any of my mom's family functions, so that was foreign to me.

"Danggg, cousin!"Qaylo exclaimed as he stared at Kaliya in awe. She was taking a third shot of Patron from one of the twins…I think it was Kyomi. It was hard to tell them apart since they were identical and the girl slash prettier versions of Kyree down to the locs. I was sure one of them was a tad bit thicker but it was hard to tell today since they both had on camo cargo pants with Mardi Gras crop tops, showing off their identical abs. They were literally perfect.

"I got this,"Kaliya smirked with flirty eyes. We both quietly agreed that Qaylo was a cutie. Out of all his cousins, Kyree resembled him the most. I guess that was a no brainer since their dads were brothers and looked just alike too. Although he hadn't said his age, it was clear that he was older because Kyree referred to him as his "big bro" and he also had a mature vibe about him. He was handsome with his light brown skin, thick lips, deep brown eyes surrounded by long lashes, and light brown locs that reached his back. I was rooting for Kaliya to get his number at the end of the day.

"I hope so, cause we ain't tryna carry nobody,"Ashton chuckled. He was one of Kyree's younger cousins at 18, but that didn't seem to matter because he was drinking right with us along with the twins who were only 20. My family had never allowed underage drinking, but nobody in Kyree's family batted an eyelash.

I thought we'd walk, but we found a spot on the neutral ground where the street car usually ran. It was obviously out of service during parades. It seemed like the entire city knew Kyree and his family, and I wasn't exaggerating. Everyone was stopping to speak to them. Some of Qaylo's friends even met up with us. These guys were what my parents called "sketchy." They'd always told me to stay clear of men like that, but I'd honestly never felt safer, and I knew Kyree would never let anything happen to me. He conversed with those guys as if he knew them his entire life and they regarded all of us ladies with respect, so they were fine with me. One thing was puzzling to me though. Maybe my eyes were playing tricks on me but I saw Qaylo accepting money from several people. Versace told me the house special daiquiri I fixed was the strongest flavor and guaranteed to hit me fast. I underestimated her expertise on the drink until it started hitting me and I began doing things I'd never done…like asking questions.

"Qaylo, who do people keep giving you money? Is it your birthday?"I asked loud enough so he could hear me over the bounce music that was blasting.

"Bruhhh,"one of his friends doubled over in hysterics. The rest of them followed up with laughter.

"Mari,"Kyree gave me a look, while stifling laughter of his own.

"What?"I asked innocently.

"It ain't his birthday, love…that man in the field,"Vance said. He was one of his other younger cousins at 21 years old.

"In the field?"I repeated in confusion. "He does farm work?"

"Yoooo,"Qaylo laughed so hard that he had to clutch his stomach. At this point everybody was laughing hysterically. Kyree laughed a little before kissing my head.

"Don't ever say that shit around anybody else, baby. Stop asking questions,"he chuckled. He suddenly grew serious and looked at Vance. "And she not your love, nigga."

"Aw, c'mon cuzzo! You know I ain't mean it like that!"

"Alright nigga, you heard me,"he chuckled.

"I'm still confused. How's Qaylo in the field if we're at a parade?"I whispered, but I guess I failed at doing so because the laughs around us increased.

"That ain't for you to worry about,"he stated, before clutching my chin and planting a kiss on my lips. I wrapped my arms around him, suddenly content with not getting a real answer to any of my questions. If I was still curious later I'd have him explain it to me once we were alone.

"Mari, you gotta hang out with me girl. You'll know more than you need to know,"Fendi giggled.

"No the hell she don't need to hang with you,"he huffed.

"Why?"I whined. "She seems fun!"

"I'm so fun! That nigga be hating bad!"

"Mannn, like I said, that ain't happening."

"We'll exchange numbers,"I said just to be defiant. He couldn't control me.

"Alright,"he nodded. He licked his lips and sported a smile that gave me chills. It was like he was daring me to try him.

"Cousin, why can't she hang with Fendi?"Cambrie laughed.

"You know why. The last time you hung with them y'all got into a gang fight."

"Boyyyy, that old shit!"Versace hollered. "And we won anyway. None of us walked away with a pimple or a scratch!"

"But y'all did walk away in handcuffs though,"Vance butted in, garnering laughter.

"We didn't go to jail though. Just central booking and then they released us to our parents. That was so long ago! I'm not even like that no more!"Fendi claimed with so much passion that I believed her.

Kyree sucked his teeth. "Girl, I just saw you fussing with somebody on instagram live last week and you was telling ole girl to pull up."

"So you saying I can't hang with your girlfriend because I defend myself? Cause that's wild."

"Nah, he not letting you hang with her because you'll corrupt her and she's obviously innocent as fuck,"Qaylo chuckled.

"Don't let her fool y'all!"Cambrie announced. "I've seen her in action and she definitely cuts up."

"Whattt?"One of the twins…I think it was Kyana, marveled. "Ion believe it."

"You definitely gotta see it to believe it because I was surprised myself."

"Everybody got that side of them. Ion know why Kyree acting like Auntie Nette and Uncle KG didn't have to get in his ass when he was running round the Calliope beating on people's children."Fendi said.

"Wait, what?"My eyes expanded in curiosity. Kyree had never mentioned this to me.

"Don't listen to her,"he said while facing me, but I was still looking at Versace and waiting for her to spill the tea.

"My sister ain't lying,"Versace giggled. "His ass was bad as fuck. He ain't really stop fighting until he was 16."

"But I stopped though! And I never did that shit in school."

"So you think you better than me?!"Fendi questioned.

"Y'all some funny ass people,"one of the twins giggled. "My brother is a changed person, so get off him."

"And that's fine! But he don't need to be acting like we gon have his girlfriend out here bad or something! Cause one thing about me, ion bother nobody!"Fendi declared.

"Anybody who says that 100% be bothering people,"one of Qaylo's friends said.

My stomach started aching from laughing so hard. Although everyone was going back and forth, everything was light hearted and humorous. Kyree's family were characters and I'd been thoroughly entertained thus far. As the bounce music commenced and people continued drinking, girls started gathering in the street to dance. Of course the twins, Versace, Fendi, and Cambrie were in the mix and they had shaking down to a science. I felt vastly inexperienced compared to them, but that only made sense. They'd probably learned when they were kids and I'd just started getting the hang of it recently.

"C'mon y'all!"Versace called me and Kaliya out. I was surprised to see Kaliya join them. She bent over and fell right in line. I'd never seen her dance to bounce music, but obviously she had plenty of experience too.

"Go ahead and have fun. I ain't gon trip,"Kyree said in my ear. "Just don't do too much."

I had to smile because he thought my hesitance was about him when it was really about me being able to keep up with his people. I heard the bounce song that was currently playing numerous times because it'd been very popular during the highschool facebook days. Back then social media was one of the main ways I was exposed to other parts of my city. I was thankful for that or else I would've been out of the loop completely. When the "bend me over, hit me with that Calliope log" part came on I literally bent over and shook my ass on Kyree. The Calliope was his hood after all, so it only made sense. Until today, I never realized how much love "Fuck Me Like a Dog" by Calliope Ceedy and Flipset Fred showed to the Calliope. It was now officially my favorite bounce song for that reason. I felt Kyree grip my hips, making it evident that he enjoyed the show I was providing him with.

"WHAT?!"I heard Versace scream, followed by a slap to my ass. I didn't know if it was her or Kyree because I didn't bother to look. I was too focused on not dropping my daiquiri and making my booty cheeks fight. That's how Essence eloquently broke down dancing to bounce music to me, and that advice has not steered me wrong so far.

"I knew she could shake that big ole booty,"Fendi cackled. "Let's go, Mari! Cut up!"

"I told y'all she wasn't that innocent,"Cambrie giggled.

The street basically turned into a block party after that. I danced on Kyree for most of the time, but for some songs I'd dance with Kaliya and the other ladies. "I Need a Hot Girl" was one of those songs. We took turns recording each other, taking shots, and dancing. I never thought of myself as even being in the realm of a hot girl, but after today I had to reconsider. This shit was fun!

"I gotta peeee!"Kyana announced, while crossing her legs. I was sure I could tell the twins apart now. Kyomi had a beauty mark under her eye that I didn't notice until like ten minutes ago.

"Me too, lowkey. I was tryna hold it until we went back to Grandma's house though,"Fendi said. "Fuck it let's go in Popeyes or something."

"Them people got their bathrooms locked. It don't even matter if you buy something."Versace divulged.

"Y'all good to go over there and pee. I know the manager,"Qaylo said. "Just say y'all my cousins and y'all gon be straight. As a matter of fact…I'll call her."

"Good! Anybody else gotta go?"Kyana asked, as Qaylo held his phone to his ear.

"Me,"Kyomi and Versace replied together.

"I do too,"Kaliya said.

"Yea, I might as well go,"I said. I'd had to pee for the past hour but I didn't say anything because Kyree had warned me about that.

"You want me to come too?"Kyree asked, placing his hands on my hips.

"No, I'll be okay,"I said, before tilting my head up so he can kiss my lips. He readily obliged.

"Alrighhhttt,"Cambrie dragged out. "We coming right back y'all."

He finally released me while telling me to call me if I needed him. Seeing as how I was only walking down the street to Popeyes, he was definitely being over the top and paranoid. I still thought it was adorable though. That extraness he displayed when it came to me was also the reason why I always felt so safe with him.

As soon as we were a safe distance from them it seemed as if niggas started coming out the wood work to talk to us. We were a nice looking group of girls, so I understood but the thirst was very real. We easily ignored everyone because we had tunnel vision to Popeyes. There was a whole line outside of Popeyes, so getting to the door was going to be eventful. Kaliya and I let the other girls attempt to lead the way to the door while we lagged behind.

"Did you see who was tryna talk to you back there?"Kaliya grinned.

"Nope,"I laughed. "Did you see any of the guys trying to talk to you?"

"Girl, if one of the star football players from LSU was trying to holler at me I would've stopped for him. That man is fine as hell."

My heart skipped a beat. Not because I was interested but because I wasn't used to grabbing the attention of big fish. I was merely flattered, but that was as far as it went.

"Of course you would've stopped. You're single and ready to mingle,"I giggled.

"Girl, I wouldn't let a boyfriend stop me either. I'd keep my options open because best believe these niggas are."

My heart raced again. This time from fear. I'd never considered the fact that Kyree may have been keeping his options open. He was young, handsome, paid, and charismatic. His job required him to interact with countless beautiful women. Was I being naive to believe that he was out here being faithful to me? The minute I questioned myself was also the moment I quickly checked myself. He'd done nothing to make me doubt him, so somebody else's lack of faith in men based on their own experiences wasn't going to get to me.

"I could see why'd you feel that way because most guys can be scum, but Kyree's not like that."I responded with confidence.

"How can you be so sur-"

"Mari and Kaliya, come on!"Versace called out to us. That's when I noticed that the manager had come to the door to get us. We walked right through with her and she led us to the bathroom and unlocked it. The bathrooms were single-stalled, so we had to take turns. It was evident Kyana had to go really bad, so she went first. While waiting for her we made small talk. In the midst of me laughing at something Versace said, I felt someone tap my shoulder. I turned around and my stomach twisted.

"Wassup, stranger? Why you looking like you seen a ghost?"Daniel smirked.

"Maybe because the last time I saw you I found out some very alarming things,"I replied. The police were literally a few feet away, so I wasn't scared. I was just shocked to see him in New Orleans. It wasn't strange though. Most BR natives would travel to New Orleans for Mardi Gras since there weren't any parades in their own city on Fat Tuesday.

"Right,"he chuckled, as if something was funny. I personally didn't find anything humorous about him being a drug dealing pimp! I felt like he put my life in danger. "I can see how that came as a shock to you since I wasn't forthcoming about it. Maybe we can have dinner and talk about i-"

"We absolutely cannot. I'm taken, and if I wasn't it would still be a *hell* no,"I emphasized. I'd never date a man who disrespected women for money, let alone for free.

"Dang,"he clutched his chest as if I broke his heart. "You taken by that nigga Kyree, huh? I heard that shit through the grapevine."

"Then why you in her face?"Versace jumped in.

"Hey,"he held his hands up. "I don't want no issues, lil mama. I just wanted to come over here and extend an apology to Kamaria for what went down the last time she was in my presence. You didn't have to run off like that, I wouldn't have let nothing happen to you and I would've got you home safely."

"My man had me, so I was good."

"See, I knew it was something more with you and that nigga,"he chuckled. "It's all good though. I ain't got no beef with you or him. I just wanted to say sorry to you and I've done that."

"Right…well I appreciate it,"I said, before giving him my back. I heard him say bye and he walked off.

"Bitch, who was that?"Cambrie asked with curious eyes. "He was hot! That's your lil trade on the side or something?"

I looked at her like she was absolutely insane.

"For me to have anything on the side that would infer that I was cheating on Kyree, and I'd never. I met him at a party and we talked for like a week. This was shortly *before* me and Kyree got together."

"So why you stopped talking to him?"Kyomi asked.

"Because he put up this facade like he was the perfect college student when he really has a double life where he's a street pharmacist and pimp."

I watched them gag at that tea before going on to tell the short story of that day. By the time Kyana was exiting the bathroom they were dying with laughter and she wanted to be clued in on the joke. Versace went to the bathroom and I repeated the story for her. Fifteen minutes later we were all done using the restroom, and we made our way back outside. The outside of Popeyes seemed to be even more packed than before. We moved through the crowd, and the cat calls resumed. This time I could see the girls giving thought to entertaining it. When a tall, dark, and handsome guy stopped Versace, she put on her best welcoming smile. That's when I noticed he was with a crew and they were just as, if not more good looking than him. They started choosing really quickly, and it seemed to be a boy for each girl. Not wanting to hate, I stood off to the side and let them get their flirt on. I looked down at my phone for the first time since in a while and I saw Kyree had texted me asking if I was okay. I quickly replied to tell him that I was good.

"Kamaria?!" A familiar voice called out to me.

I looked up and instantly recognized who was in front of me.

"Elliot?!"I smiled. "Long time no see."

"Right?"He grinned before leaning in to initiate a hug. I made it a half hug only because the last time I saw this guy his face was between my legs. Elliot was my prom date who's mom was a friend of my mom. I was sure his mom bribed him with something to get him to go to prom with me. He was a freshman in college at the time and probably had way better stuff to be doing. But he'd made my night enjoyable by talking, dancing, and laughing with me. Then he ended it even better by giving me my first sexual experience and orgasm. I naively assumed that would lead to us dating but turns out the nigga had a girlfriend at the time. My feelings were hurt but I quickly got over it. That's why I was able to see him today and be cool. It was all water under the bridge.

"You look good, girl. What you been up t-"

"What's going on over here?!"

Elliot jolted a few feet away out of nowhere because Kyree had popped up and *pushed* him from in front of me.

"Aye, what's your problem?!"

In my highschool days I thought Elliot was so cool but he sounded like a complete square trying to defend himself against Kyree. I guess that was the difference in being from the hood and merely having a little swag.

"You gon have a problem if you don't take yo' long neck ass on!"

"This nigga,"Qaylo laughed in an instigating manner. I couldn't lie...Elliot's neck was long now that Kyree had pointed it out. Now that I was looking at him he wasn't even as handsome as I remembered. He was probably considered cute to most girls with his red skin, light eyes, and soft curly fro that was lined to perfection. But he didn't have shit on my man.

"Say, we don't want no issues. We just out here tryna have a good time,"the boy who stopped Versace spoke up.

"Mannn, I know you ain't entertaining this lame, cuzzo,"Qaylo laughed.

"Lame?! We ain't never been lame! Kamaria certainly didn't think I was lame when I had her scre-"

Goosebumps formed on my arms before he could even finish his statement because I had a feeling where he was about to take things. He never got the chance though because Kyree punched him dead in his face. It was a knockout. All of his male cousins and Qaylo's friends stepped forward because maybe they thought his crew would be ready to fight. They scattered instead, leaving everybody laughing. Everybody except Kyree.

"C'mon y'all,"Qaylo chuckled. "We been out here for a few hours and I'm hungry again."

We walked off with urgency before a crowd could form around Elliot, who was still on the ground now holding his nose.

"You alright, Kyr-"Versace began to ask, while touching his shoulder but he jerked away from her.

"Don't fucking touching me!"He glared at her and then glared at me before storming off. One angry look from him had hurt my feelings. He was obviously mad at me, but why? I hadn't done anything wrong! I wanted to explain that to him but I wasn't going to do that while he was steaming hot. The last thing I wanted to do was give his family a show. But when he shot me another look of disgust I couldn't help myself. I had to say something!

"Why are you looking at me like that?"

"What you mean?! You over here entertaining niggas!"

"No I wasn't! I went to prom with that boy!"

"Bruh..."Vance scratched his head as if that was the worst thing in the world.

"I knew you had to know that nigga with the way you was smiling in his face. Y'all still be talking or something?!"

"What? No! You doing way too much right now!"

"I'm doing too much?!"He stalked towards me.

"Aye, I think y'all need some space right now,"Qaylo jumped in between us. "Y'all too hype and we far from the house."

"I'm not hype. That's him!"

"Say, chill Kamaria,"Qaylo urged. "Talk to him when he calms down."

I was going to take his advice because it seemed that I'd made things worse by admitting I'd gone to prom with Elliot.

I was hoping that this old shit didn't interfere with my Mardi Gras when it'd been going so good.

Kyree

We'd been back at my Grandma's house for an hour now and I still hadn't talked to Kamaria. The last time I saw her she was fixing a plate of food like everything was copacetic. I was initially pissed because I felt like she was letting my people and her cousin influence her. Since they were entertaining niggas, she felt like she had to do the same. I started looking at everything differently once I found out that she actually knew the nigga. I was under the impression that she had little to no male interaction before me. I knew she kissed other niggas and shit, but ole boy was about to blurt something out to me about her *screaming*. I'd cut him off with my fist but I didn't miss that shit at all. I also noticed the spooked look on her face when he was about to say it, which led me to believe it was true. I hadn't asked her about it yet because I knew she'd tell the truth and I wasn't sure how I'd handle it. Since it was before my time it shouldn't have been a big deal. However, Kamaria had made it seem like I was her first in every aspect sexually. If I learned otherwise I'd feel worse than I felt right now.

"Aye, you good?"Qaylo asked, as he stepped outside. I was chilling on my Grandma's back porch where nobody really hung out on Mardi Gras unless they wanted privacy. All of the action was on the front porch.

"I'm straight,"I said evenly while looking forward.

"Nigga no you not,"he tittered. "Lil mama got you in your feelings."

"Alright, I feel some type of way. That's why I'm tryna calm down before I talk to her about what happened."

I already regretted coming at her sideways in front of other people. If I was going to check her it should've been in private. That was one thing I'd be apologizing to her about for sure, but she still needed to explain to me why she thought it was okay to be skinning and grinning in one of her old nigga's faces.

"As you should, cause you got at her kinda crazy and you know you was down bad for knocking that nigga out."

"Man, fuck that nigga. He was about to say some foul shit."

"Yea, I don't doubt that but you know I got weed and an illegal gun on me. Police was all around us, lil bro."

"Damn," I muttered when I came to the realization that I'd put my family in jeopardy because I didn't check my emotions. That was some bitch shit.

"You good," he chuckled. "I had already sold all the weed I brought out there so I really would've just gone down for the gun. I would've ate that bullshit ass charge." He said confidently. His nonchalance when it came to jail was really mind boggling. I wasn't scared to admit that I never wanted to be behind bars. That was a big reason why I stopped fighting in my high school years. I'd only got put in cuffs and sat in the back of the police car, and that shit got my mind right. Meanwhile this nigga had done two whole years in jail before and acted like it was nothing.

"I'm bouta say, it ain't look like you was tripping too hard since you was on the sideline's instigating and shit."

"Never that...sometimes it's just funny hoeing niggas,"he laughed. "But you think you and Kamaria will be straight?"

"Definitely, we just gotta clear some things up fir-"

The back door flew open, and Cambrie stumbled out with a purple cup in her hand. Everybody had been drinking all day, so alcohol had been a factor in everything. It's what made me punch that nigga without even thinking about it. If I'd been sober I would've tried harder to practice self control, but with liquor in my system I just reacted.

It probably played a part in how I handled Mari too, but I wouldn't be using that as a cop out whenever I apologized.

"You mad at us, cousin?"She slurred.

"He probably is. Y'all had that man girl around bukoo niggas. That's fake and it's why he ain't want her hanging with y'all in the first place,"Qaylo grinned.

I shook my head because he wasn't doing shit but stirring the pot and trying to draw a reaction out of Cambrie. I'd never told that nigga I was mad with anybody for what went down. Nobody could make Kamaria do shit. I did snap on Versace a little but that's because she was asking me a dumb ass question while I was heated. I made a mental note to say sorry to her too. Like I'd already expressed earlier, I did have an issue with Mari potentially hanging with Fendi and Versace alone but that's because I knew they were always in mess. It's like no matter where they went it found them. They were good people, but just ratchet as fuck and always with the shit. Why would I willingly send my girl into a situation like that unless I wanted her to be fighting for her life?

"I *know* Kyree don't feel that way about me! I always got his back! I'm single, so I was in my rights to stop! I thought Kamaria would walk off and find you or just stand to the side and let us do our thing. It's not my fault that she did the opposite."

"Alright, Cam," I mumbled, hoping she'd get the hint and leave. It felt like she was going out of her way to rub the shit in.

"That means take yo' ass on somewhere. He ain't tryna hear that bullshit,"Qaylo sniggered.

"I'm sure he'd say that if that's what he meant, but cousin, if you feel some type of way then my bad. If I knew Kamaria better I probably would've said something or told her to chill out. But after what happened inside Popeyes I knew it was best to fall back and just fill you in on everything lat-"

"Wait,"my head bounced up and I looked at her intently. "What happened inside Popeyes?"

"Mannn,"Qaylo shook his head. "Kyree, don't listen to he-"

"Nah, what happened?"I asked again.

"She was flirting with some guy she used to talk to. She entertained him a little too long in my opinion."

"You being messy as fuck, bruh,"Qaylo grumbled.

"Call it what you want. I'm looking out for my cousin, and you should be doing the same."

"I'm gon always do that. That don't even gotta be said, but it seems like you going out of your way to start shit. Even if that is true you could wait until tomorrow to tell him. Kamaria is with us for the rest of the day, yea."

"And?"

"And, their drama could easily fuck up the whole day...but that must be what you want."

Qaylo was making valid points, but everything he was saying was already at the back of my head. I wasn't stupid, so I knew Cambrie hadn't put down her pom poms for Hailey overnight. Her motives were extremely questionable, but that didn't dictate the validity of what she was telling me. I planned on getting clarity from Kamaria and Kamaria only.

The back door opened again, and this time Versace stepped out.

"Dang,"she frowned. "I thought yall was back here smoking."

"Shit, we can make that happen asap,"Qaylo responded.

"Yea, let's do that,"she clasped her hands before looking at me. "You still mad at me?"

"I never was mad at you. Tell me what happened inside Popeyes though…"

"Inside Popeyes?"She frowned. "Not a damn thing from what I can recall besides us taking turns to piss."

"Cambrie claims Kamaria was flirting with a nigga,"Qaylo relayed.

"Girlahhh,"Versace drawled while shooting Cambrie a menacing look. "That girl was not flirting with no nigga. She actually gave him her ass to kiss. It was *your* cousin who asked the damn girl once the nigga walked off was he her side nigga as if that would be cool."

"That was my way of trying to get the tea!"Cambrie screeched defensively.

"It was stupid because let's say that was the case, why would that girl be comfortable enough to tell you of all people? You was obviously being shady and trying to start shit on the behalf of your lil friend."

"No, I'm looking out for my cousin!"

"Girl, you was just trying to fight Kamria two weeks ago. You ain't riding for him that hard, and now I see why Kamaria slapped your friend. You better chill or you gon be next,"she tittered.

One thing about Fendi and Versace, they were straight shooters. They got that shit from their mama. Even my grandma would brag about how they may have offended many, but they never told any lies. That's why I believed Versace's version of the story 100%.

"So what did she say after Cambrie asked that dumb ass question?"I questioned, not really caring about offending Cambrie. I loved her to death, but she couldn't be trusted when it came to my relationship. I'd be sure to relay this message to Kamaria too. To keep the confusion down, I wouldn't go into full detail about how she attempted to sabotage us. But I'd definitely let it be known that she was against us so Mari could know how to move around her going forward.

"She said that he was a guy she talked to right before she and you made it official."

"Oh, okay,"I nodded. Right away I knew it was Daniel. He was nothing for me to worry about. Mari had cut him off cold turkey after learning that he was a drug dealing pimp. I knew for a fact she wasn't flirting with his ass.

"Thanks for the info, cousin,"I stood up and gave her a half hug.

"How you gon take her word against mine?"Cambrie questioned.

"Girl shut up. You know your ass way lying down,"Versace snapped. Cambrie wasn't a punk, but she couldn't see Versace and she knew it. That's why I wasn't surprised that she sealed her lips and didn't respond.

"Smoke one with us, Ky,"Qaylo insisted, as he rolled up.

"Maybe later,"I said before walking back in the house. There were a couple of people inside but Kamaria wasn't one. Even her cousin had made herself comfortable on my granny's couch by taking a nap. I walked outside, and Mari was sitting on the front lawn not to my Grandma. They were chatting away like old friends while drinking. I was sure Mari had refilled her Daiquiri by now.

"Don't wait too long to have kids, baby. Do it while your body is still young and up for the challenge,"I heard my grandma say as I invaded their space. I had no idea why that was the topic of conversation, but I was cool with it.

"Hey,"she smiled up at me goofily before giggling. My baby was so drunk.

"Grandma, let me borrow her for a minute,"I pulled her out of the chair.

"Alright, you make sure you return her. We were having a very important conversation,"she winked at her.

"I'll be right back, Grandma,"she giggled, as I pulled her to the beginning of the long driveway where my car was parked. I sat on the hood and pulled her between my legs. I couldn't help myself as I stole a kiss off her pretty lips.

"Oh, you love me again?"She laughed.

"I always love you. My bad for flipping out on you in front of everybody like that. I was in fact tripping like you said."

"You were,"she breathed heavily. "You hurt my feelings."

"And that's the last thing I want to do."

"All I said was hello to that boy, Kyree."

"From my perspective I saw you smiling all big and hugging that nigga."

"I barely hugged him and I did smile because I was surprised to see an old friend."

"That's all he is?"I gave her a look.

"Okay, we were never friends. But we did kinda grow up together because our mom's were tight. My mom set us up to go to my prom. Everything was very platonic until the end of night..."

"What happened?"I braced myself.

"You sure you wanna know?"

"Yes."

"Okay...he gave me head."

"Mannn,"I looked off in agony.

"Really Kyree? That was forever ago,"she laughed.

"I really don't see what's funny! What happened to me being your first?"

"You are. That wasn't a lie!"

"Yea, I'm the first nigga to penetrate you but you obviously had experience in some other areas."

"Okay?"Her eyes danced around in bewilderment. "Is that a crime? I never told you I was completely innocent. That's something you assumed and ran with. Either way, I haven't done nearly as much as you! So can I start questioning you about every bitch you've kissed, touched, or fucked? Let me know so I can have a field day!"

As much as I wanted to be stubborn on the matter, she had a point. I was just so drunk of Kamaria's love that I wanted to be the only man who'd gotten a taste, but I couldn't control the past. I was the only nigga in her present and future, so that was all that mattered.

"Alright…you right, bruh. I still say it's down bad how you used to fuck with other niggas though."I joked. I kissed her deeply while "Halfway" by S-8ighty blasted from a distance. That was a sign to me that no weapons formed against us would prosper.

"You're pushing it,"she giggled. "Oh yea, that reminds me…I ran into Daniel at Popeyes. He tried to offer me an apology date. I shot that fool down so fast."

"Forreal?"I chuckled as if she was actually revealing something to me.

This was why nobody could get in my head when it came to her. She was real and I knew she'd never do me dirty or take what we shared for granted. I never did return her to my grandma. She stayed right under me for the rest of the day.

Chapter 11

Kyree

March 13, 2020

"Yessss! Yessss!"Kamaria chanted as I long stroked her center vigorously. She was clawing at my back with her thick legs wrapped around me. That shit brought me so much warmth and comfort. Funnily, "Say Yes" by Lil Corey was playing as she literally screamed it. Yesterday we made a month of being together but I swear it felt like it'd been longer. I didn't have to question shit about how I felt because I was wearing my heart on my sleeve with her. The deep feelings I'd developed had me doing things I'd never done. In the past, I'd never remembered special dates or anniversaries. If I did remember it was last minute or because I was reminded. With her I was planning a week in advance because our relationship was turning one month old. I didn't go over the top. We just drove back to New Orleans so she could get a Louis Vuitton bag she'd been wanting from Canal Place, and then we had dinner at Landry's. She said she felt bad because she didn't know we were exchanging gifts, but honestly, I didn't care about receiving gifts. I wanted to spoil her. As long as she was good to me and never took that pussy away then we were even.

"I'm finna nut,"I grunted. "Where you want it at?"

"I-in my pussyyy,"she moaned. I wasted no time giving her what she asked for. Hearing her talk nasty was my weakness because I knew it wasn't in her regular personality. Sex with me was bringing it out of her. I also liked to hear her tell me to nut in her, so if something happened she couldn't act brand new. The chances of something happening was low though. Last month she'd had a few instances where she was sloppy with her birth control, but her period had come on time right at the beginning of this month. Now she'd gotten used to taking the birth control pills, leaving no room for slip ups. It was cool because I was going to get her one day. For now I was just going to dream about the day she had my child.

"Damn, that was good,"I expressed, after pulling out and collapsing on top of her. "Give me a kiss."

Our lips collided and it wasn't long before we were tonguing each other down. My dick was growing hard again, and she felt it because it was grinding against her wet pussy. I was about to slide back into her, when her phone started ringing.

"Ignore it."

I already knew who it was and they didn't want shit of importance. Probably was looking for a turn up since it was the weekend, but we were doing us right now.

"She called me earlier and I ignored it. I'm not gonna ignore her again. Sorry, Ky,"she kissed me sweetly, before grabbing her phone off the nightstand. Just as I suspected, it was Kaliya.

Before Mardi Gras break, I'd never heard of this cousin. All of a sudden they were two peas in a pod. I found it odd how she had a first cousin close by at Southern University this whole time and they hadn't been hanging out for the past few years. They were seemingly velcroed together now. That wasn't an issue for me. Kaliya was cool, and being a family guy myself, I liked the idea of Mari having family members she could depend on. Her parents already weren't shit. I just questioned the timing of this blossoming relationship. They'd know each other all their lives and now Kaliya wanted to be up her ass? It felt like it was very convenient but it wasn't my place to say anything.

"Wassup, cous?"

"You tell me, I texted you and called today and you didn't reply."

The volume on Kamaria's phone must've been all the way up because I heard Kaliya clearly on the other line.

"Girl, I had two hard ass tests today and came straight to my man's place to lay up."

"Oh...so y'all not getting into nothing tonight?"

"No, we usually chill on Friday nights."

"Y'all wasn't chilling last Friday night,"she pointed out. That was it. I couldn't stay quiet any longer.

"That's because a good business opportunity came by that I couldn't pass up on,"I relayed loud enough so she'd hear. I'd been waiting to throw a party at this popular club in Downtown Baton Rouge but they always hosted their own events every Friday through Sunday. Last Friday opened up for some mysterious reason, but I didn't question it. I thanked God, accepted the blessing, and my bank account took a major win. Kaliya had tagged along and she turnt up all night long. She was undoubtedly looking for a repeat this weekend, but wasn't shit moving until tomorrow. Including Kamaria.

"I'm on speaker?!"

"No, you just talking loud,"Mari giggled.

"No, bitch, your volume is too high. Anyways, let's do something cousin."

"Man,"I took the phone and put it on speaker. "We busy, cousin. We gon all link tomorrow."

"And that sounds cool...but would it be okay if I just hung out with my cousin alone tonight?"

"I mean, that's up to her,"I said, handing the phone back to her. After a hectic week we'd both expressed how we wanted to spend Friday night together so I was trusting that she'd honor that.

"So what we doing, cuz?"

"I'm sorry, but I'm in for the night with my man. But I'll see you tomorrow and maybe we can do brunch on Sunday."

"Girl, I'm tryna be outside tonight,"she whined. "Don't let no nigga keep you locked up."

"Where you friends at, Kaliya?"I interjected once again. Shit, I needed answers at this point because she was acting like Kamaria's absence was holding her up.

"Kyree…"she gave me an antagonizing look.

"Wow,"Kaliya giggled. "You trying to play on my top, Kyree? I thought we were better than that."

"We cool and all, I'm just tryna see something. I'm not coming at you no type of way. It's always nothing but respect on my end."

"Okay, well my friends are around…I just wanted to hang with my favorite cousin."

"Hang with those friends tonight. I'm sure they're feeling neglected since you've been with us every weekend for the past few weeks."

"Actually, they've been neglecting me. Everybody's either tied up with school or work."

"Oh, so that's why you've been hanging with us?"I asked for further clarity.

"No, I'm making up for lost time with my cousin,"she said. Feeling satisfied with that answer, I was about to fall back. Maybe I was judging her unfairly. "And it's fun partying with y'all. There's endless perks, the number one thing is everything being free."

Just like that she killed any little bit of credit I was about to give her. She suddenly wanted to be Kamaria's friend so she could reap the benefits of my party promotions and I couldn't be convinced otherwise.

"Bitch, you play too much,"Kamaria laughed. Clearly that user ass comment flew over her head and she took it as a joke. They talked for a few more minutes before Mari ended the call.

"Now why were you acting like that with my cousin? What if I treated your cousins like that?"

"Like what? I ain't do that girl nothing, and my cousins don't be bothering us while we laid up."

"You were giving her a hard time, Ky. Don't play crazy."

"I was just tryna get in her head and see why she was acting like her night couldn't go on without you. Shit."

"But that wasn't your place. I already shot her down on the strength of us agreeing to stay in earlier. But you have a hard time letting me handle things by myself. You just gotta intervene at all times."

"What?"My neck jerked back so I could gauge if she was forreal right now.

"You heard me loud and clear,"she batted her eyelashes.

It sounded like she was trying to infer that I was controlling, and that wasn't the case. Kamaria was very smart, but sometimes she didn't know shit from sugar. This was one of those times. I had to just let her see on her own though because she obviously wouldn't be receptive to what I thought about her cousin. It was also a small possibility that I was wrong. Who knows…only time would tell. She would never stop me from looking out for her though. She or anybody else could call me whatever they wanted.

Chapter 12

Kamaria

March 27, 2020 (Spring Break)

"Heard your top good, let me see, boo. Pussy so fat, I wanna feed you. If your head game fire, I might keep you," I rapped along to "Sweet Tooth" by the city girls as I flat ironed my 30 inch bright red bus down wig. I was lowkey feeling like a thick ass version of JT, and since we were in Miami that was very appropriate. Miami was very predictable for Spring Break but I'd never been, so I was excited. We'd just landed an hour ago and we were going to go eat at some restaurant called Big Pink and then go to the beach. Later on that night we were going to King of Diamonds.

"Where them niggas who gon' eat it? Fuck it all night. 'Cause I'm nasty and good pussy don't get tired," I rapped while turning in the mirror to get a glimpse of my booty in my brown string bikini. It wasn't meant to be a thong, but it was giving that the way my ass was swallowing. I didn't care because I looked fine as hell and I had a two piece brown crochet cover up that consisted of a mini skirt and crop blouse that tied in the front. I'd tried on all my outfits for Kyree a week ago and this one was his favorite. He could get jealous at times but he never tripped about what I wore. I think he liked how comfortable I'd gotten with my body and showing it off.

"Girl, what you know about this?"Kaliya sniggered, as she walked into the bathroom. This was a friend's trip, so the whole UBR gang was here as well as Kaliya. SU Spring break was the same week as ours, so it worked out perfectly. I was starting to think that Kaliya went to UBR though with how much she had been hanging with us for the past month. We'd gotten so close and it was honestly a breath of fresh air. It made me wish we'd made up sooner.

The guys had split the price of the six bedroom house, and all us ladies had to do was purchase our flights. Well Kyree got my flight and Shad had gotten Essence's. We were the only couples on the trip. No, Essence and Shad weren't officially together but they were obviously on great terms if he'd paid for her flight and they chose to stay in the second master bedroom together. Kyree and I got the first master. Lark and Zion had a Jack and Jill style bedroom. Then there was Dale, Tysean, and Kaliya who had their own modest bedrooms.

"Huh?"I asked in confusion.

"I said what you know about this? You a City Girl now or something?"She reiterated. That's when I realized she was talking about the song coming from my playlist. Kyree was downstairs with his guys. Naturally, they finished first so they were waiting on us. All the girls had gathered in our bathroom because we had a big mirror and a lot of counter space.

"I think that's my business,"I replied playfully.

"Don't let the innocent face fool you. My friend got Kyree sprung for a reason,"Essence said before slapping my booty.

"What she said,"I giggled, before putting on more of my Fenty gloss bomb in the shade Sweet Mouth.

"I just can't see Kamaria doing certain stuff,"she laughed. "I imagine her as a pillow princess."

"Uh-uh, you got her messed up,"Lark looked at her out the side of her eyes.

"There's nothing wrong with being a pillow princess. Some niggas like that,"she noted.

"While mine don't,"I tittered.

"Well how's he in bed?"

My laughter instantly stopped. I knew she didn't mean any harm and this was simply girl talk, but Kyree's dick was not up for discussion.

"I think that's my business,"I said firmly, repeating the exact words I'd uttered at the beginning of this conversation. The shift in my energy was apparent, making things awkward. Thankfully, there was a knock at the bathroom door putting an end to that.

"Y'all hurry up!"Shad shouted. "We hungry!"

Kyree

Spring Break/ Day 2

Spring break was right on time. Between school and throwing parties I was worn out and in need of a serious break. With it officially being Spring, students were back partying in droves. They didn't care if the semester was going to be over in two short months. That usually gave them more of a reason to party. I was taking full advantage of people's desperation for turn ups but I was also keeping up with what was important. Namely school and Kamaria. I heavily considered just chilling for Spring Break and resting, but my baby was excited to celebrate it for the first time in her college career so I couldn't let her down. Being here in Miami with her made me realize I'd made the right decision. Laying under a Cabana at Nikki Beach with a cup of D'usse on the rocks in my hand and Mari laying across my chest was the perfect remedy for all my stress. She was on her second strawberry lemon drop. I'd rented our own Cabana next to our friends who had a big section. They were taking back to back shots and dancing to the popular music the DJ was spinning. Yesterday was a lot with traveling, checking into our Airbnb, South Beach, and KOD. We had fun, but we were all exhausted. We needed today to sleep in and then do something chill. This beach club was definitely chill but still a vibe.

"Why did my mom text me in the family group chat saying I should remove my bikini pictures from instagram?"

"What? She put that in the family group chat?"

"Yes…the group chat that has my dad, aunts, uncles, grandparents, and cousins. If she had a problem she could've texted me separately."

"Right, but I'm trying to see what's the problem. You grown and I took those pictures myself, you looked fine as hell."

She really had the internet in a frenzy. Twitter loved her so much that they migrated over to her instagram to keep up with her. She went from having 900 followers to 10,000 within a month. In this day and age, her body type was sought after and women were paying for it. What her mom tried picking apart was now a part of the influencer starter package. With Mari it was admired even more because she was all natural. There were girls asking her for her meal plans and work routines, not knowing that neither existed. I was telling her to take advantage of that love because it could be quite lucrative, but she had her head in the books. She would just post her pictures, respond to a few compliments from women, and go about her business. Her bathing suit pictures from yesterday and today had blown up on twitter. I thought the bathing suit yesterday was fire, but her get-up today was lethal. She wore an orange high cut one piece that was completely backless with a plunging neckline that showcased her perfect breasts. Over it she wore an orange netted skirt knee length skirt that had two long splits up the sides. She paired the look with a brown and orange Tory Burch tote and matching slides. Right after she took her pictures, I handed my phone off Essence to snap us up. I always made it a point to post us together so nobody could ever get it twisted, but we also looked good together with our coordinating fits today . I sported an orange Burberry t-shirt, orange Burberry plaid swim shorts, and matching slides. I made sure to post pictures of us kissing, her sitting in my lap, and me grabbing her big ole ass. I'm sure that didn't stop thirsty niggas from sliding in her dm's, but it wasn't like she was going to respond anyway.

"She said it's distasteful for me to be on the internet with my body out, and my dad was quick to agree."

"Oh, forreal? That nigga had something to say?"I asked in awe.

"Yea, he said I've always carried myself with respect and I shouldn't stop now."

"I'm trying to see the correlation between that and bikini pictures."

I hated the notion that if a female posted sexy pictures on social media that she was classless or didn't respect herself. Why couldn't a woman just be proud of their body and want to show off? There was no reason Kamaria should've been getting judged by her family for posting pictures in bathing suits while in Miami. It was like judging a dog for barking.

"Me too because Kaliya posted pictures in her bathing suit. They didn't say shit about her."

"That's suspect."

"Not really. It's been like this. Only she's speaking up for me now, which I appreciate."

"What did she say?"

"She said 'what's the big deal, I posted pictures in my bathing suit too.' My mom had the audacity to say 'but you weren't turned with your back to the camera, showing off your backside. Your pictures were tasteful.' So apparently her pictures are acceptable and mine aren't. My other family members cosigned by liking that text message."

"Man, you don't have to put up with that shit."

The worst part about everything was that her mom was doing all this shit in front of an audience who felt the need to chime in.

"I know, which is why I just left the chat. They won't annoy me while I'm enjoying myself,"she snuggled up closer to me.

"Good,"I kissed her forehead, and squeezed her booty. " And you better not remove one picture."

"I definitely won't be doing th-...what the fuck?This lady is absolutely positively insane."She held her phone up to my face. "Look."

I see you removed yourself from the family group chat. Running from the truth won't work in your favor and neither will posting those salacious photos. I don't know who you're trying to impress, but no real man would approve of his woman exposing herself to the world like that. I also think you're forgetting everything I taught you. Certain things look a lot more inappropriate because of your size. You can't get away with stuff that girls that are Kaliya's size can get away with. This is not me criticizing you or your body. This is reality. I love you and have fun on your trip. Please respect your fathers and I's wishes as we are the ones who support you.

"Okay, everything I read is some bullshit but this last line got me. Is she tryna say that you should do whatever she says because she funds your life?"

"That's what it looks like to me...and I'm thinking maybe I should take heed."

"No, fuck that. Don't let nobody control you like that with money. Parent or not."

"Kyree, I'm not trying to get cut off right now so close to gradua-"

"You with me so you'll never be down bad. I can easily take care of you financially up to graduation."

"My life doesn't end after graduation."

"No shit. That's why I've been looking at apartments and condos in New Orleans for us."

"For us?"She smirked. "Well, when were you gonna tell me this?"

"Shit, we practically live together now. I thought it was something that was understood. Did I jump the gun or something? You can let me know if you have other plans set in stone."

"Honestly, I don't...well, I did have a plan but I'm not comfortable with it anymore."

"Why not?"

"Because it involves going home and staying with my parents. That's not happening."

"So what were you going to do?"

"I was going to get my own apartment and work,"she shrugged. "I even thought about asking my auntie to stay with her. She also has two other properties that I'm sure she would've allowed me to stay in for a discounted price."

"And just fuck me right?"I quizzed. I admired her ambition, but I wasn't feeling how I'd been left out of her plans. She obviously wasn't planning on telling me unless I asked.

"Don't do that, Ky. One thing's for certain, I'm always thinking about you."

Peering into her eyes as she said that shit gave me butterflies, but I quickly brushed it off. If she ever wanted to play on my emotions she could do it with ease because when it came to her I was cotton soft.

"So what happened this time?"

"I'm not a mind reader. Sure, we live in each other's skin now. But this is college. I didn't know if you wanted to be on the same thing in the real world and I wasn't going to assume. "

"Mannn, you say that like college is some sort of fantasy worl-"

"No, I'm not saying that, but post college is real adulthood. This is just a teaser."

"Well I want to do *real* adulthood with you."

"And had I known that then we would've been on the same page. I would love to live with you."

"Cool,"I grinned, not being able to hide my happiness when it came to our future together. "Oh yea, and I meant what I said about money too. I got you."

"I hear you, but I still don't know how comfortable I am with th-"

"Why not? I give you money all the time."

"Yea for my upkeep like hair and nails. But that's a huge leap into completely taking care of me."

"I disagree…as a matter of fact, what do you need for the next two months that's so big that I can't take care of? Your tuition and housing is already paid. That's the only major shit I can think of. I can give you that monthly allowance your parents give you for the next two months right now, plus more.

Your phone bill? That's light work. I'm already paying for your upkeep as you call it, so what's the issue?"

"I don't know, I guess I don't like the idea of being completely dependent on anyone. What if something happens?"

"I just told you I'll put the money in your hands, so no matter what happens you'll be straight. But I ain't no lame ass nigga. As long as you don't straight up shit on me, I'll stand on my word. Either way, you'll never be completely assed out and you know it, so there's no harm in accepting what I'm offering."

"And how do you know that?"

"Mari, you barely spend money like that. All the designer shit you got comes from other people spoiling your ass. When you shop it be from them cheap, online fast fashi-"

"Okay, not too much,"she cut her eyes at me evilly.

"Nah,"I chuckled. "I'm not tryna play on you because you dress your ass off regardless and the price of shit don't mean nothing. My point was you're always able to save a nice chunk of that monthly allowance your parents give you. You can probably afford to take care of yourself for these next two months with no job or without my help."

The guilty look on her face was a clear sign that I was correct.

"Yea, I know what the real issue is here."

"Enlighten me."

"You don't want your parents to cut you off because you love them. No matter how they treat you or talk to you, you still yearn for their love and acceptance."

"And you think that's pathetic right?"

"No, any child would want that from their parents. I think you just have to do what's best for you. But ion fuck with them people at all."

"My parents or my whole family?"She sniggered.

"Based on what you just told me about them cosigning her negativity I say fuck em all. Why the auntie you love so much didn't defend you?"

"She left that group message over a disagreement about where Christmas should be held last year. Everybody agreed we'd do it at her house, but my mama went above her and got everybody to agree to have it at our house at the last minute. My auntie cursed all her brothers and sisters out before leaving the gm."

"That's so childish on your mama's part,"I laughed. "But I bet Auntie still showed up on Christmas day, huh?"

"Of course, family is still family."

"And that mindset is why your mama is the monster that she is. She knows nobody will ever really stand up to her or put their foot down."

"After Mardi Gras I learned there's really no changing her...it's like the more I spoke up for myself the more she gaslighted me. That's when I decided that I couldn't stay with them after graduation."

"But you have no plans on permanently cutting them off, right?"

"Nope, because I love my parents at the end of the day. I just can't take them in large doses and that's fine."

I wanted to say that she shouldn't have had to take them in small doses either. None of that shit was healthy for her. She was way in Miami at a luxurious beach club and they'd found a way to fuck with her. Those people were cancerous and needed to be chopped from her life altogether. But it wasn't my place to tell her what to do. I'd offered my opinion and that was all I could do.

Kamaria

Spring Break/ Day 3

"I like it! I love it! Boy lick it, flip me, shove it! I want it! You know it! So come put that dick on me!" Treety's "I Like It" blasted from the Yacht's speaker. Once again, the boys had come through. They booked and paid for the yacht we were currently turning up on. This whole trip had been showing me what I'd been missing out on for the past few years, but I was just grateful to be experiencing now and I was definitely making up for lost time. I hadn't touched Cognac since my first and last sloppy drunk experience during Mardi Gras break, but I was back on it today. Only this time I'd opted for D'usse because Essence told me it was way better than Hennessy. She introduced me to the D'usse and Lemonade

combo, and I was hooked. Wanting to take it slow, I was only on my second cup. I would've been okay if Kaliya wasn't pouring shots down everyone's throats, making them "drive the boat." I was undoubtedly on the verge of being fucked up, but everybody was. Even Kyree was on a level that I hadn't seen him on before. Before we left the airbnb he'd urged me not to take off my cover up because my bikini bottom was an actual thong. All of us girls had planned on wearing metallic gold bikinis on the boat. I got mine right from Shein, but I didn't realize it was literally a thong until I tried it on for the first time today. I ordered last minute so it came the day before we left. I ordered swimsuits from Shein a lot, so I knew it would fit. I had a gold mesh mini skirt for a cover up and it looked cute, so I didn't mind leaving it on. However, as soon as the liquor got in my system and I started dancing, the skirt rode up and my entire ass was out. I realized Kyree was drunk when he simply got behind and slapped my ass while egging me on. Now my skirt was off and I'd posted several photos on instagram in my thong. I was sure I'd hear my mom's mouth about it, but I wasn't worrying about that. I was just living in the moment.

"Damn bitch, you strong,"Essence gawked at Kaliya taking yet another shot from the Patron bottle she'd bought for the day.

"Girl, any Tequila is like water to me. I'm a pro at this."

"Shit, obviously!"Zion squawked, making us all laugh. All of us girls had migrated to the front of the boat to take each other's pictures, but now we were running our mouths and getting comfortable.

"Here cousin,"Kaliya put the Patron bottle to my mouth. I liked Patron too, so I opened my mouth.

"Hell na! You tripping, Kaliya! Mari you better not drink that shit!"A deep voice roared, resulting in me snapping my mouth shut.

Kyree must've been watching us like a hawk for him to see us from the back of the boat. The boat wasn't huge, but it wasn't tiny either. I looked back and he was standing right by the captain with a mean mug on his face. His playful demeanor had vanished.

"Dang, I thought your father was back in New Orleans Kamaria..."she said loud enough for him to hear.

"Ion gotta be her daddy to know she can't be mixing liquors! Shit, you want her to die or something? Kamaria, don't drink that shit!"

"I'm not!"I snapped, now irritated. He was embarrassing the hell out of me. Okay, so maybe I was about to drink it...but what was the big deal? What was the hysteria about mixing liquors? Kyree's strong reaction was enough for me to just assume it had to be a huge no no.

"Kyree, come hop in this picture!"Shad called out to him. He shot me one last glare before he reluctantly walked off.

"Bitch, do you still want the shot?"Kaliya questioned.

"Honestly, I'm with Kyree on this,"Essence said. "She been on D'usse all day. If she starts drinking Tequila she'll get sick. She's already a light weight."

"I am not,"I said defensively.

"Friend, you are,"Zion giggled. "It's only because you just started really drinking. I think your tolerance will grow over time."

"I mix liquors all the time. Besides, we're here to watch her. What's the worst that could happen?"Kaliya opened her arms.

"Gee, I don't know…alcohol poisoning?"Lark rebutted sarcastically.

"And I don't see you mixing liquors *today*,"Essence added on. "Don't try to make her do something that you ain't even doing."

"Okay, first off, I'm grown so nobody can't make me do anything. Secondly, I was not going to get alcohol poisoning from one shot of Tequila. Y'all are doing the most just like Kyree."

"Maybe so, but I see your ass didn't take that shit,"Zion tittered.

"Exactly,"Lark laughed.

"So you just gon let that nigga control you?"Kaliya questioned. That question, followed by my friends' comments bothered me. I had a point to prove. That point being that Kyree didn't run me. I grabbed the Patron bottle and took a nice swig.

"Bitchhhhh,"Essence marveled as I quickly handed Kaliya her bottle back. I looked behind me to make sure Kyree wasn't looking. Thankfully he was still preoccupied with his boys.

"You then drank that shit to prove something and you still watching your back to make sure that nigga not looking. Point not proven, bitch,"Lark laughed. "But watch your ass gon be fucked up."

"And that's my business,"I snapped, before taking a long sip of my D'usse and lemonade. That Patron had my throat burning. Now that I'd experienced both, I was probably more of a brown girl.

"She just gotta learn the hard way I guess,"Essence rolled her eyes. "Thank God *we're* here."

"Enough of that, I noticed there's nothing on the itinerary for tonight."Kaliya said.

"Probably because we got two more hours on this boat and the sun is about to set. This is our night time turn up. We won't have energy for shit else after this,"Essence replied. I wasn't feeling her tone with my cousin. She just seemed so combative and that wasn't like her. All Kaliya was doing was having fun.

"Well this Miami Dolphins football player invited us to his section tonight at The Office,"Kaliya said discreetly. I didn't blame her considering how Kyree was lurking around and could pop out any second.

"Ouuu, I'll go,"Lark said excitedly.

"Me too. I'm down for whatever,"Zion said.

"What about you, cousin?"Kaliya asked while looking directly at me.

"Uhhhh,"I twisted my hair around my finger nervously. "I don't know…"

I was honestly looking forward to staying in with my man and riding his dick all night. The alcohol I'd been consuming was going straight to my vagina. I didn't want to be around niggas that weren't Kyree, and I wasn't sure how he'd feel about it. I certainly wouldn't be cool with him kicking it in a section with a bunch of big booty instagram models. So it didn't take a genius to know that he would most likely trip if I even mentioned it.

"I hope you ain't hesitating because of Kyree. He doesn't even have to know where we're goi-"

"Friend, if you are hesitating because of your man who treats you like a princess then so be it,"Essence aggressively cut her off. "Bitches would kill to have a nigga who adores them like Kyree adores you. Don't jeopardize that to go hang around some dusty ass, run through professional athletes. It's not even that serious."

"Facts,"Lark co-signed. "This seems like an outing for the single ladies. So I guess you gotta sit out too, Essence."

"Lies,"Essence scoffed. "I am not taken. If y'all outside tonight then so am I."

"I thought it wasn't that serious?"Kaliya asked mockingly. She'd played it off well, but I could tell Essence's words had gotten to her.

"It's not, but shit, I'm not against partying on thirsty niggas dimes. It sounds like a cool lil time."

"Well…I don't know how he'll feel about us showing up without Kamaria."

"Why would he care about that if he invited you?"I blinked my eyes rapidly.

She smacked her teeth. "He slid in my dm's because he said you never opened his. I told him I'd try to get you there tonight."

"Oh no, you tripping,"I laughed. "Were you gonna mention that if I readily agreed? Or were you gonna leave me in the blind?"

"It really doesn't matter. My plan was just for us to go out and have a good time on his dime. It wasn't like you had to mess with him if we showed up."

"But he would've been under that impression,"Essence said. "A nigga with expectations is dangerous."

"I doubt he would've been hounding Kamaria with all the females he's going to have around him tonight."

"What you mean by that?"Essence asked with a stank face.

"Absolutely nothing except the man has options. He's not giving he'll throw a temper tantrum if he doesn't get his way."

"No shade Kaliya, but you giving a man you don't know wayyyy too much credit,"Zion giggled. "I guess tonight ain't happening after all. I wouldn't even feel comfortable going now."

"Same,"Lark agreed.

"So we just gon turn down a free turn up?"Kaliya quizzed.

"Girl, you haven't had to touch your wallet this whole trip,"Essence said. "The boys have been covering everything down to the tabs at the restaurants we've been eating at. You can't be that hard up for a free section and alcohol."

"Essence I'm really not feeling your tone with me. You coming on wayyy to strong when all I'm trying to do is provide fun experiences. My friends appreciate my connections."

"What connections? This so-called connect only came to you because Mari paid him dust. So who are you supposed to be?"Essence asked with her hand on her hip.

"Okay,"I said, feeling the need to speak up. Things were going too far now. "Relax Essence because you're doing a lot right now. It's not even that deep."

"Relax?"Essence's head bounced back. It looked like she wanted to go off, but she just shook her head and laughed. "Let me just separate myself chile…"

She made her way to the back of the boat, while I downed the rest of my drink. I was going to drink until nobody could get on my nerves anymore.

Kyree

The boat was about to dock soon and I was praying Kamaria didn't throw up a second before it did. She was out of her body. She was sitting down with her eyes closed. I knew I was going to have to carry her ass off this mutherfucker. I had already sobered up an hour ago because I saw where she was headed. A clear sign was her twerking to Come Through by Summer Walker. Wasn't shit about that song twerkable. Her blacking out when she was with me wasn't a big issue because I was going to make sure she was straight. But she wouldn't always be with me. She just didn't know how to drink yet and I wanted her to learn immediately. I'd learned my limits by the end of my freshman year of college. Kamaria was late to the party for sure, and her dumb ass cousin made it no better. She was obviously drunk too but she knew how to handle her shit because she was still standing after taking countless shots. That wasn't my issue though. My problem with her was serving Mari shot after shot. I'd let it rock all day. I only stepped in when I saw her trying to give her Tequila. I was cool with her taking D'usse shots, but that changed an hour ago when I noticed her stumbling around the boat. When she almost fell in the damn water, I told everybody she was officially cut off. That's why I didn't understand why Kaliya was currently walking towards her with a new bottle of D'usse that she'd just popped open.

"One more shot, cousin!"She screamed, while gripping her jaw.

Before I could even think I pushed her hand away and knocked the bottle from her hand. It fell and spilled everywhere. Essence quickly picked it up and threw a towel on the alcohol so it wouldn't spread. Meanwhile Kaliya had the nerve to be looking at me like I'd violated her or something. The audacity.

"Did you just touch me?!"She screamed.

"No, I'm pretty sure he slapped the bottle from your hand and stopped you from serving somebody who's blacked out more alcohol,"Tysean explained calmly.

"No! He put his hands on me and I want an apology!"

"Bitch, I ain't apologizing for shit! You out your top!"I shouted.

"Bitch?! That's so disrespectful!"

"Oh…my bad. I apologize, *Miss* Bitch."

"Bruh,"Shad doubled over with laughter. "Calm down, Kyree."

"Nah! I don't know what this dumb hoe on, but she weird as fuck! Mari over her damn near passed out and she still trying to give her alcohol! I wasn't all the way serious when I asked if you were trying to kill her earlier but now I'm really starting to wonder!"

"Fuck you! Bitch ass nigga!"Kaliya screamed, before roughly palming my face. My anger skyrocketed as Essence pulled her away and Shad stepped in front of me.

"Man, I ain't bouta do that stupid bitch nothing," I grumbled. "She ain't even worth it."

I meant that wholeheartedly. It never crossed my mind to reach out and put my hands on her. I'd only pushed her hand away from Kamaria's face because she was trying to force a damn shot down her throat. After today this bitch was officially on my shit list and I was going to let Mari know it as soon as she sobered up. Right now the only thing on my mind was watching her and making sure she was good.

Kamaria

"Ugh," I groaned as I woke up. My head was *pounding.* I sat up holding it while looking around at the dark room. The only light was coming from the tv. I sat there for a minute trying to piece together the day because I was having a hard time recalling the last time I was conscious. The first thing I remembered was the yacht and then everything else started coming to me. Now I understand why mixing liquors was a big no-no. After Essence and Kaliya's argument, I took more shots of Tequila. That had definitely been my downfall and I didn't plan on admitting it to anyone out loud. I'd learned my lesson the hard way. Damn, I guess Essence was right afterall. Not just her, but Kyree as well.

I located my phone on the charger on the nightstand right next to me. I picked it up to check the time. It was only 12 AM which meant I'd been asleep for a few hours because the boat docked at 8 pm. I had no recollection of the boat docking or the ride home. But I was glad to see that I was here in one piece. I may have had a painful headache, but I had on my pajamas and my headscarf. I even smelled fresh, making it evident that Kyree had bathed me. I had to be awake for that but I didn't remember it. A bunch of instagram notifications from my last post flooded my lock screen. I scrolled all the way to the bottom and saw a lengthy message from Kaliya. I knew it was long because the entire thing wasn't showing. But the first few sentences already had me feeling a way, so I quickly unlocked my phone to read it in its entirety.

Cousin, your boyfriend disrespected the fuck out of me on the boat. You were out of it so I know you don't

remember what happened, and I want to explain myself before he gets all in your head. I was trying to give you another shot of D'usse and he pushed me before slapping the bottle from my hand. He also called me out my name multiple times. I know you like him a lot, but he went too far. I'd never let anybody I was dealing with handle you like that. All I want is an apology and I think I deserve one. Love you, and I don't want any of this to come between us.

Right after I finished reading the message the door opened and Kyree swaggered in.

"You're up,"he smiled. "You was throwing up bad earlier. You scared the shit out of me."

He walked over to the nightstand on his side of the bed, grabbed a little white pack that read "goodie," and a glass of water. He tore the pack open, and gave it to me along with the water.

"Take this. I already know you got a headache. This will help."

Although I wanted to dig into him about what happened with my cousin, I chose to take the goodie first. I needed something to combat this excruciating headache. After swallowing the bitter powder and taking a big gulp of water, I was ready to talk about whatever the hell happened.

"How you feeling?"He touched my forehead like I had a fever or something. "You hungry? We ordered pizza. Eating something greasy will make you feel better too. I'm finna go get you so-"

"Kyree, what happened with you and my cousin on the boat?"

He paused, obviously caught off guard.

"You remember that?"

"No, but she texted me saying you disrespected he-"

"I did because she had no business trying to give you more alcohol when you clearly had surpassed your limit."

"So that gives you a right to push her and curse her out multiple times?"

"Pushed her? Yea, fuck that hoe forreal,"he chuckled. "Cause now she lying. You can ask anybody, I didn't push that bit-"

"Stop calling her out her name!"

"Ion gotta do shit. I don't respect that bitch, so fuck her. She don't have your best interest at heart and it's evident. If it was just you and her on that boat she would've allowed you to drink yourself to death! That's who you going hard for?"

"Yea I'm going hard because I'm not going to cosign you disrespecting my cousin who's a female! You're a man so you had no business touching her in any way or cursing her out!"

"So the only way I can intervene if somebody's trying to hurt you is if it's a man? You sound stupid as fuck, Mari."

"Stupid?"My heart dropped. He'd never flat out insulted me in that way.

"Yea, stupid,"he said without an ounce of remorse. "I'm telling you I stopped somebody from giving you alcohol while you were blacked out and couldn't even consent to it but you more worried about my choice of words."

"It isn't just about your choice of words if you put your hands on he-"

"STOP SAYING THAT LIKE I BEAT THAT BITCH UP OR SOMETHING!"He roared angrily, making me flinch. "SHE GRABBED YOUR FACE TO FORCE A SHOT DOWN YOUR THROAT AND I MOVED HER HAND AWAY. THAT'S ALL! The only thing that got hurt was the bottle of D'usse because it fell when I knocked it from her hand!"

"Do you think all that was called for though? All you had to do was tell her no and she would've backed off."

"I did that once before when she tried to give you that damn Tequila. And your stupid ass was ready to drink it!"

He was right about the Tequila situation but I couldn't get past him calling me stupid. That just made me want to defend myself because he was insulting the fuck out of me.

"I don't give a fuck! I'm tired of you policing me anytime I drink! I'm an adult! I can handle myself! You act like you my damn daddy or something!"

"I can't be that nigga! He damn sure wouldn't speak up for you!"

I gasped as my heart dropped. That was a sore spot and he knew it. I didn't have a comeback for that, but I wanted him to pay. My water was still in my hand. The next thing I knew it was splashing in his face and I threw the cup at his head too.

"I can't believe you'd say that!"I screamed as I hopped off the bed and swung on him furiously. I had blacked out again but this time there was no liquor involved. It was just me and my hurt feelings.

"What the fuck?! Say, chill out Kamaria!"

I didn't know where Shad came from, but he pulled me away.

"The fuck y'all got going on?!"Dale asked.

"Man, get her stupid ass out of my face before she get me out of character. Real shit,"Kyree gritted, as he licked blood from his lip. He stormed off to the bathroom and slammed the door. I tried to go after him because he was going to pay for cursing me out in front of his friends.

"Nahhh,"Shad pulled me back. "That nigga heated right now, so give him his space. Go holler at the girls or something."

I took heed, and went to go find the girls. I went to Kaliya's room first but she was knocked out. Everybody else wasn't in their rooms so I went downstairs. In the living room there was a huge glass door that led to the huge backyard where there was a pool and jacuzzi. That's where Essence, Lark, and Zion were. I quickly walked back there, anxious as ever to vent to someone.

"Look who's risen from the dead,"Essence smirked but as I stepped closer to them her smile fell. "What's wrong with you, friend?"

"Me and Kyree got into a fight,"my voice cracked.

"An argument right?!"She questioned like she was ready to go to war.

"No, it got physical,"I divulged as tears ran down my face. I couldn't believe that things had gone this far. My emotions were all over the place and I was desperately wishing I had a time machine.

"He put his hands on you?"Lark gasped.

"No, I put my hands on him! UGH!"I dropped down on the lounge chair and threw my head in my hands.

"What? Why, Mari?"Essence questioned. "He took such good care of you tonight. What reason would y'all have to be arguing in the first place?"

"Because he disrespected my cousin and stood on it. Can y'all believe that?!"

I expected them to be in an uproar with me. As women and my friends I was sure they'd see my point of view. But the silence was so loud. I had to look up at them to read their faces and body language. It didn't take long for me to decipher that they would be siding with him.

"Friend...I wouldn't even lie to you, your cousin was out of line. You was faded and she was trying to give you more alcohol. Straight up, I don't like the bitch and I think she's jealous of your relationship. I was side-eyeing her from the minute she asked about how Kyree was in bed."

"Oh my God, Essence,"I groaned. "I don't think she meant it that way."

"And I gave her the benefit of the doubt but then she was basically going to deliver you to a nigga like you're not in a happy relationship. That girl wants you to be miserable and single with her, and you drinking the kool-aid. I'm convinced."

I rolled my eyes and didn't even give thought to what she was saying. Those were two instances and I wasn't sold that Kaliya had bad intentions. Bad judgment? Maybe. Not thinking things through? Sure. But I wasn't convinced that she was out to get me or my relationship. I couldn't even see it being that deep for Kaliya. She was a beautiful girl who could have pretty much any guy she wanted. Why would she be jealous of me?

"That theory aside, she was doing too much today on the boat. She knows you're a beginner with drinking and she got you past your limit. Then when you were blacked out, she tried to pour more alcohol down your throat. That was insane,"Zion shook her head.

"Okay, that does sound insane,"I admitted. "If she did that then she was wrong, b-"

"Ain't no if,"Essence twisted her neck. "None of us have any reason to lie. She did it."

"Alright,"I breathed heavily. "Still, did that give Kyree a right to come at her so strongly? He could've simply removed the bottle from her hand."

"He could've,"Lark shrugged. "But I think he just reacted fast without thinking. He went straight into protective mode and I can't say I blame him."

"I just don't think Kaliya had intentions to hurt me. She was drinking all day too, so she probably wasn't thinking strait-"

"The credit you're giving her needs to be given to the nigga who took care of you while Kaliya didn't do so much as hold your hair while you threw up,"Essence huffed.

"Why do you have such an attitude with me?"I snapped.

"Because you sound dumb defending this hoe like your life is depending on it."

"Yea because that's my family!"

"And blood don't mean shit! But okay, Mari. You got it. I don't wanna fuss with you about this because that ain't even like us. We better than that. I'm sure her true colors will be revealed to you one day, and if I'm wrong…I won't be too prideful to admit that. In the meantime, you owe Kyree an apology. Because he was truly looking out for you and you sided with somebody who was bringing you harm, regardless of what you think her intentions were. Had she given you more alcohol while you were already blacked out that could've really been detrimental to you."

"Agreed. We can go back and forth about her intentions all day. Nobody besides her knows what's going on in her brain. What can't be argued is her actions and she was about to do some fucked up shit. Kyree stepped in…yea, his reaction probably was a lot but I bet she never tries that shit again,"Lark tittered.

Deep down, I knew they were right and it made me feel even worse for how I handled Kyree. He didn't deserve that reaction from me. I could only hope that he was willing to hear my apology and make amends. If the shoe was on the other foot I'd be breaking up with him. Domestic violence was always something I said I'd never tolerate and here I was putting my hands on him because he said some mean things. It was all so stupid.

"So, friend…you really hit him? I can't even see you doing that,"Zion said in disbelief.

"Right,"Lark agreed. "I'm trying to picture it."

"Well he called me stupid and threw my family issues in my face, so yea, that sent me over the edge."

"Ouuu, now see, I didn't know that. Maybe he deserved a lick or two,"Essence said with her hand on her chin.

"No he didn't. Domestic violence is never okay,"I said.

"Bitch we know that. It's clear you don't,"Zion giggled. "Kyree loves you though. He won't stay mad."

"I can only hope…"I hugged myself for comfort. As I started to think of what I'd say to apologize, the glass door slid open. I turned around and goosebumps covered my body. It was Kyree, and he looked just as upset as he did when he told Shad to get me away from him. My nerves went into a frenzy.

Kyree

"Let's go inside y'all,"Essence said to Lark and Zion.

"Y'all can stay out here. I was about to tell Mari to come upstairs,"I said. I'd told Shad to get her away from me, but wanting my distance from her didn't last long. This was unlike us, and I refused to let her cousin's influence turn us into something we weren't. Kaliya had obviously gotten to Kamaria first with her version of what had taken place. I was mad that she would just take her word for it. But beyond Kaliya exaggerating about me putting my hands on her, I had disrespected her. I could see why Kamaria wouldn't root for me cursing her cousin out like a bitch off the streets, but what she failed to realize was that Kaliya wasn't acting like a cousin. My cousins stepped for me and were extremely protective, and it was a good feeling. I think that was the overall feeling Mari craved with her own family. That's why she failed to see Kaliya for the fake bitch she was and that's why she refused to cut her parents off despite them constantly beating her down. It also didn't help that Kaliya was all of a sudden an ally for her within her family. That probably made her feel like she finally had a blood relative that would ride for her. Since family was everything to me, I could empathize with

Mari and why she wanted that. She would have to realize on her own that she would never get that from her family. The angry part of me that was mad with how she lashed out on me wanted to make her sweat it out. My evil side was saying to punish her for how she came at me. But my heart wouldn't even let me move like that. She'd been punished her whole life and she didn't need to be beat down by me too. However, this wasn't about to be a recurring thing with us. So it was time to nip some shit in the bud.

"No, we were about to go inside anyway,"Lark said, as they all got out of the pool and grabbed their towels. I sat down on the lounge chair next to Kamaria as they walked in the house. She was avoiding my face and I could tell it was out of guilt.

"You then mixed on me and can't even look me in my eyes? That's crazy,"I chuckled, before brushing my locs back so I could get in her face. I leaned forward and stared at her intensely until she had no choice but to match my gaze.

"I'm sorry,"her voice cracked, as her eyes filled with tears. I'm not going to lie, that got to me but I had to stay strong. I couldn't let her break me down with the waterworks. "But you hurt my feelings by throwing my family stuff in my face."

"I know."

"You know?"

"Yea, bruh. That was the reason I did."

She was visibly stunned, and she blinked back more tears.

"That's really fucked up, Kyree."

"It is fucked up, and I was wrong. I'm not proud of that shit…but you think you're the only one whose feelings were hurt? All I did was look out for you just for you to turn around and spit in my face. Was I not owed a conversation before you just took your cousin's side?"

"I tried to have a conversation. I didn't just start going off on you."

"You weren't genuinely coming to me to get clarity on the situation. Your mind was made up. It was in your tone and your demeanor. I'm lying?"

She hesitated before releasing a heavy sigh.

".....no, you're not lying. But when you basically confirmed that you unapologetically cursed my cousin out that made me upset. I'd never disrespect someone in your family."

"You were about to fist fight my cousin, girl. What are you talking about?"

"Because she disrespected me first. Kaliya didn't do you anything."

"Wrong again,"I snapped, growing agitated. "She was trying to hurt you in my presence. That's disrespectful as fuck. I would hope that if you saw one of my family members on some flaw shit with me that you would speak up. If not, maybe we should rethink this relationship."

A look of terror consumed her face. That shit made me feel bad, but I wasn't bluffing. If our relationship was going to consist of her upholding her family while they were wrong and expecting me to deal with it then there'd be no relationship. As much as that would hurt me too, I had to set boundaries.

"Is that what you want?"

"Fuck no, but I can't take you going to bat for somebody who don't mean you no well while shitting on me. Again, I was dead ass wrong for bringing up your family but right before that you accused me of acting like I was your daddy. As if I was on some dry, controlling shit. Do you really think that?"

"No...I know you were just looking out for me and you weren't wrong. I need to learn my limits with alcohol and after today I really learned my lesson. All of this could've been avoided if I just took the advice you gave me...but you could work on your delivery."

"I will...and looking back, I could've just taken the bottle from Kaliya. I didn't have to curse her out or knock the bottle from her hand."

"So you're going to apologize?"She asked with a hopeful smile. My poor baby was so naive.

"Hell no! I'm just willing to acknowledge that I could've done things differently."

"Well will you at least work on that moving forward?"

"Going forward I don't want your cousin in our mix anymore. I don't trust her, and after today I want you to really think about what everybody has told you. Blood doesn't make somebody your family, Mari."

I could see the irritation flash across her face but she didn't act on that emotion. She held it back and nodded her head instead. She heard what I was saying, she just didn't want to hear it. That was fine. As long as I put it on her mind. If it was there it meant she'd think about it for days to come. Right now everything was fresh and her head wasn't clear. She was smart and I believed her judgment would eventually come down from the clouds.

"I will however work on my delivery with you. Maybe if I didn't snap on you about that tequila you would've received what I was actually saying. Even though I notice that anytime I try to school you on something you get kind of defensive, and my delivery don't always be harsh."

"Because you're *always* trying to school me. It makes me feel like you think I'm stupid, and you confirmed that by calling me that in the midst of an argument."

"You're far from stupid, man. It's just…your street smarts not up there with your book smarts. You grew up sheltered and in the burbs. You're nobody's pushover and you stand up for yourself if somebody is overtly coming for you.

But if it's underhanded shit going on you don't catch on right away. You can't tell sugar from shit and that's dangerous. That's what I'm trying to protect you from. I'm not trying to control shit and despite what I said, I don't think you're stupid. You just haven't been exposed to a lot to know enough."

"I can't tell shit from sugar? You're talking about Kaliya, right?"

"Shit, really your whole family…"

"What? I realize I have issues with my parents tho-"

"It's beyond that. It's the way you deal with it but I'm off that. That's a touchy subject and I don't want it affecting our relationship."

"Neither do I,"she sighed. " And regardless of what you said I should've kept my hands to myself. That'll never happen again."

"Girl, I ate that shit,"I laughed. Her licks packed power but compared to my strength, that wasn't bout nothing. I was more mad about her throwing water and a glass at me. "Come here…"

I pulled her off her chair and into my lap. I laid back on the lounge chair, so she was laying on top of me.

"You really forgive me?"

"Yup,"I kissed her forehead.

"Why so fast?"

"Because I love you. Flaws and all. We locked in."

"But you just threatened to break up with me."

"Cause you need to know how serious I am about keeping your cousin from me."

"I definitely got the memo. I'm sorry again."

"I know, Mari. I'm sorry, too,"I pressed my lips against hers and kissed her deeply.

"So you not mad at me anymore?"

"No, I'm still kinda mad…but you can make it up to me."

She smiled mischievously before leaning back in to resume our kiss. She slipped her tongue into my mouth at the same time her hand entered my Gallery Dept shorts. Her soft hand located my dick and she wasted no time stroking it up and down. I was nice and hard in record time. She slid down and engulfed my entire dick at once. My breath was momentarily lodged in my throat. This was a first for her. She'd achieved getting my whole dick in her mouth since the first time she gave me head, but it always took her a minute to get there. She always had to work her way down. I guess her fucking up tonight was all the ammo she needed to step her shit up...and damn, was she stepping her shit up. She had already learned how to please me with her mouth, but this shit she was doing now was on a new level. She'd mastered the art of giving head.

"Alright, alright,"I grunted, as I literally grabbed her hair to make her stop. I'd snatched that bonnet off the minute she started deep throating me while simultaneously playing with my balls. It was a possibility I would have nothing left to give with the way she was eating me up, and I didn't want to chance that. "Come ride this dick."

Like the good girl she was at heart, she readily listened. She climbed into my lap and prepared to gently slide herself down my dick. She had me fucked up though. I usually let her have control whenever she rode me, but not this time. I was about to fuck the shit out of her ass. This was a form of punishment I could get with for her actions.

"Kyreee!"She shouted, as I abruptly pushed her all the way down on my dick and started pounding in her shit.

"Shut and take this dick."

"I-I-I'm t-trying! Slow downnnn, please,"she begged. Funnily enough, she was still trying to desperately match my thrusts, but she was no match for the type of time I was on.

"I ain't slowing down shit. You gon stop playing with me?"

I knew I took her by surprise when I slipped a finger inside her ass. I'd only done that while eating her pussy. Never while fucking her.

"Ughhh!"She moaned as her head flew back.

"Yea, you love that shit don't you?"I gritted before sloshing my tongue all over her neck.

"Yessss!"

"What else you love?"

"I love you! I love you so much, Kyree!"

As crazy as this day was, ending it inside her under the stars in Miami was enough for me to say that everything had turned out perfectly. Make up sex had never been better. I bet she didn't even know that I was just getting started with her. It also hadn't slipped my mind that her ass had gotten so drunk today that she forgot to take her birth control, so she was getting filled up repeatedly tonight.

Chapter 13

Kamaria

April 18, 2020

*"You lookin' good but I can't wait to see you naked. If you give it to me, I won't say shit. Baby, it's our time, it's what we make it. And when it's over. You gon' be droppin' on me..."*The DJ spun a brand new Fredo Bang song that featured a female bounce artist, which meant it was perfect for booty shaking. Considering that it was my birthday, that's all I really wanted to do. I wasn't expecting much today. Kyree told me we were going to dinner and then to the club that he had an event at. I was with that because I knew we'd have fun. We always had fun at his parties. But with my boyfriend I should've known better.

My birthday conveniently fell on a Saturday this year, so I didn't have to be bothered with school. I had one last week of classes before final exams started and I was more than prepared. After Spring Break I locked in with school and I was doing so good that I could barely get by on my tests and still pass with B's. But I already knew I was ending this semester with straight A's, and I had a few job interviews lined up right before graduation. Kyree and I had even looked at some places in New Orleans. We'd narrowed down our choices and planned on signing a lease by May. I was super excited about our future. We may have hit a bumpy road in Miami, but things couldn't have been better between us now. If I ever questioned his love for me, the way he went out for my birthday was enough for me to never do that again.

After classes on Friday, he told me to pack a bag. I had no idea where we were going but I was ready for whatever he had planned. When we arrived at a nice mansion in Bocage Citi Place Estates I was stunned. The house put my parents to shame and that was saying a lot. He revealed that we were staying here for the weekend. I thought the house was just for us to sleep at and live it up. I would've never guessed that he planned a pool party for me the following day. Not just any pool party either, a Bratz themed pool party.

On Friday night all of our friends showed up with overnight bags. I was happy because this house was way too big for just me and Kyree to enjoy alone. We had a little kickback with just us and had a blast. Essence had made a pink Hennessy lemonade drink that everybody loved and Kyree ordered food. By 12 am we were all drunk and they presented me with a pretty pink sheet cake with balloons that read "Happy Birthday Mari!" No lie, I was satisfied with that night alone. I had so much fun that I slept in until 1 pm. I guess that was enough time for a decorator and her whole team to sneak in and decorate the interior and exterior of the house Bratz themed. When I woke up and saw it I was honestly moved to tears. I told Kyree how I'd always wanted a Bratz party as a little girl but my mom never approved despite me having numerous Bratz dolls and toys. My whole room was even Bratz at one point, but she never gave me that Bratz party. One time she gave me a Barbie party, claiming that's what she thought I said. By the time I was 11, I was over my Bratz obsession but still disappointed that I never got my Bratz party. Now I finally had it.

It took me a minute to realize I was actually having a party though. I saw the decorations, but I just figured Kyree did that to make me feel special. It still didn't register when my usual hairstylist and makeup artist, Traci and Chyna, showed up to doll me up. Feeling like doing something extreme like a Bratz doll, I got a 30 inch burgundy sew in with a wispy bang. Wanting the length to show, I wore it bone straight. My beat for the day was just as dramatic as my hair in true Bratz doll fashion. The decorations around the house were purple, black, and gold so I opted for a glitter gold cut crease with a nude lip lined in dark brown lip liner. I even let Chyna convince me to add face bling. It wasn't much, just a few rhinestones around my eyes, but it really enhanced the look. I couldn't get enough of myself as I took numerous selfies. It didn't dawn on me that I was having a pool party until Kyree's sisters and cousins showed up. It seemed like everyone who was there on Mardi

Gras was here today except Cambrie, which I was okay with. After Mardi Gras Kyree told me how she couldn't be trusted. I wanted him to go into detail but he didn't. Either way, that was his cousin so I'd follow his lead. I assumed they were coming out that night with us until Fendi handed Kyree a bag. He presented me with something else I'd expressed wanting; a Daisie Martelle original. It was a custom made purple and gold latex swimsuit. It came with a high cut bottom, a bikini top, and a mini skirt. He'd also taken the liberty to get me some matching gold YSL platform heels. The entire outfit easily gave Bratz and that's when Kyree had to tell me I was having a pool party.

When I went to the kitchen I realized that his people had arrived with car loads of food and party supplies. Apparently his mom and grandma had cooked all the food and it was enough to feed the whole UBR. They called me to wish me a happy birthday but they made no mention of this. I immediately called them to say thankyou. I hated to make comparisons but this was more than my own family had ever attempted to do for me. My mom gave me a long, drawn out Facebook post where she bragged about me being the perfect person and student. All the things she never said to my face. My dad texted me a sweet happy birthday message that morning, and sent $500 via Cash App. It was appreciated but it also felt dry. My auntie had called ten minutes after 12 AM the night before screaming happy birthday like she did every year. Then we made plans to get together for lunch whenever I got back to the city. I was looking forward to my gifts from her because she never skimmed back when it came to me. My parents always got me nice gifts too. I couldn't lie about that...but it wasn't just about gifts. It was about showing up for me. Kyree and his family were doing that and I hadn't even known any of them for that long. I could've made excuses for them since Kyree was in charge of this event and most likely didn't invite them, but for the past three years until now I'd spent my birthday at UBR *alone*. So making comparisons was easy.

I felt bad because Kaliya gave me the nicest and sweetest birthday post on instagram with pictures we'd taken between Mardi Gras and Spring Break. She even sent me $100 through Cash App and texted me to ask what I was doing today. I tried to stay strong and have my own mind when it came to her, but my friends and Kyree had undoubtedly gotten in my head. The more I thought about what they said the more I felt like there was some truth to it. They had no reason to lie on her or hate on our relationship. It would be hella random if they were, so I knew that wasn't the case. But it was also possible that Kaliya was just misunderstood and that she didn't mean any harm. Maybe it just all came across wrong and looked bad. I don't know, but either way, I felt so bad ignoring her today when she asked me what my plans were. I wouldn't say I fell back from her completely since Spring Break, we just weren't hanging out or talking as much. There were times when I'd get something to eat with her or we'd catch a movie together. But our turning up days had come to an abrupt halt after Miami and I know she noticed it. I did appreciate the fact that she didn't run to our family and tell them anything though. That also led me to believe that she didn't have bad intentions like everyone thought. Regardless, my boyfriend or my friends didn't like her so I just had to keep those worlds separate for now.

Kaliya became an afterthought as my pool party kicked into full swing. I quickly learned that it was invite only and that was for the best. I was surrounded by people I was actually cool with and not people who just wanted to party. Everybody came with gifts or money for me. By the time the sun was setting the party had a total of about forty people and we were lit. Versace had bought Daiquiris all the way from New Orleans and kept them frozen in an ice chest, and I loved her for that. I finally learned my limits with alcohol, so I was drunk but I had it under control. I was bouncing around from dancing on my man, to mingling with my friends, swimming in the pool, and even dancing by myself. I was currently standing next to the pool singing my heart out to Karina Pasian's "The Love We Got." Kyomi had requested some throwback bops to the

DJ Kyree had hired for the night and he complied. It set the mood since a lot of people that came through were boo'd up.

"You dancing without me,"Kyree walked up behind me and wrapped his arms around me. He just got out of the pool so he was soaking wet, but I didn't care. I wanted him close to me. I turned around and wrapped my arms around him so I could start singing to him.

"He's embedded in my space. Every time he speaks he blows me away. Don't care what people say. As long as he's in the same place where I lay. See, I'll be his echo. I'm his princess, he's my general. And no matter what you think about love. Time won't outlast us..."

"Oh yea?"He laughed. "That's how you feel?"

"You already know how I feel. Thank you for making my day special, baby."

"This was light. Just wait until the year I can afford to buy you that G-Wagon."

"Whew,"my heart skipped a beat. "Can we get to your birthday *this* year first? It's your Kobe year so I'm going to do something special."

"That's way at the end of December. Today is about you, Mari. You know it's okay for everything to be about you right?" He asked, before sensually kissing me. He didn't allow me to answer the question, but it made me think. Growing up, I always had to share my birthday love with Kaliya since we were a week apart. I was always in her shadow. So I didn't know what it felt like for it to be all about me. As vain as it may have sounded, I loved it and I could get used to it. But the way my heart was set up, I couldn't wait to reciprocate this same energy for Kyree. He deserved the world and more.

Chapter 14

Kyree

April 24, 2020

"We need one last end of the year blow out here in BR. You need to plan something Kyree,"Tysean ordered.

My head bounced back. "I don't need to do shit but pass my exams and stay black."

"So you not throwing no more parties? That's it?"He asked like he couldn't believe it.

"Ty, we have two more weeks left in school and final exams start on Monday. You should be done with partying,"Lark laughed. It was a Friday noon, and we were all chilling in the quad waiting for our next class.

"Shit, my first exam is tonight at 7 pm,"I divulged. "The last thing on my mind is parties. I threw enough this Spring."

"So you not doing no end of the year bash?"Ty questioned.

"I mean, you know I'ma do the big graduation party in New Orleans at Masquerade at the end of May. Other than that, I'm done out here."

"That's fucked up, you know I'm going back to Atlanta after graduation."

"That sounds like a you problem,"I chuckled. "Nigga you can always drive to New Orleans for the par..."

I lost my train of thought mid sentence when I saw Kamaria approaching us. She looked fine as hell today in a gray Skims set that consisted of a crop top and tights. She tied a gray and white plaid flannel around her waist that she most likely put on in her classes because it could get cold inside, and her top was basically a glorified bra. She paired the outfit with gray, white, and silver Chanel sneakers that I gifted her for her birthday. She was also rocking a vintage Louis Vuitton silver monogram Speedy 35. Her auntie gave that to her for her birthday along with a bunch of other vintage designer pieces. I didn't know Auntie Sana that well yet, but she was the goat for that alone.

"Damn, this nigga really loose his mind whenever this girl come around,"Shad laughed and everybody else followed suit.

"Man, fuck all y'all,"I chuckled as Kamaria twisted into our space and sat right where she belonged; in my lap. I gripped her chin and kissed her with all tongue. Maybe I should've been mindful of our audience, but I wasn't worried about them people.

"Ewww,"Essence giggled. "Y'all need to get a room doing all that."

"We can. Shit,"I huffed.

"Anyways, I loveee that outfit Mari. Where'd you get it?"Zion asked.

"Fendi and Versace got me this along with two other Skims sets."

"Ouuu, that's Skims? I be seeing the girls going up for it on Twitter but I thought they were just talking. I see I'ma have to give Miss Kim my coins,"Essence snapped her fingers.

"Same, cause that fits like a glove,"Zion said. "And it looks comfortable."

"It's *so* comfortable,"Mari stressed.

"Yea, y'all should all get it,"Ty offered in a tone that made it clear that he could care less. "Mari, tell your man to throw one last party here in BR."

"My man needs to focus on his classes and graduating,"she asserted. That shit made my dick jump and I know she felt it. "He currently has two C's, so he needs to do extremely well on his final exams to finish strong."

"I told you nigga,"I shrugged.

"C'mon sis,"he begged. "Y'all moving into that nice house…I know y'all could use the extra money."

"No, actually we're good,"she giggled. On Wednesday we drove to New Orleans to have dinner with her Auntie and her husband. But before that we signed our lease for our three bedroom Avondale home. It was modest, but modern and brand new with all up to date appliances. What really sold Mari was the big rooms and even bigger closets. It was the perfect start for us until we moved into our dream home down the line. I could see us bringing our first and second child back to that house and getting our careers off the ground. The rent wasn't cheap but it also wasn't outrageous. Wanting to get ahead of things and show Mari how serious I was about providing, I went into my savings and paid the rent up for a year. The lease was for two years, so that was more than enough security for now. We told Mari's Aunt and Uncle the news at dinner, and she offered us some barely used furniture she had in storage. Apparently she had just cleared out one of her properties because she had started renting it out. I was on the fence about it until she started showing us pictures. Everything was in impeccable condition and it was neutral colors that would allow Mari to still add her own touches. I could honestly care less about the decorating process, but I knew she was excited about that. We happily accepted the furniture and I was grateful that it was one less thing I had to pay for. I was still in a safe space money wise, but I was ready to start making all that money I'd spent back. I had tunnel vision to graduation though and Mari was helping me stay focused. We'd been studying non-stop together.

"Mari, I love this color on you. You should try orange in the fall,"Essence said as she touched her long red hair. She had curled it today. She'd been experimenting with a lot of hair styles and colors for the past few months and it showed how versatile she was. She could pull off anything. With a face as pretty as hers that wasn't surprising.

"I was thinking about that, but I gotta find the perfect shade…and I need to find a New Orleans stylist because I'm not about to be driving out here."

"Girl, I got a few. I'ma send em to you."

"Send em to me too, girl,"Shad jested in a girly voice, making us laugh. Essence swung on him and they started play fighting. They still weren't together, but they hadn't been going back and forth as much as they usually did. Essence had even been at our apartment with him a lot since Miami. I was lowkey rooting for them two fools to stop playing games.

"You done for the day, huh?"I asked Mari as our friends carried on.

"Yup."

"So what you bouta do? You going back to my apartment?"I asked. I'd long ago given her a copy of my key so she could let herself in whenever our schedules conflicted.

"Dang, I can't go back to my own shit?"

"Girl that's the campus shit."

"And your apartment is ours?"

"Nah, our shit is in New Orleans, but for now my apartment is our meeting grounds and I want you there when I'm done with my day."

"I have somewhere to go Kyree..."

Based on the way she said it I knew some bullshit was on the horizon.

"Where you going? Actually...I have a better question, when was you gon let me know that you was going somewhere?"

"I just got invited like an hour ago so I was going to tell you whenever I saw you."

"Invited where?"

"Kaliya's having a kickback at her apartment for her birthday. She asked me to help her set up, so I was going to head there around 5 or 6. It starts at 7 and I was only planning on staying for an hour tops."

Off rip, I wanted to say hell no but I knew that wouldn't be received well. Kamaria was liable to go and stay longer just because I said no just to prove I didn't control her. I didn't want no smoke with her behind this, but I wasn't comfortable with her partying with Kaliya.

"You gon take one of the girls with you?"I asked. If Essence, Lark, or Zion went I would be able to breathe easier.

"After Miami?"She laughed. "Yea right. Let me guess, you don't want to go?"

"No, but I know I can't stop you from doing what you want to. Clearly your mind is already made up. Just do me a favor."

"What's that?"

"Don't drink."

"I honestly wasn't planning on it."

"Forreal? Why?"

"I'm just not in the mood,"she shrugged. "After last weekend I realized I need to chill for a while."

"Why? Because you had a hangover on Sunday?"I laughed.

"That's funny? I was fighting for my life."

"You so dramatic, bruh."

"You know I was going through it, and it was weird because I drank way more in Miami and I wasn't that sick the next day."

"Probably because I gave you a Goodie in Miami."

"Yea, probably. But I'm definitely not getting drunk tonight and like I said, I'm not staying long."

"You better not or I'ma pull up and get you myself…as a matter of fact, share your location with me."

"Okay,"she shrugged. "If it's that serious."

"It is, and let me go follow Kaliya on instagram so I can tune in tonight."

"You need to focus on your exam that's tonight."

"I can focus on that and make sure you straight."

"I'll be fine,"she rolled her eyes and then kissed my lips. I wanted to believe that and I wasn't trying to put negativity in the air but I didn't trust Kaliya as far as I could throw her. Being vigilant wouldn't hurt anything. If nothing happened, then cool. But if something was to happen, I could pull up with

the quickness.

Kamaria

"Well look who it is, my funny acting cousin,"Kaliya grinned as she let me in her apartment. Her parents had her set up nice in her own off campus apartment. Everything was extremely girly from the pink and silver color scheme to the mirrored furniture. This was the type of apartment I envisioned for myself for my senior year, but my parents refused. She had a few girls in her living room. I said a general hello to them as I entered before focusing on Kaliya.

"Funny acting?"I feigned confusion. She wasn't lying though. I had been funny acting, which is why I made it a point to come through for her today. I even sent her some money to get a few bottles. It was her birthday gift but also a guilt gift.

"You heard me, bitch,"she giggled, before hugging me tightly. "I'm glad you came though....especially since my invitation got lost in the mail to your party."

"Don't do that, Kaliya,"I shook my head. "I told you that party was a surprise and I had no control over who was invit-"

"You could've told me to pull up though once you realized what was going on."

I definitely could have if I had wanted to. The issue was I didn't want to for obvious reasons.

"Blame it on my mind, not my heart."

"I ain't mad at you, cous. I know your friends and boyfriend don't like me for whatever reason,"she rolled her eyes. "I guess I'm too lit for them."

I could've explained why they *really* didn't like her but I didn't even want to open that can of worms. It was her birthday and it wasn't the time to rock the boat.

"Anyways, what do you need help with?"I asked as we walked to her kitchen. She had every liquor you could think of and numerous boxes of Pizza stacked up. There were also cute DIY pink birthday decorations everywhere. It was a nice set up and a perfect college party.

"Bitch, it's 6:45. All the work is done."

"My bad,"I giggled, while playing with my freshly curled hair. "I fell asleep after my classes and when I woke up I had to do my makeup and redo my hair."

I kept on the same outfit I wore to my classes because it was cute as hell.

Kaliya looked me up and down. "You look cute."

"Thanks, so do you."

She was rocking a pink two piece pink set that consisted of a mesh mini skirt with fur at the bottom along with the matching bikini top. Her pink pasties and underwear underneath didn't leave much to the imagination but it screamed birthday girl. She paired it with pink stripper heels. Her makeup appeared to be done professionally and she looked really pretty. The only thing I didn't like was her hair. She switched it up with a blonde wig but whoever installed it didn't know what the hell they were doing. It was bulky and her lace was waving at me. The baby hairs were even worse. They barely stuck to her forehead and they were touching her brows. It was kind of bringing her whole look down a few notches, but I definitely wasn't going to tell her that. Perhaps if I'd gotten here earlier I would've built up the courage to say something.

"Oh, I know," she flipped her hair. I knew she was joking but that cockiness while her hair looked a mess was so unbecoming of her. She looked down at my purse. "I saw you post that Auntie Sana got you that."

"Yea. I love it. Ever since I saw this on celebrities as a kid I have wanted it."

"Hmmp, well she only bought me a measly Tory Burch bag with matching sneakers. She sent me a picture of it after she called to tell me happy birthday."

"Tory Burch is measly?"I frowned. Last time I checked, that was high fashion as well. It was on the lower end compared to other brands, but it was far from cheap and they had quality items. I loved me a good pair of Tory Burch slides.

"Compared to vintage Louis Vuitton it is…but I don't expect you to call out the blatant favoritism since it's benefiting you."

I frowned. "Kaliya, don't get me started on favoritism. My mama made you a slideshow for your birthday today. She called you the prettiest girl in the world and the daughter she always wanted. Please. If Auntie Sana does favor me it's because she sees shit like that and feels for me."

"I mean…that was kind of messed up, but imagine how Auntie Kathy felt last weekend when you had a whole party and nobody from your family was invited. Then *you* wrote a whole paragraph thanking Kyree and his family for making your day special. You don't think that was kinda shady?"

"No! They did make my day special. If anybody took that as shade then they should've stepped up. Prior to me and Kyree being a thing I don't recall my parents throwing me surprise parties or driving out to BR to celebrate my day with me. You were right across town and you never even hit me up. So I could care less how anybody felt last weekend because did anybody care about how I felt all these years?"

All that guilt I was feeling about giving Kaliya the cold shoulder on Kyree's behalf was vanishing the more she talked. Her thoughts aligned a lot more with my family than I thought. Since she'd been defending me for the past few months I thought she saw the things I went through in this family and empathized with me. I had it all wrong.

"C'mon cousin…it's not a secret we weren't close and I thought we talked about that on Mardi Gras."

"We did, and I'm not mad at you about that but you not about to stand here in my face and make me feel bad for having *one* person in this family who favors me. Because while your dad may have made comments that made you feel a way, he never let it show in his actions. He doesn't talk down to you in front of the rest of the family, he gives you whatever you want, and he treats you like you're his most prized possession. I have no idea what that feels like."

"Ya know what…I don't wanna argue about this. Your feelings are valid and maybe I overstepped."

"Maybe?"I raised a brow.

"Okay, I'm sorry bitch. I guess I'm just a little jealous of that bag,"she giggled. If she was jealous of the bag then I wasn't even going to tell her about all the other stuff Auntie Sana got me. "You gotta let me borrow it sometime."

"We'll see…"I uttered before twisting out the kitchen and to the little dining room area to sit at her glass table. The couch was full and after the conversation I'd just had I wasn't in the mood to mingle. My nerves were bad. I hated having to constantly defend myself in this family. I was dreading sticking around her for at least an hour. I was so ready to go.

"You want a shot, cousin?"Kaliya asked from the kitchen. Her back was turned to me, but I could see her setting up pink cups on the countertop to make drinks.

I said I wouldn't drink but after dealing with her I needed something. It would certainly take the edge off. One shot wouldn't hurt.

"Yea, Hennessy please."

A few seconds later she walked over with a tray full of pink cups. She sat it down and handed me my cup. Her friends walked over and started grabbing the other cups off the trap.

"Damn, this is a big shot,"I said while looking down inside the cup. "You don't have any little shot cups?"

"We couldn't find any at the store,"one of her friends said. "These will do though."

"Yea, don't be boring bitch,"Kaliya snickered.

"I'm far from boring,"I contended. "I was just acknowledging the obvious."

I threw the shot back because if I didn't I would have probably cursed her out next.

"Damn, why didn't you wait for us?"One of her friends snickered. "Give her another one, Kaliya!"

"No, I'm good,"I stated. That one shot already had me feeling sick which was weird because I thought I had become one with Cognac.

"Boringggg,"Kaliya sang.

"Ok, well bitch, I'll be that,"I snapped.

"Ou, she's feisty. I like that,"another girl giggled.

I rolled my eyes, wanting them all to shut the fuck up.

"I think she's really feeling some type of way, so let's step over here to the living room,"Kaliya mumbled. When they left my space, the doorbell rang. Other people had started arriving. I remained by the kitchen watching the clock and wishing I could text Kyree, but he was taking his test. I started tapping my feet as "Best You Ever Had" by Megan Thee Stallion played. The party was now in full swing and I felt myself getting into the groove. I started recording myself rapping the song word for word on my instagram story.

"This your song huh?"A random guy asked.

"Yup!"I shouted excitedly. I didn't know what was going on but I suddenly had all the energy in the world and I felt like turning up. So I stood up to start dancing.

"Ayeee!"Kaliya screamed. "Get it cousin!"

Kaliya

My kickback had only been going on for an hour and I had more than enough footage of this bitch making a fool of herself. She was such an idiot to think shit was good between us after she played me to the left for her boyfriend and her new friends. When I made amends with her on Mardi Gras, I actually had genuine intentions. I noticed her new found popularity due to who she was dating and I wanted in on the action! Since she was my cousin I was willing to bury our childhood rivalry so we could have fun together. I also wanted to witness her and Kyree up close. His name was larger than life on the college scene in BR. He'd fucked several popular girls here at Southern. I'd been to plenty of his parties but I'd never been in close proximity to him. I was curious about who he was and why the hell he was with Kamaria. I thought she was giving him money or doing his homework. Shit, something. I just knew he couldn't seriously be interested in my chubby nerd ass cousin. That's why I tricked my Auntie Kathy into making Kamaria take me with her on Mardi Gras. She lived up my ass so it took no effort for me to get my way with her. That day I learned that he was actually head over hills for my cousin, and that annoyed the fuck out of me. I'd witnessed them together at dinner prior to that but I thought he was putting on a show for my aunt and uncle. It turns out he was really a great guy and he was giving my undeserving cousin the princess treatment. I had the worst luck with guys for the past four years. I had fallen in love three times and every situation blew up in my face. The first guy was DL and got aired out on a campus burn page. The second guy gave me Chlamydia and Gonorrhea on two separate occasions. Then the third guy, Rome, just straight up told me that he wasn't interested in a serious relationship with me. I was still having sex with him till this day because it was obvious he felt something for me if he kept coming back. Either way, it was frustrating seeing Kamaria get the world from Kyree while I waited on my nigga to wake up and treat me how I deserved to be treated. Keeping it real, Kamaria did not deserve a guy like Kyree. He was way out of her league. I was on a mission to show him that too. My plans were derailed after Miami, but I was back in business after that bitch showed up today.

Maybe if she didn't start acting funny with me I would've taken it easy on her. But I was over this bitch. She thought she was better than me just because the last few months of her life were lit. It didn't matter that she was graduating on time while I had flunked out of nursing school. I'd bounce back in no time and show her how to really do it. In the meantime, she was definitely going to lose her perfect boyfriend. That ecstasy I slipped in her drink was going to ensure that. Her dumb ass was currently giving a nigga a lap dance while I recorded it all and posted it in my close friends. I'd added Kyree today after he followed me on instagram. He made things easier for me because now I didn't have to go out of my way to send it to him. I would've posted it on my main story to further embarrass her but I didn't want our family to see it. I wasn't posting anything from this party on my story because they wouldn't approve and I had a certain image to uphold in their eyes.

"TAKE YOUR CLOTHES OFF KAMARIA!"I shouted.

Sure enough, this bitch started to pull her pants down while screaming like a lunatic.

"Woahhh, no!"My frenemy, Ashley stepped in and physically stopped her. "What the hell is she drinking? She was not like this an hour ago."

"Man move and let this hoe do whatever she wants,"Rhino, Rome's friend, said. Rome was here too and he was staring at Kamaria's ass a little too hard for my liking. "She's off that Hennessy and obviously feeling freaky."

I'd fixed her two cups of Hennessy and she was in the middle of her second one. I knew after that Ecstasy kicked in that she'd want more alcohol. She practically begged me to give her more.

"Move, Ashley! We're all grown. Let her have fun."

"Bitch isn't this your cousin?"Ashley snapped. "You gon let her strip in a room full of people?"

"She can do whatever she wants! If you have a problem with it you can leave!"

Ashley was the reason I found it easy to stop hanging with my normal group of friends this semester. We constantly butted heads because she always had something to tell me. That bitch thought she was better than me and I hated that. She's lucky I didn't slip something in her drink.

"Let's just all get naked!"Kamaria screamed. She went to pull off her top, and I excitedly started recording. I was anxious for the money shit. Unfortunately, I never got it because she stopped like she was having a spasm and just started throwing up. My eyes expanded in horror because it looked like she was having an exorcism as she fell to the ground throwing up.

"Oh hell no! I don't know what y'all gave this bitch, but I ain't bouta be here when she dies!"Rome shouted, as he jumped up and ran out the door and his friends followed.

"Kamaria, get up!"I screamed, as she sat on her knees throwing up. I had no idea how this bitch had gone from being full of life to being sick so fast. It usually took longer to come down from that ecstasy high. I knew first hand. Everybody else started seeing themselves out too, and that pissed me off. The only people who stayed behind were my friends, including Ashley. She was trying to get Kamaria off the floor and take her to the bathroom, but she seemingly couldn't move. She had ruined my party with her antics! I was about to tell her she had to go, when my front door literally burst open. I had one of my friends lock it after everybody left. My heart dropped into my ass when I saw Kyree at the door with a gun in his hand and his UBR crew behind him. I didn't anticipate him showing his face here or popping up like he was ready for war. I wanted him to see those videos and think Kamaria was violating him. I mean, I'd record multiple niggas feeling her up and her dancing provocatively on them. Why did it look like he showed up to kill everybody except the bitch he was in a relationship with?

"Beat that bitch up. Now." He turned to those UBR rats and gave them a direct order. Before I knew it, they swarmed me like a pack of wild hyenas and started jumping me. Not one of my friends jumped in while they dragged me across the floor. I tried to cover my face to the best of my ability but I felt the impact of several powerful blows. Around my eyes felt numb and I tasted blood coming from my mouth and nose. It was safe to say that my mastermind plan had backfired terribly.

Chapter 15

Kyree

April 25, 2020

I tried my best to live my life with no regrets, but man, I wished I could go back in time to tell Kamaria that she wasn't going to that party. I would've stolen her keys or held her hostage just so she wouldn't have gone to that fucking kickback. If I could somehow go back in time to say fuck that exam just to be by her side I would've done that too. That was the *only* reason why I didn't see those stories that Kaliya had posted in her close friends right away. Phone use wasn't allowed in the testing center, so my phone was off for a whole hour while I took my test. Kamaria told me she was only staying at Kaliya's kickback for an hour, so I fully expected her to be at my apartment when I arrived back. When I walked in and didn't see her face amongst all of our friends that were hanging out with Shad and Essence, I assumed she was in my room but she wasn't. For the first time since leaving the testing center, I checked my text messages. There I saw that she sent me a short video of her singing some Megan Thee Stallion song. Call me paranoid, but I could look at her and just see something wasn't right. She seemed jumpy and over the top. Her eyes were also doing some weird shit that I couldn't really explain. I called her repeatedly with no answer, so I went to instagram to see if she'd posted anything. The first thing I saw was Kaliya's profile picture on my story feed with the green circle around it. That meant I was in her close friends. Not only was that shit odd, but inappropriate. I only followed her on instagram so I could watch her stories and make sure her party was an environment that Mari should be in. I didn't know what her reasoning was for putting me in her close friends, but I clicked on it to watch anyway. I needed to see what the fuck was going on and Mari hadn't posted anything. Let's just say I got more than what I bargained for when I watched them damn stories. I went to my closet, grabbed one of my legally registered guns, and stormed out of my room. My boys asked me what was up immediately. All I said was Mari was at Kaliya's party and she needed me. They all jumped up and followed me out the house. We hopped in two separate cars and made it to the other side of town in record time. When I kicked the door in I expected to still see those niggas who were clearly taking advantage of Mari while she was under the influence. That's why I brought my gun. I didn't think the party would be damn near cleared out and I didn't expect to see Mari on the floor fighting for her life. Then there was Kaliya standing over her looking like she could care less and not even helping her. Right then everything I was thinking was confirmed and I ordered an ass whooping for her. Essence, Lark, and Zion unleashed on her and none of her friends attempted to jump in or even stop it. That was a clear sign of how dirty that bitch was. Or maybe my gun was making them stand down. I didn't know for sure and I didn't care. I handed my gun off to Dale and went straight for Kamaria who had finally stopped throwing up and was laying out like she was ready to go to sleep.

"Mari, come on," I said, as I scooped her up. I turned to those other bitches who had to be Kaliya's friends. "Where the fuck her purse and phone at?"

The girl who'd been standing next to Kaliya when I first walked in shakily pointed her finger towards the kitchen table on the other side of the room. Dale walked over and sure enough it was over there. I had no idea who called the girls off Kaliya because I'd been focused on Mari who was in the midst of blacking out. I assumed it was Ty and Shad because they were holding Zion and Essence back. Lark was busy questioning Kaliya's friends.

"What the fuck did y'all do to her?!"

"What?! We didn't do anything!" One of the girls backed away with her hands up. "She's obviously drunk and that's not our fault."

"Bitch you know damn well alcohol didn't have her acting how she was acting," I gritted.

"Well…Kaliya fixed the shots," the girl who told me where her purse and phone was spoke up.

"Ashley, really?" A girl scoffed.

"Yes, really. After tonight I'm good on this bitch Kaliya. She put all of us in a dangerous position and she would obviously do us dirty if she did it to her own cousin,"she said with a straight face before focusing on me. "I can't say anything for a fact because I didn't see her fix those shots, but I do know that Kaliya has a thing for party pills. Mainly ecstasy and molly. Considering I didn't see Kamaria take a pill I can only assume that it was in her shot. All she had was one shot and thirty minutes later she wasn't the same person. Kaliya was recording her the whole time and amping her up to do degrading shit. I had to step in at that point. When she started throwing up like she was having a seizure everybody got scared and left."

"Bitch,"Kaliya coughed up blood while climbing on her knees. It looked like she'd been run over by a bulldozer. Her wig was a thing of the past. She normally wore her real hair and I recalled her having edges the last time I saw it so I could only assume that she'd lost them in the fight. Her mouth was gushing blood along with her nose. She also had two black eyes and bruises all over her light skin. It was nothing less than what that evil bitch deserved.

"Yo-you don't know what you're talking about. She just had too much to drink and I can't control a grown woman,"she said weakly. "I always knew you were a fucking hater! Jealous bitch!"

I couldn't believe she was using her energy to lie. Before her former friend broke it down I already knew something like that had happened. Anybody who saw those videos I saw with her encouraging Mari to do crazy shit would know that she was conspiring against her. She wasn't even low with her shit. She actually put me in her close friends just so I could see it. I could've sworn she wanted me to know that she'd set Mari up. I wasn't sure what else she could've wanted me to get from those videos.

"Jealous of what? You flunking out of nursing school? These niggas fucking you and leaving you with nothing but a wet ass?! Your multiple abortions? Nooo…maybe I'm jealous of your pussy always being on fire with all those STDs you *then had! Bitch, you are a bottom of the barrel whore! A pretty face or your family's money won't change that!"*

Kaliya broke down into tears and didn't respond. That was all the confirmation I needed to know that everything ole girl said was true.

"Whew!"Zion called out. That's when I realized she was recording.

"Girl, why are you recording this?"Essence questioned.

"Insurance,"I answered the question for her. With a manipulative bitch like Kaliya we needed that. I turned to all the girls except Ashley.

"If any of y'all go to the police I'm posting this shit and I bet it ruins all of y'all lives,"I glowered down at Kaliya. "Especially yours, bitch. So I'd think about my next move if I were you."

With that, we were out the door. Mari didn't just have alcohol in her system so I was scared out of my mind to take her back to my apartment. Anything could happen through the night, so I made the executive decision to take her to the hospital. Everybody agreed that was the best decision. When we brought her to the emergency room and divulged how she may have been drugged, they took her away immediately. Of course they came questioning us and we gave a different version of what actually happened. We also completely left Kaliya's name out of it. We'd already gotten justice for the situation in the form of a beat down. The last thing I wanted was for my friends to get arrested right before finals and graduation because of this shit. They all had bright futures and I wouldn't put that in jeopardy. So we simply said that we were at a party, Kamaria started acting unlike herself, and then she got really sick. We had our story straight and we were all sober, so it was received.

I had to call Kaliya's parents in case anything happened because I wasn't a blood relative nor were we married for me to make decisions. I also may have not liked them, but they deserved to be here. Shit, I was hoping this would make them love their daughter more and cling to her. If they gave her the affection and attention she needed growing up she wouldn't have been so desperate to make certain relationships work in the first place. Kaliya was rotten to her core but Mari gave her the benefit of the doubt because she wanted that family love so damn bad. I hated that the shit had to blow up in her face like this, but everything happened for a reason. But if Kaliya knew what was best for her she'd disappear because I was seriously thinking about getting a shooter in my family to smoke her ass.

Mari's parents sounded distraught when I told them what happened and promised to be there right away. Therefore, I was optimistic that they'd show up and act like they had some sense. I was thinking about calling my mama to fill her in. I needed to talk to someone who could calm me down and make me feel better. It wasn't like Mari was in surgery or anything but the thought of her being examined was still scary for me. I stood up to go find a private area to call my mom and I ran into the doctor who'd questioned us. I stood in his way to stop him.

"Can you tell me anything about Kamaria Laurent?"I asked. We'd been at the hospital for over an hour at that point so I knew his ass knew something.

"What's your relationship to Ms. Laurent?"

"I'm...I'm her brother."

He gave me a look.

"Look man, I really love her and I'm worried about it. I just need to know what's going on. Trust me, she'd want me to know."

"Well she's going to be fine. She's stabilized and resting right now. We could only do the drug screening. We couldn't conduct a rape kit without her conse-"

"She wasn't raped,"I stated because I knew that shit for a fact. Somebody would've died if that had happened.

"I don't think so either. It doesn't appear like she was assaulted at all but it is a part of the procedure whenever someone is slipped drugs."

"So what was she slipped?"

"Ecstasy."

I got chills because Ashley was spot on about her evil ass friend.

"It's a classic date rape drug, but Ms.Laurents body rejected it quickly. Considering her current condition it makes sense."

"Her current condition?"

"Son, I've already said too much. You'll be able to see Ms. Laurent and speak with her soon. She should tell you."

My heart was beating so fast it felt like I might pass out. I didn't need Mari to tell me shit. I already knew what it was because I'd been deliberately trying to make it happen. I just didn't think I'd gotten lucky yet. This was a hell of a time for me and her to find out. I couldn't believe this shit. Now I really wanted Kaliya buried six feet deep.

"At least tell me this…did the ecstasy ruin her current condition?"

"No, it didn't. It's a good thing you got her to us when you did,"he patted my shoulder and walked off.

Now I really needed to call my damn mama.

Kamaria

I opened my eyes to a bunch of blurry figures standing around me. I was cold, my head hurt, nausea consumed me, and I literally felt sick to my stomach. All of that was bad, but what was really bad was that I had no memory of anything. I recalled arriving at Kaliya's party with the plan to only stay there for an hour. Something else had to happen because if I had the uneventful night I planned on having I wouldn't have woken up feeling unlike myself. When my full vision finally came to me I saw my parents and Kyree's parents standing around me. I looked down at myself and saw the dress I was wearing along with the white bedding. I was in the hospital! The fact that something grievous had happened to me finally settled in and I started to panic.

"Calm down, baby."

I relaxed the second I felt Kyree's hand cover mine. I looked over and he was standing right next to me wearing the same clothes I'd seen him in last. He leaned down, moved my hair out of my face, and kissed my forehead. He then handed me ice water which was appreciated because my mouth was dry like a cotton ball.

"How you feeling?"He asked me after I took a long sip of water.

"Terrible,"I choked out.

"Get used to it,"my mom glared down at me. "Morning sickness is prevalent in the first few months of *pregnancy*."

My heart plummeted and that panicking feeling that went away came right away.

"W-w-w-what?"I choked out.

"You're pregnant, Kamaria,"my dad looked at me with contempt.

"I thought we agreed to explain to her why she was here first before dropping that bomb on her?"Kyree questioned them while holding on to my hand. He was giving me the comfort that I desperately needed right now. I didn't even know why I was in the hospital and the first thing I heard was that I'm pregnant? I'd been taking my birth control religiously! I'd bled earlier this month!

"You suggested that, young man. We didn't agree to anything,"my dad said, surprising me. He seemed so confrontational and that was unlike him. He must've been really upset with me.

"And we don't even know what happened to really tell her,"my mom rolled her eyes.

"Woah,"Ms.Nette uttered. "What do you mean we don't know? I could've sworn my son told you in great detail that y'all niece drugged Kamaria and could've killed my fucking grandbaby in the process."

"I don't see why I would trust your son's word about something he wasn't there to see. You also shouldn't be repeating that because you didn't see it either."

"Bitch, if it wasn't for my son who knows what would've happened to *your* daughter!"

"Is all that really necessary?"My dad asked.

"Hell yea, nigga,"Mr.Kylo said. "If this was one of my daughters laid up in this bed I'd be at my nieces doorstep demanding answers."

"We facetimed Kaliya after Kyree gave his version of what happened and she swore she did no such thing! Hell, I wanted to call the police when I saw her bruised and battered!"My mom voiced passionately.

I had no words as everybody went back and forth. I was getting an earful and my mind was reeling. Details that I was missing were suddenly coming back to me. Like the back and forth I had with Kaliya that made me want to leave altogether. I stupidly stuck around, trying to prove that I was supportive to somebody who was undeserving. That's why I was in the predicament I was in now. I didn't doubt anything Kyree said because the first and only drink I remember having was that big ass shot she'd made for me. After that everything was a real blur.

"You wanted to call the police for that but not your daughter being drugged?"Ms.Nette squinted at her like she was stupid.

"Why would I call the police and we don't know what happened? She could've taken ecstasy on her own for all we kno-"

"I did not,"I cut her off in a shaky but firm voice. "I've never done drugs in my life."

"Your tox screen says something differently my dear."

"That's because your niece drugged her!"Kyree shouted.

"Okay, since you know so much tell us who beat my niece up to a bloody pulp and why she's so scared to go to the authorities?"She quizzed.

"Mannn, I don't know but she had that shit coming,"he replied with zero remorse. "And maybe she doesn't want to go to the police because she ain't living right."

"What's that supposed to mean?"

"Shit, he keep telling you she drugged your damn daughter. The fuck is wrong with y'all people? Ion even want y'all around my grandchild the way y'all treating y'all own daughter,"Mr.Kylo grumbled.

"Well I don't just blindly believe anyone. If Kamaria could tell me that Kaliya drugged her it would make a world of difference but she doesn't remember anything. I don't want to persecute Kaliya if she's being falsely accused,"my mom explained. At this point nothing she said surprised me. She had to *hate* me.

"I actually do remember Kaliya making me a big shot of Hennessy. After that I don't remember anything,"I said.

"Hmmp, what now?"Ms.Nette glanced at my mom.

"That's not a gotcha moment,"she scoffed. "If Kamaria took it on her own she's not going to own up to it."

I was stumped into silence. I couldn't believe she was blaming *me* for this.

"Yea, we might not ever know what really happened at that party. All I know is that Kamaria or Kaliya have never gotten into this type of trouble. I've never known either one of them to be party girls,"my dad said while looking at Kyree. The mental gymnastics my parents were doing to make sense of something that was being laid out for them was sickening. These people were no good for me.

"Hold up, I know you not trying to blame this shit on *my* baby!"Ms. Nette hollered with her arms crossed.

"He must be trying to get his shit knocked back,"Mr.Kylo said in a calm voice that gave me chills. My dad's body shifted in a way that made me think that he was scared.

"Hey, we not even bouta do all that,"Kyree interrupted, while holding up his phone. "Everybody be quiet and open y'all ears while I play this audio."

If my mom wanted proof then she certainly got it from the audio Kyree played of Kaliya's friend relaying what happened from her point of view. I tried my hardest not to gag when she started revealing Kaliya's tea. All that shit was news to me but it was no wonder why she'd stoop so low. She clearly hated her own life and was miserable so she took it out on me. I hated that I'd ever given her a fair shot. When we made up I gave her a clean slate. Now I wished I'd held every weird thing she'd ever done when we were kids against her. Holding a grudge would've paid off big time in this situation. At least I could say that I'd tried though. There was no room to question anything anymore. Now I knew exactly who she was and could permanently cut her diabolical ass off.

"Well there we have it. Obviously y'all niece is not as innocent as y'all think,"Ms. Nette fluttered her eyes.

"She's denying it in that video too…her story about not doing it hasn't changed."

That did it for me.

"Really mom?! Her word means more to you than mine! I'm your daughter!"I shouted through tears.

"Are you?! Because the daughter I raised doesn't behave the way you've been behaving these past few months! My daughter was taught that marriage comes before babies! My daughter would also never go against her blood for a man! You certainly aren't acting like the daughter I raised!"

"Bitch, fuck all that!"Ms.Nette exclaimed. "This girl is 22 years fucking old! She's about to graduate college next month! She's grown and she has a great support system. She'll be a great mother. Who cares if she did things out of the order you preferred?! You ain't God to be judging her! This girl got your blood pumping through her veins and you're treating her like a hoe off the streets! Something scary happened to her and you've found every angle to blame her except focusing on the obvious culprit. Who came out of your pussy; Kaliya or Kamaria?"

My mom's light skin turned red. She was enraged. I could count on one hand how many times she got like this and her mouth got deadly everytime. I wanted to duck for cover.

"Neither of them came out of my pussy."

The room fell silent and the tension was thick. The hairs on the back of my neck stood up and goosebumps formed on my arms.

"Katheline,"my dad gritted discreetly, but it was useless. She'd already said what she said loud and proud. She jerked away from him when he tried to touch her.

"No, Lionel! I've had enough of this shit! I've tried my hardest to embrace your bastard child from day one but now she's trying to ruin *my* family with wild allegations and I won't allow it! I'm washing my hands with her. She ain't no daughter of mine and never will be."

It was like an asteroid had dropped right on my heart and broke it into a million pieces. My whole life had been a lie. This lady was the only mother I'd ever known. We had family portraits with her holding me as a baby. To learn that I'd been lied to from the very beginning hurt. But now her hatred for me made so much sense. I was a reminder of my dads betrayal. I had vivid memories of my mom...I mean Katheline trying her hardest to have a second child but it never happened. That undoubtedly aided her dislike for me and the poor way she treated me. She couldn't have her own baby but had to raise an outside child. This shit was rich.

"Yo, you really are an evil ass bitch."Kyree stated.

My dad looked at Mr.Kylo. "You're going to let your son curse out a woman like tha-"

"Say, shut your bitch ass up,"Mr.Kylo said. "You a weak ass nigga for allowing your wife to treat your daughter like shit. Y'all don't deserve no respect and my son can call y'all whatever he wants."

That silenced my cowardly father. He didn't even try to explain his wife's claims to me or comfort me. I was on the verge of tears and his only concern was Kyree cursing out Katheline. Everything was starting to add up. My dad never stood up for me because he didn't want to rock the boat with his marriage. I was obviously a mistake so he was never going to go too hard for me. He allowed me to be his wifes punching bag.

"And this is the family of the person you let knock you up,"Katheline scoffed. "If you had any sense you'd get rid of that little mutherfucker."

I protectively clutched my stomach. With everything going on, I didn't have time to think about how I felt about being pregnant. But the second my mom said I should kill my child I wanted to kill her. I hadn't planned this, and the timing wasn't ideal but this baby was *mine*. I vowed to be a better parent than she or my dad ever was. I'd put that on my life. I already loved what was growing in me unconditionally.

"Bitch, I'll kill you playing with my fucking child!"Kyree released my hand to charge toward my mom. His dad stopped him dead in his tracks.

"Nah, that's what we won't do, son. Fuck that hoe. She ain't never gon have no blessings talking like that. You don't gotta deal with her because karma got her."

"No, let him try to deal with me!"Katheline walked around to the other side of the bed but Ms.Nette stood in front of her.

"Where you think you going?"

"Get out my way!"Katheline pushed her and the next thing I knew she was laid out on the ground. Ms.Nette had cocked back and punched her dead in the face so fast that she never saw it coming. I didn't even see it coming. It was an effective blow because it echoed and knocked the wind out of Katheline.

"Kathy!"My dad exclaimed, before picking her off the ground.

"You bitch! You going to jail for that shit! Punching people in the face is a crime! You going down for assault!"

"You pushed her first!"I screamed. "You don't even have a reason to be here! You're not family! Leave and take your husband with you!"

"Oh bitch, please! I raised your dumb ass and we take great care of you until this day! You'll need us before we need you!"

"That's where you're sadly mistaken! I don't need you, him, or anybody else in that damn family! Y'all can take y'all money and shove it up y'all asse-"

"Kamaria!"My dad gasped. "Don't talk to your mother like that!"

"Nigga, that's not her mother!"Kyree clamored.

"Maybe not biologically! But she took her in the moment her mother died during childbirth! I know she loves Kamaria, she's just disappointed in her right now!"

Bomb after bomb was being dropped on me. Not only was the only mom I'd ever known not my mom but my biological mom was dead. Wow. This had to be a sick joke.

"Disappointment would've never made her reveal some shit like that in this way! And she don't love shit. She's always treated Mari like a red headed step child and your coward ass let her for all these years. But all that shit is dead. You heard her, she don't need y'all. She gon be super straight. Now get the fuck out before I call security on y'all asses."

Chapter 16

Kyree

May 16, 2020

I watched Kamaria intently as she looked over two different white dresses that were hanging from hooks on my closet. She had "Cranes in the Sky" by Solange blasting from my tv. I knew the song by heart because she'd been wearing it out. My room at my apartment was flooded with boxes that contained all of her stuff from her dorm. Move out day for everyone on campus had been yesterday, so me and Shad brought all of her stuff here. My lease wasn't up on this apartment until the end of June which was perfect because our lease agreement for the house didn't start until July. We had two weeks in the midst of that where we wouldn't have a place to stay but my parents already made it clear that my old room was always open for us, so we were good. For now though, this apartment was ours and her stuff being everywhere was oddly comforting to me. We were really in this thing called life together and it was a great feeling.

"Why do you keep staring at me?"She broke her gaze from the dresses to look at me.

"Because it's fun watching you go back and forth between those two dresses like we're walking across the stage tomorrow or something,"I laughed lightly. "Come here."

"We may not be walking tomorrow but we will be next weekend,"she said as she twisted over to where I was sitting on the edge of my bed. Once she was in front of me, I wrapped my arms around her waist and kissed her belly.

"Why do you keep doing that? I'm not even showing yet,"she mumbled.

"So...my son is still in there, girl."

"Your son?"She offered a small smile. "Okay, if that's what you think."

"What do you think?"I asked anxiously. Yesterday was two weeks since she'd been drugged and we hadn't discussed the baby a whole lot. It wasn't that I didn't want to. If anybody was happy about our child it was me. I'd wanted and prayed for this. It's just that too much was going on and I didn't want to burden her with something else. Kaliya had betrayed her in a way that would understandably have her feeling down. Then to add insult to injury her mother wasn't actually her mother and that had my baby's head all the way fucked up. She couldn't even properly cope with the situation though. The hospital kept her for one night and a half a day to ensure that the baby was okay. She was released Saturday evening. I wanted her to take some time to just sit with what happened to her, so I urged her to contact her professors and tell them what happened so she could reschedule her tests. With her high GPA and perfect track record as a student some of them probably would've let her slide under the circumstances. Kamaria wasn't going for that though. She was drugged on Friday and aced her first final on Monday. She flew through finals week with A after A as if nothing had happened to her. I was proud of her but also worried about her mental health. It was like she'd just brushed everything off and kept it moving. That wasn't normal. I didn't want her moping around and feeling sorry for herself, but I did want her to express how she was really feeling. Because no matter how hard she tried to hide it I didn't miss the sadness in her eyes.

"I don't know or care. I just want a healthy baby."

To hear her say that she actually wanted the baby made my heart swell. My initial thoughts after learning she was pregnant was that I'd have to convince her to keep it. Then when her "mom" said that evil shit about her getting rid of it I thought she'd let that get in her head. But she hadn't. She obviously wanted this baby just like I did. Maybe not as much, but that didn't matter. As long as she was on board.

"You're gonna get that healthy baby in the form of a boy,"I kissed her belly again. She had to get pregnant in Miami because she was a month and a half along. She swore she got her period after Miami. It just happened to be lighter than usual. The doctor said some women experienced period-like symptoms during the first trimester, but it was impossible to have an actual period. Considering how she hadn't bled this month at all, he was right.

"If it is a boy, I want him to be a junior,"I said.

"Done,"she wrapped her arms around my neck.

"That easy, huh?"

"Yup."

"Why?"

"Because I love you,"she leaned down to kiss my lips. When she pulled away she just stared at me.

"Wassup?"

"Nothing, just…thank you, for everything."

"What you thanking me for?"

She took a heavy breath. "For putting up with me. I know me and my family drama has to get on your last nerves. Then I was defending Kaliya when you were right about her the whole time. I feel so damn stupid…so thank you for not holding any of this against me."

"Mari, I would have no right to hold any of this shit against you because it's not your fault. You can't choose the shit you were born into."

"Maybe not, but I could've used better judgeme-"

"No."

"No?"

"No. Every move you made was because of the way you were brought up. Now going forward I do expect you to know better and move better. Only because this situation was too extreme for you not to have learned from it. But before this nothing so severe happened for you to just be up on game and know that your blood cousin would drug you. Shit, I would've never thought that in my wildest imagination and I was vocal about not liking the bitch. If anything I thought she was gon try to get you to overdrink like last time. That's why I was uneasy about you going. If I would've known what was on her mind you wouldn't have been going nowhere."

"She's not even my blood cousin…,"she laughed like she was still in disbelief. She probably was. If somebody told me my mom wasn't my mom and her whole side of the family wasn't my blood relatives I would've been in shock for the rest of my life. Learning that you didn't come from where you thought you came from had to be an out of body experience. "That's insane but I guess I should feel relieved right?"

"Don't worry about how you should feel. Tell me how you really feel."

"I feellll…hurt, betrayed,and unwanted but I've always felt that way. Katheline always treated me terribly so I was always hurt. My dad never defended me and let her have her way with me so I always felt betrayed. And they…they just never gave me the love and support I needed outside of material things, so that left me feeling unwanted. I guess those feelings are just amplified now that I know the truth. I also *do* feel kind of relieved that Katheline is not my real mom. Outside of my auntie, I never felt real love from her side of the family. This all explains why and that gives me closure. Because if Katheline was my blood mother and she just hated me for no reason that would hurt a lot more. It just sucks that I'll never know my real mom."

"She has to have a family. Maybe you can ask your dad for that information"

"I don't think I want to do that. At least not now or any time soon."

"Why?"

"Because my mom's family had to have seen her pregnant and they were definitely aware when she died after giving birth. They just let my dad take me."

"He's your dad. They couldn't stop him."

"I didn't say they should've, but if they were interested in having a relationship with me they would've tried."

"Do you think Katheline's family knew you weren't hers?"

"They had to know. She was obviously never pregnant with me. That's why I've been ignoring my auntie."

I got quiet and looked off.

"What?"

"I don't know…I just feel like you should talk to her about it and give her a chance to explain. You never know what she might say."

"That's what scares me."

"What?"

"I don't know what she might say,"her voice cracked. "The thought of everybody knowing something important about me while I was in the dark is the ultimate betrayal. I don't want to think that one of my favorite people would do that to me."

"Aw, Mari," I pulled her closer and hugged her waist tighter. "I can't sit up here and say that won't be the case because I don't know. But at least let her tell you that herself if it's true. Don't just assume."

"And if it is true?"

"Then you tell her how that hurt you. She can explain why she kept the secret and maybe it'll make you feel better. Or maybe not. Either way, at least you got it off your chest and can move on. You don't gotta wonder what if."

"You're right, maybe I should unblock her and finally call her back."

"You blocked that lady?" I laughed.

"I blocked the entire family. I don't have nothing to say to those people."

"And you shouldn't, but I feel like your Auntie really loves you."

"I know she loves me. I can't even question that."

"Then holler at her, Mari. It's not healthy to be holding shit in. And you don't gotta face none of this shit alone because I'm right here."

She dropped down into my lap and kissed me with what felt like every fiber of passion in her body.

"I love you so much."

"I love you more,"I kissed her again.

Kamaria

There were three days left until graduation and it was one of the few things that had me clinging to my sanity. It was something to look forward to when I just wanted to give up. Something else I had that kept me pushing was my baby. I had to be okay for the life that was growing inside of me. It was bad enough I'd started off the pregnancy rocky with drinking. Then being drugged could've caused me to lose the baby. I thanked God everyday for sparing me and my child. Now I just wanted to be at peace for him. I'd been referring to the baby as a boy ever since Kyree told me that's what he wanted. But I had a good feeling that it actually would be a boy. I'd been looking up baby shower ideas and nursery themes so we could properly prepare for baby KJ.

The timing of everything worked out in my favor because had I gone through this shit at the beginning of the fall semester I probably would've either dropped my classes or flunked out. The cards I'd been dealt at this stage in my life forced me to be strong. My childhood had broken me down so much but I was being built back up day by day. I felt like a new person. Not only was I more self aware but I was also more aware of others. I'd put all my issues on the back burner to ensure that I breezed through finals week stress free. Now that I'd conquered that I was ready to deal with everything accordingly. The first order of business I had was work related. I was in New Orleans because I had two job interviews. Kyree told me I didn't have to work and with the way morning sickness had started kicking my ass I'd probably take heed. I didn't see any harm in exploring my options though.

The next thing on my to do list was a lunch date with Auntie Sana at Morrows. At first I was completely against talking to her. I'd ruled the entire side of my mom's family out because I'd declared that they were guilty by association. They had to know and that's why they treated me like an afterthought. However, my auntie and I had always been better than that. She didn't deserve the treatment I was rightfully giving the rest of them. She was the only one who'd found other ways to reach out to me despite being blocked, which showed how much she cared about me. So I finally unblocked her and agreed to meet up with her. I couldn't act like I'd come to this decision on my own though. Kyree had persuaded me with his words of encouragement.

The way he worded things made me want to put on my big girl panties and address the situation head on. "CPR" by Summer Walker played from the car speaker making me think about him even more. We rode to New Orleans in his car but he went to his parents house. He let me drive his car so I could handle my business. He'd hinted at wanting to sleep at his parents house tonight and I didn't mind. I'd slept there before and I was more comfortable there than I was in the house I grew up in. I guess that was the difference between being sincerely welcomed versus being tolerated.

When I approached Auntie Sana at the table she was sitting at in Morrows she stood up nervously and watched me walk up with sorrow in her eyes. I stood strong because I didn't want her to feel bad for me. I just wanted her to give me answers that the people who I thought were parents didn't seem pressed to give. When I reached her, she embraced me in a tight hug. The news in my "family" had evidently traveled fast about me being pregnant and Kaliya getting jumped. When my auntie reached out to me she was only inquiring about my pregnancy. Other family members attempted to question me about Kaliya getting jumped because I was sure they'd gotten some half ass story Katheline had given them. I blocked them all because I didn't owe them an explanation, especially where Kaliya was concerned. I was certain that bitch was being tight lipped because she didn't want her real business aired out. I don't think anybody knew that Katheline had revealed to me that she wasn't my real mom or that I'd been drugged. If she did tell them anything related to that it was probably that lie she'd made up about me taking ecstasy on my own and blaming Kaliya which resulted in her getting jumped. I didn't know for a fact and I didn't care to clear it up with people who didn't love me anyway. Things were different with Auntie Sana though. If she was willing to listen then I was more than ready to tell her what really happened.

"I already ordered all of your favorites, baby girl. You're eating for two,"she grinned at me with watery eyes.

"Oh God, are you about to cry?"I cracked a smile against my will.

"My baby is having a baby. It's emotional so of course I'm going to cry."

I just looked at her, unsure of what to say. She probably wanted to have lunch to merely assure me that she'd be here for me regardless of the rest of the family standing by Kaliya. But things were so much more deeper than that.

"You hear me, Kamaria? I don't care what's going on with you, your mama,your dad, or Kaliya. I'm here for whatever you ne-"

"Auntie Sana, that lady is *not* my mama."

A surprised look overcame her face and it seemed real. I just wasn't sure if she was surprised because she didn't know or because she didn't know how I knew. Her next question cleared things up for me expeditiously.

"W-who told you that?"

My heart dropped. That was the only confirmation I needed to know that she knew and never bothered to tell me. Instead of reacting off of emotion, I held my composure. I needed answers and I wouldn't get them if I just blew up.

"Let's start with this, why did you want to sit down and talk to me?"

"Well...Kathy texted the whole family a long paragraph about how we were to stay away from you because your poor decisions got Kaliya jumped. She also revealed that you were pregnant out of wedlock and asked us to back her and Lionel up in not supporting you. I tried to fish for more details with the Kaliya situation, but she refused to explain the situation in depth. I automatically knew it was bullshit at that point and I have a strong feeling that Kaliya has never been as innocent as they think. They put that girl on a pedestal like she's perfection and they make excuses whenever she doesn't get her way. For example, she tried out for the SU Dancing Dolls four damn times and never made it past the first round. Her mom and dad tried calling the dean to pay for a private audition. They think their money can buy her the perfect life and that's why she walks around feeling like everybody should bow down to her. I don't believe for a second that she got jumped for absolutely no reason. Am I wrong?"

"No, you're not. The truth is that she slipped ecstasy into my drink at her birthday party. If it wasn't for my boyfriend seeing her instagram story where she was hyping me up to do embarrassing things, who knows how that night would've ended for me. Kyree also has a video of her friend explaining what happened from her point of view if you need further proo-
"

"I don't, baby girl. I believe you. Now let's talk about how you know Kathy isn't your biological mom."

"Please, let's talk about it," I crossed my arms.

She sighed heavily. "I'm sure you're upset that I knew and never told you, but it wasn't my place, baby. I couldn't just go against your guardians and tell you something that they didn't want you to know. When they brought you home as a newborn Kathy made it seem like she would be a good mother to you and treat you like her own. I couldn't do anything but respect that. And honestly, when you were a baby and even through your toddler years she treated you fine. I felt like everything worked out for the best even though Lionel cheated. Your real mother passed away and that was a tragedy but Kathy was having trouble having kids so I figured you were her blessing. It seemed to change as you got older though. I think a lot of it had to do with the fact that she couldn't have a child of her own..."

"So she started resenting me."

"Yes,"she responded, thinking that I was asking a question. I knew that shit for a fact though. I had gone through it.

"And that's when you stepped in and started showing me extra special attention, right?"

"Kamaria, I've loved you from the very beginning. You're my niece."

My heart pounded.

"I appreciate that you took on that role so seriously despite us not being bloo-"

"No babygirl, we are blood."

My heart beat sped up.

"W-what?"

"You know that I don't have the same dad as my other siblings, right?"

"Yes I know that. But what does that have to do with anything?"

I didn't know where she was going with this but my heart was racing with anticipation.

"When my mom got pregnant with me she thought her baby making days were over and she was fresh off a divorce. I think she was just trying to have fun which is how she ended up with my dad who was nothing like my siblings father. He was a struggling musician, so my mom was ashamed. She never let him have full access to me and I guess he never pushed for it since his career always had him on the go anyway. He'd come around seldomly and we'd spend time together. He passed away from cancer when I was 20 and that's when I finally met the other side of my family. He had one other child and his death brought us super close. She was two years younger than me and her name was *Samaria.*"

"Auntie Sana…"my eyes grew misty. "What are you telling me?"

"I'm telling you that my little sister is your biological mother,"she teared up. "Living with this has been hard because I feel like it's partially my fault. I bought Samaria around my mom's side of the family. I always felt like an outcast growing up so I was thrilled to show off a piece of me, and Samaria was my mini me in every way. We were the same height, we had the same hair, and we had the same face. The only differences we had was that she was way thicker and darker…she passed that down to you."

Tears ran down my face as my heart ached for something I'd never have.

"Everywhere we went men had eyes for her and Lionel was no different but Katheline had eyes for her too. That's what they used to do, bring other women into their bedroom,"she divulged, blowing my mind. As much as Katheline carried on like she was perfect I would've never thought that she would be down for threesomes. The visual in my head was actually disturbing.

"Only Samaria wasn't a woman,"she continued. "She was a naive 18 year old girl who wasn't mature enough to be in a 33 year olds bed. I only found out because I saw Lionel and Samaria at the movies together. Naturally, I went off and threatened to tell Katheline. That's when I learned from Samaria that she knew because it had all started in her house. I was even more livid because I felt like it was low-down of them to do that with my sister. I called up Katheline for confirmation and I learned that they had been all having sex together, but she did not approve of them seeing each other outside of her. That's where all the drama started. Katheline didn't like the fact that her husband had seemed to fall for somebody that was just supposed to be fun for them. She made him choose and he claimed to choose her, but he'd still see Samaria behind her back. It got to a point where I separated myself from all of them because there was too much going on."

"What happened when she got pregnant with me?"

"The whole family ostracized me because your dad fully left Katheline to be by Samaria's side through the pregnancy. They felt like I was at fault for bringing her around as if Kathy didn't bring her into her bedroom…"

"Kind of how they blamed me for Kaliya's actions."

"Right."

"So why do you still fool with them?" I asked incredulously. For the life of me I couldn't understand how she could even be amicable with Katheline and my dad for all these years when they were terrible people.

"Because of *you*, Kamaria. When Samaria died after having you, your father was there and he had rights to you. It wasn't like I could take you and just run off. So I had to play nice just so I could stay in your life. My sister would've wanted that."

Her response made me feel warm. She was looking in my eyes and I could feel her love for me bouncing off of every word. She genuinely cared about being here for me and I'd always appreciate that.

"How'd you get back on everyone's good side though? I thought they shunned you."

"Lionel went running right back to Katheline with you after Samaria passed away. She was hesitant at first but she allowed our older sister and our mother to get in her head. They were urging her to fight for her marriage, including taking care of you. Obviously she gave in and it seemed like she really loved you when you were a baby. I guess she faked until she couldn't fake anymore. It probably always ate her up that she couldn't have Lionel's children despite him desperately wanting them. It also had to hurt knowing that he'd settled for her and that he would've been somewhere else if it weren't for *death*."

"Wow, no wonder she hates me,"I sniffled while shaking my head. "It makes me feel a little better to know that nothing was actually never wrong with *me*."

"Of course nothing was wrong with you, baby girl,"she grabbed my hands. "Haven't I always told you that you were beautiful and smart?"

"Yes, but my self esteem was shot because the woman I believed to be my mother made it her mission to tell me the opposite."

"I'm sorry you had to endure that and it makes me feel like shit that I didn't do more. It just felt like my hands were tied because had I said something they would've cut me out of your life completely. I figured it was better for me to be there for you in some capacity than to not be there at all. You needed someone in your corner. I had no one growing up and it made me feel unworthy. I think that's the main reason why it took me so long to allow a man to love me. I could've been married in my early 20's but I sabotaged anything that came my way. I didn't start healing until I was in my thirties and that's when I met your Uncle Jaryn."

"Everything happens for a reason because I couldn't imagine you with anyone else."

"You're right about that, sweetie. Everything happens for a reason. Including all of this. You might be asking God why right now but it'll all start to make sense soon."

"I think it's already starting to make sense. It's messed up that I had to go through all of that but I probably wouldn't be where I am now with Kyree and our baby."

"So you're happy about being pregnant?"

"Yes. It wasn't planned but I'm excited."

"As you should be. This should be one of the happiest times in your life. Enjoy it to the fullest and be thankful that you have an Aunt on the same journey as you,"she grinned.

I gasped. "Auntie Sana you're pregnant?"

She nodded as happy tears ran down her cheeks. "Almost three months along and high risk, but I know God will bless us with a happy and healthy baby."

Once Auntie Sana hit 35 everyone ruled her out when it came to having kids. She was 43 years old now so I'm sure no one was expecting this, but she deserved it. I knew she was going to be a perfect mom.

"I know so too," I sniffled. "And Auntie, I just want to say thankyou."

"For what?"

"For always being here for me. I'm not going to lie, I was mad with you at first because I felt like you helped pull the wool over my eyes but after listening to you I know you had no ill intent. The only thing you ever tried to do was look out for me and that's more than my father has ever tried to do…so I appreciate you for that."

"Awww, thank you, baby girl. But you don't have to thank me for that. We're family. That's what I was supposed to do and I'll continue doing it as long as I have breath in my body."

Just like that I knew I would be alright. I'd probably never have the mother or father I'd always yearned for, but I had people who loved me and wanted to be there for me. Therefore, I didn't need some fake ass mom or a cowardly father. I had everything I needed and unlike my father, I'd never settle for less.

Chapter 17

Kyree

Graduation Day

"Congratulations!"My mom screamed as Kamaria and I walked to them hand in hand. I couldn't believe that I was a college graduate. The journey had been everything but easy for me and I questioned if I'd really make it several times. But I stuck with it and it all paid off. College was more than what I expected it to be. The ultimate goal was to get my degree and have fun, but I'd done that and then some. I was leaving here with a career, full pockets, the love of my life, and a baby on the way. God had shown out big time and I couldn't stop thanking him.

"Thank y'all so much,"Mari gushed. For the first time she was seeing the signs my family got made with both of our faces on them. We decided to do a graduation photoshoot last minute last week with a popular photographer in the city named Kiyor Patel. I had to pay an arm and a leg for a rush fee, but it was worth it to have our memories documented professionally. My people put those pictures to use today. They had posters, fans of our faces, and even the balloons they carried had our pictures on them. I expected nothing less from my family but for Mari this was new and she loved it.

"Let's take pictures!"Auntie Sana clapped. She and her husband were the only ones who'd shown up from Mari's family today and that's how she wanted it. I would've been looking at her sideways if she wanted it another way. If anybody thought I was protective before then they hadn't seen anything yet. With Kamaria being pregnant she didn't need anyone stressing her out and I wanted to keep her away from negative energy. That's why I was relieved that she decided to wash her hands with her family, and I use the word family loosely. She gave me a full rundown of everything Auntie Sana told her about Katheline, her dad, and her real mom. Those people had a lot of nerve acting like Mari getting pregnant out of wedlock was such a disgrace when their whole marriage was a joke. They were the epitome of throwing stones from a glass house.

I already knew we had about 20 minutes worth of picture taking because people from my mom and dad's side of the family showed up. Like most college graduations, ours didn't have formal tickets, so it was free for all. That made my life easy because I would've hated having to choose. Thankfully our reservations at Landry's weren't for another two hours. The graduation was in BR, but we wanted to eat in New Orleans because we like our city's food way better.

"Alright, it's our turn!"My mom announced as she pulled my dad over to us. We'd only taken pictures with my grandparents and Auntie Sana so far. Auntie Sana's husband had been taking the pictures on his professional camera.

"Can we get in the picture?"

I thought I was hallucinating when I looked off to the side and saw Katheline and Lionel's bitch ass. He had a bouquet of roses in his hand and she stood next to him smiling awkwardly. I'd feel stupid too if I showed up unwanted, asking dumb ass questions. Mari looked over at them, scoffed, and then looked back at the camera.

"Smile, family,"she instructed in a jovial voice. I wanted to burst out laughing but I kept it cool. If we ignored them then maybe they'd go away.

"I know she's not ignoring us as if we didn't put her through school!"

Of course Katheline's ignorant ass wasn't going to go down without a fight. That's how her ass got knocked out last time. She didn't know when to quit.

"Look, we're not doing all that today. Unless you want a repeat of last time I advise you to shut up and leave. Kamaria obviously doesn't want you here,"my mom asserted. I knew she'd be the first to speak up. She was probably eager to put hands on that lady again.

"I'm not trying to do anything. I'm here to support my daughter but I see y'all then brainwashed her."

Several people in my family made comments wondering what the hell she was talking about. Everyone knew Mari was pregnant because I'd called around to share the good news. I didn't however divulge Mari's family issue because that wasn't everybody's business. They were about to get an earful now though.

"Brainwash?"My mom's head jerked back. "Bitch, if you mad about Mari not fucking with you then blame yourself! Cause it didn't even have to be like this."

"Hey, we're just here to support,"Lionel finally said something. "I just wanted to tell my daughter congratulations because I really am proud of her."

Mari just looked at him blankly making it clear that she wasn't impressed by the words coming from his mouth.

"So you're going to look at him crazy?!"Katheline questioned, before looking at her sister. "Sana, you better get your niece."

"I don't gotta get shit. What you need to do is stay away from my niece."

"What?"Katheline uttered as if she were appalled. "This is my child. If anything I have more of a right to be here than anybod-"

This time, Kamaria cut her off."Girl, you are not my mother and you made that clear a few weeks ago. Maybe you didn't mean everything you said, but I meant everything I said. I'm done with both of y'all."

"Oh girl, don't be ridiculous! You know you need us to help you out. What are you going to do? Bring a baby back to his apartment that he shares with another person?"

"Bitch, don't play with my fucking cousin!"Versace hollered as she stepped towards her. Katheline jumped back in fear, making a few of my family members snicker. Lucky for her, Qaylo pulled Versace back.

"This whole family is obviously violent! You're going to raise a baby in this, Kamaria?!"Katheline held her chest in horror.

"Yes. I'm going to raise *my* child surrounded by real love. Not forced love. You know the kind where I had to raise a child that wasn't mine in order to keep a man who would've really preferred somebody else but couldn't have her because she died."

Katheline looked like she saw a ghost. She slowly turned to Auntie Sana.

"While you were running your mouth did you mention that the home wrecker was your half sister from your father?"

Sana laughed. "I sure did. I also told her how you and Lionel both welcomed her into y'alls bed with open arms."

"Oop…"my mom covered her mouth with her hand.

"Bitch, this is teaaaa. What the fuck?"Fendi marveled.

Katheline's light skin turned red as everyone openly reacted to her business being out in the open. As a woman who obviously cared about appearances this had to be humiliating for her but it was exactly what she deserved. She'd been coming down on Mari like her shit didn't stink when she was really the funkiest bitch around.

"Ya know what? I don't need this! I tried to be the bigger person but I guess it's really time to throw in the towel."

"Please do! I don't want or need you in my life! By the way, when my baby comes home from the hospital he'll be going to a house that his daddy is paying every bill in! We'll be well taken care of!"

I guess that dig about me sharing an apartment with Shad got to her but it didn't bother me. Most college students had roommates. I knew that I was making big moves for my family so I saw no need to prove something to anyone who wouldn't be a part of our lives. I guess Mari just had to let that hoe know though and I wasn't mad at it. I was actually proud of her and that's why I'd remained quiet. She needed to address them and let them know that she was done so there'd be no confusion moving forward. They wouldn't be popping up unexpectedly anywhere else.

Katheline stormed off in anger demanding that Lionel follow her. I was surprised when he stepped towards Kamaria. I protectively stepped forward making him step back with his hands up.

"I'm not trying to cause trouble. I just wanted to say that I'm sorry Kamaria. From the bottom of my heart. Here, take this,"he said discreetly as if Kathy was still lurking around. He handed her off an envelope at the speed of lightning and then shuffled away.

"What's that?"My Granny noisily asked.

"It's money,"Mari said with a stank face. "I'm gonna go give this back to him."

"Girl hell no,"my mom looked at her crazily. "Put that up for a rainy day. Don't give no money back. Now if that bitch Katheline gave it to you I'd be telling you to be prideful. You don't accept shit from somebody like that. But that's your dad and he owes you for bringing you into this world, so take it as a parting gift."

"Yea, I'm with Nette on this,"Auntie Sana. "All his sorry ass can offer is money anyway and you do have a little one on the way."

"Our little one is straight,"I declared, although I wouldn't have felt a way about her accepting the money. Unlike Katheline, her dad hadn't made comments about her needing him, so there was no need to be prideful where he was concerned. He gave her that money out of guilt. He didn't want anything in return.

"We all know that and we're all going to make sure of that,"my dad said. "But as a parent I fell on hard times where I wished I had money stashed somewhere. So Mari should keep the money and put it up."

"Wait…there's a necklace in here."

Mari pulled out a small diamond necklace with the letter "K" attached to it.

Auntie Sana gasped. "That was your mom's, baby girl. She got that when she found out she was having a girl. She named you right away."

"You want me to put it on you?"I asked after she just stood there not saying anything. She just stared at the necklace. I felt like it was a symbol of "what if" for her. Mainly "what if" her mom hadn't died? She'd never know and that undoubtedly took a toll on her but she'd never have a shortage of love moving forward. I'd lay down and bet my last dollar on that shit. She would always be enough for me.

"Yes, please,"she whispered.

After I clasped the necklace around her neck I kissed the side of her face.

"I love you, Ky."She turned her face and pecked my lips.

"I love you way more, Mari."

Epilogue

Kamaria

December 22, 2021

"Happy Birthday to you! Happy Birthday to you! Happy Birthday to KJ! Happy Birthday to you!"

I couldn't believe it had been a year since my heart outside of my body had been born. Just like Kyree and I predicted, we had a boy. Kyree Genesis Pierre Junior was a beautiful, healthy, playful, and cuddly baby boy. Not only did he inherit his dad's name but he inherited his looks too. Everything from his complexion to his face was *all* Kyree. I loved it. My baby was the apple of everybody's eyes. Everyone from his grandparents, big cousins, and aunties spoiled him. Nobody had Kyree beat though. When we officially learned we were having a boy at our gender reveal dinner party, Kyree shed real tears. I already knew he'd be a great father, but that sealed the deal for me. After that he went out and bought everything our son needed from clothes, shoes, and even blue furniture for his nursery. We'd already talked about doing the nursery in a blue elephant theme if it was a boy and I had a mood board going, so he knew exactly what I wanted and he got it. He left no line uncrossed. He even made my pregnancy a breeze. The first trimester got harder for me towards the end. I could hardly keep anything down and I was always so tired. That made my decision to not work easy and I felt stable in doing so because my dad had gifted me $50,000 in that big envelope on my graduation day. Therefore, I knew I could keep us afloat if things didn't go as planned with him and his job. It wasn't necessary though because business took off for him in New Orleans. I was his unofficial bookkeeper so I could say with confidence that he was killing it. It was safe to say New Orleans night life was way more popping than Baton Rouge's. With money rolling in like a flood, I was able to kick my feet up during my pregnancy. I was waited on hand and foot by Kyree. Anything I wanted I got whether it was food, a massage, a shopping spree, or space to rest. He gave it to me with no hesitation. His parents were on the same type of timing because they were always calling me to ask if I needed anything. They were also at every hospital visit with me and Kyree. If it weren't for the big belly holding me down I would've loved to stay pregnant forever. I guess that's why I was pregnant again. I loved it so much the first time around that I rushed back in for a second time. Or it was because Kyree couldn't stay off me and refused to pull out. It also could've been me not staying on top of my birth control. Or maybe it was the fact that me and Kyree had baby girl fever because of Auntie Sana's daughter, Jamaria Sky. She resembled me and she was so damn beautiful that I wanted a daughter of my own. Whatever it was, I was anticipating our baby girl who was set to arrive in mid February. Kylee Genesis Pierre was going to be just as perfect as her big brother.

"Blow the candles out, man,"Kyree said with a big smile while bringing KJ close to his Spiderman cake. My baby looked adorable in his personalized birthday spiderman shirt, Balmain jeans, and his red, black, and white jordan ones. Kyree had taken him to get a lining at the barbershop and

Ms.Nette had started his locs. I cried when I saw him after he got it done because he was getting so big.

Kyree ended up blowing the candles out for him and we both kissed each side of his cheeks while he smiled from ear to ear. I'd never seen a baby so smiley but that was a testament to how much love he got on a daily basis. Even the people at his daycare adored him and they would send me pictures throughout the day while I was at work. That's right, I'd finally started putting my degree to use. I was the Staff Accountant at the Four Seasons. I was certain that my internships from college had scored me the job, and I was happy with it. I could sit all day and just be one with numbers. For me, it was a low maintenance job because math had always come easy to me. I didn't even think about quitting when I got pregnant a few months after starting. Kyree encouraged me to work because he saw that it made me happy. Staying at home with KJ for the first two months was cool but I was restless and needed something of my own to do. So Kyree found KJ a daycare while I sought out a job. One thing he put his foot down about was me helping with any bills.

He would just urge me to put my money up for whenever I wanted to use it or if we fell on hard times. I didn't see any issue with that, so I obliged.

"Hold that ring up, cousin!"Fendi screamed, making everybody laugh. She was referring to my seven carat engagement ring. It was a stunner. Kyree had proposed to me at KJ's Toy Story themed baby shower. It was beautiful and I still remembered everything so vividly. If I ever did forget anything it was professionally videographed for my memories. He let the room full of our loved ones know that he started loving me early on in our friendship but he was scared to take it to the next level because he didn't want to mess it up. But he refused to let the fear of the unknown keep him from the best thing that ever happened to him. The best thing being me. That made my heart combust. We set a date for the fall of 2021…but I got pregnant during the summer derailing those plans. I refused to be a pregnant bride, so we rescheduled for the fall of 2022 and I fully planned on getting a birth control shot that was good for at least a year. Baby number three wasn't coming for at least another three or four years if it was up to me. Meanwhile, Kyree kept telling everyone that he wanted to have all five of his kids back to back. That's right. *Five.* I loved being pregnant but not that damn much. For now I was perfectly okay with my boy and girl.

After we finished taking pictures with the birthday cake, we stepped aside so Ms.Nette could cut it. I shifted from side to side because my feet were starting to hurt. I was dressed down in jeans, a spiderman shirt that read "Mommy of the birthday boy," and Jordans. Kyree had on the same exact outfit except his shirt said "Daddy of the birthday boy."

"Come sit down,"Kyree ordered as he pulled me to the closest table nearby. The spacious event hall was decorated to perfection and we paid the price for it.

"We getting down to the wire with this pregnancy. When you go on maternity leave again?"

"January, Ky."

He'd asked this before and it was the same answer every time.

"Mannn, that's too late, Mari."

I burst into giggles. "Kyree, January is literally next week. What did you want me to say? Tomorrow?"

"Yea, if that's possible."

"Well it's not and I love my job."

"And I love that you love your job but I want you off your feet asap so you can get ready for my baby girl."

"All I do at work is sit at my desk," I laughed. "I'll be okay once I get home and elevate my feet. I've just been moving around all day."

"Da-Da!" KJ shouted as he ran over. We left him with his Auntie Kyana by the cake table but he was always going to find his daddy. He'd started walking a month ago and now all he did was run. 95% of the time he'd be looking for his daddy. I was hoping Kylee would be a mama's girl because Kyree had KJ on lock.

"What's up, man? I thought you was about to get some cake."

KJ reached for him and we laughed.

"You know he wants you," I giggled. "The only way he's going to get cake is if you take him."

"Ma-ma,"KJ leaned over and kissed my belly. He was a sponge, constantly soaking up everything around him. He'd seen his dad kiss my belly multiple times a day and he'd started doing it too. I never got tired of it either.

"Awwww, give mommy a kiss,"I scooped him up and kissed all over his chubby cheeks. Out of the corner of my eye I saw Kyree smiling at us like an idiot.

"Why you so happy?"I laughed.

"Really? You holding my son with my daughter in your belly and an engagement ring on your finger. I'm finna get up and start doing back flips in a minute."

"You so crazy,"I tittered.

"Crazy over you, Mrs.Pierre."

"Pump your brakes. We have to make it down the aisle first."

"I'm ready to run down that muthafucker. You the one talking bout you don't wanna be pregnant at your wedding."

"I don't! A big belly just doesn't go with the dress I have in mind."

"The belly only makes you more beautiful in my eyes."

"That's why you got me again, huh?"

"I couldn't help it, baby. It was too easy. But I'ma chill out next year because I'm ready to get married. After our wedding, it's up."

"Lies you tell,"I chortled. My mouth was saying one thing, but I was turned on by everything he said. It made me want to gladly give him however many babies he wanted. They'd be loved and well taken care of, so why not?

"Girl, you know you gon give me whatever I want."

"Oh, really?"

"Hell yea. That's what we do. We give each other whatever we want."

"Well if I'm going to keep having babies I'm going to need a new and bigger house."

"Done. Shit, that might be your push present. I was wondering how I was going to top the G-Wagon and now I got it. A house...I'ma hit up a realtor after Christmas. Cause I think we're ready to own a home."

He'd kept his word from our senior year and got me that G-Wagon exactly three weeks after I gave birth to his son.

That's how I knew I'd have a new house by the end of next Spring. One thing Kyree was going to do was make shit happen. If it was coming from his mouth then I could believe it would become a reality. That's how I knew I'd be his wife and be pregnant with child number 3 by the time 2022 was coming to an end.

"Okay, daddy. It's your world,"I relented.

His eyes sparkled, before he grabbed me up by my throat.

"Gimme them lips, my love."

We kissed passionately while "Hold You Down" by DJ Khaled conveniently played. He'd definitely held me down through my toughest times. A lot of other guys wouldn't have been able to handle my naivety along with my family drama. But Kyree was ten toes down through it all. Thankfully my dad and Katheline had left me alone like I asked, so they weren't an issue. I had recently seen Kaliya's instagram against my will because that hoe tried to follow me from her new page. She was stripping in Houston now and I could care less. I blocked her and went about my day.

I recognized how blessed I was to never be subjected to struggle love like most girls my age. One of Kyree's favorite songs to dedicate to me was Faithful by Drake, and I understood why. When he promised to commit to me, he stood by that. He respected our relationship to the fullest. I never felt like I was in competition with other women for his attention or that he'd wander off. That's why it would have to take God himself to get me away from this man. I knew things were still fresh in the relationship and that it could potentially change but I prayed for the best outcome everyday. Even if things ever got rocky I just hoped that we could work through it and still raise our kids in a healthy environment. But I didn't want to speak or think anything less than positive about our future. We loved being together and I didn't foresee that changing anytime soon. The University of Baton Rouge didn't just give me an education, it gave me the love of my life and I couldn't be more grateful.

THE END.

For updates,visuals, and sneak peeks join my reading group on Facebook, "That's All Cee Reading Group."